Granada

Middle East Literature in Translation
Michael Beard *and* Adnan Haydar, *Series Editors*

Other titles in Middle East Literature in Translation

The Author and His Doubles: Essays on Classical Arabic Culture
Abdelfattah Kilito; Michael Cooperson, trans.

The Committee
Sonallah Ibrahim; Mary St. Germain and Charlene Constable, trans.

A Cup of Sin: Selected Poems
Simin Behbahani; Farzaneh Milani and Kaveh Safa, trans.

Fatma: A Novel of Arabia
Raja Alem with Tom McDonough

Fugitive Light: A Novel
Mohammed Berrada; Issa J. Boullata, trans.

In Search of Walid Masoud: A Novel
Jabra Ibrahim Jabra; Roger Allen and Adnan Haydar, trans.

Moroccan Folktales
Jilali El Koudia, trans.; Roger Allen, ed.

Three Tales of Love and Death
Out El Kouloub

Women Without Men: A Novella
Shahrnush Parsipur; Kamran Talattof and Jocelyn Sharlet, trans.

Yasar Kemal on His Life and Art
Eugene Lyons Hébert and Barry Tharaud, trans.

Zanouba: A Novel
Out El Kouloub; Nayra Atiya, trans.

Granada

A Novel

Radwa Ashour

Translated from the Arabic by William Granara

With a Foreword by Maria Rosa Menocal

Syracuse University Press

First Edition 2003
04 05 06 07 08   6 5 4 3 2

This translation is based on the Arabic edition, *Granata*,
which is volume 1 of *Thulathiyat Gharnata* (The Granada Trilogy)
(Beirut: Al-Muassassa al-arabiyya lil-dirasat wa al-nashr, 1998).

Mohamad El-Hindi Books on Arab Culture and Islamic Civilization
are published with the assistance of a grant from Ahmad El-Hindi.

The paper used in this publication meets the minimum requirements
of American National Standard for Information Sciences—Permanence
of Paper for Printed Library Materials, ANSI Z39.48–1984.∞™

Library of Congress Cataloging-in-Publication Data
'Ashūr, Raḍwa
[Gharnāṭah. English]
Granada : a novel / Radwa Ashour ; translated by William Granara.—
1st ed.
p. cm.—(Middle East literature in translation)
ISBN 0-8156-0765-2
1. Granada (Spain)—History—Fiction. I. Granara, William. II. Title.
III. Series.
PJ7814.S514 G4813 2003
892.7'36—dc22   2003018502

Manufactured in the United States of America

Contents

Egyptian writer **Radwa Ashour** is a novelist, critic, and professor of English literature at Ain Shams University, in Egypt. After studying English Literature at Cairo University, graduating in 1967, she earned her doctorate in African-American literature in 1975 from Massachusetts University. She then joined the faculty at Ain Shams University, where she has taught ever since, except for brief periods. Ashour has written several novels and short stories; the trilogy of which *Granada* forms the first part was named Best Book of the Year by the General Egyptian Book Organization in 1994, and won first prize in the first Arab Women's Book Fair two years later.

William Granara is a translator, writer, and professor of Arabic language and literature at Harvard University, where he also directs the Arabic language program. He studied Arabic at Georgetown University and received his Ph.D. in Arabic and Islamic Studies at the University of Pennsylvania. He formerly served as the executive director of the Center for Arabic Study at the American University in Cairo and as director of the Arabic Field School of the U.S. Department of State in Tunis, Tunisia. Professor Granara specializes in the history and culture of Muslim Sicily, and has written on cross-cultural encounters between Islam and Christendom throughout the Middle Ages. In addition, he lectures and writes on contemporary Arabic literature and has published translations of Egyptian and North African fiction.

Foreword
Ways of Remembering Granada

I n Arabic letters, the tradition of remembering the lost shards of Islamic Spain is an old and venerable one. The destruction of Cordoba itself—the Caliphate politically dismembered and the venerable city sacked, along with the nearby palatine city of Madinat al-Zahra, *One Thousand and One Nights*-like in its architectural wonders—was the subject of what is perhaps the best-known work of Andalusian literature, *Tauq al-Hamam* (The neck-ring of the dove), by Ibn Hazm of Cordoba. Not unlike the extended family of characters so lovingly created by Radwa Ashour in this novel, Ibn Hazm was himself of a generation that lived through the transition from one universe to another, a personal witness to the unimaginable losses that followed the political debacles of his time. The Cordoban's celebrated work about love, and about its ways of shaping the human condition, and about the sorrows of loss in love, easily elides the love of a woman with that of his homeland. When he says "My love for her blotted out all that went before, and made anathema to me all that came after" he might as easily be describing one as the other. And it is precisely this kind of crucial interdependence of public and personal histories, and the ways in which life and love must indeed go on, and yet are unbearably transfigured by earth-shaking historical events, that is on vivid display in *Granada*.

A work of historical fiction set in the aftermath of the Castilian takeover of the lone Islamic kingdom of Granada in 1492, *Granada* tells the story of an extended family grappling with the consequences of that political catastrophe for the Muslim community. Granada at that moment recreated here by the Egyptian novelist Radwa Ashour, the turn of the sixteenth century in a Spain where the New World has just barely been discovered, is removed by about five hundred years from Ibn Hazm's devastated Cordoba—almost exactly as long and far as it is removed from us, and from the "interesting times" in which we ourselves live. One is tempted to argue that while the details of history change—and the textures and colors of everyday life are more or less exotic to a reader—the personal remains the same, and that the love stories and the family sagas that come to us superimposed on the narrative of the sack of Madinat al-Zahra by fundamentalist Berbers in 1009 are, at the end of the day, love stories and family sagas like all others, whether five or fifty or five hundred years later.

But in fact all history is not created equal, and the Arabs and many other Muslims have long harbored a complex nostalgia for an al-Andalus remembered, iconically, as both the best of times and the worst of times in their history. From Ibn Hazm through Radwa Ashour—with everyone from Ibn al-Khatib to Salman Rushdie in between—to evoke any given chapter within the longue duree of Andalusian history, no matter how seemingly domestic or how formally poetic, is to call forth the complex specter of how much a culture can achieve, how fragile such achievement is, and most of all, how much it can lose. Ashour has chosen 1492, the most easily lamentable moment in this history, and by far the most often chosen as a setting for historical novels [1]—it is, after all, one of those moments

---

1. In relatively recent years one notes two prominent and best-selling 1492 novels: Tariq Ali's *Shadows of the Pomegranate Tree,* with a setting just outside the city of Granada but at the same moment Ashour has chosen, and Noah Gordon's *The Last Jew,* whose eponymous hero is, instead, from Toledo, but who shares with the Muslim characters—as the Jews did indeed share historically, in Spain, with the Muslims—their struggles with the choices of adaptation and conversion versus resistance or exile. Far less common are historical novels set in earlier moments in the very rich landscape that is the seven-hundred-some year history that begins in the

of history whose various dramas, like those of the French Revolu-
tion, seem to have already been written by a melodramatic novelist.
Nevertheless, in *Granada* she tells a story that is fresh in many ways,
and whose relevance to contemporary issues does not obtrusively
call attention to itself. In telling the story of an extended family on
this cusp of history she leaves no doubt about the unmitigated evils
that follow the revocation of rights at first granted to Muslims under
Christian rule, without, however, leaving us with characters who
are little more than mouthpieces for righteous ideology.

On the contrary, part of the genuine pathos of the novel—and I
strongly believe the historical as well as personal verisimilitude—lies
in the many different paths taken by the different members of the
family, and in the equal love the novelist has for these very different
children of her imagination. From those who became members of
the violent resistance in the Alpujarras (that mountainous region to
the southeast of Granada where Muslim refugees waged a ferocious
struggle for dozens of years, until they were finally, brutally, re-
pressed) to those who were not only willing to convert to Christianity, but even loath to give shelter, in the family house, to other
family members suspected by the Inquisition authorities, all of her
characters are first and foremost complex human beings and not
easily judged. Driven by different ways of expressing their love for
each other, for their culture, and for their children, these men and
women (and the women have center stage a great deal of the time,
as the enduring centers of a social world that is increasingly hidden
and domestic, and this too she shares with Ibn Hazm, whose love-
treatise is set inside the harem where he was brought up) struggle to
make the best decisions they can, when no decision seems quite
good enough, under the circumstances. So the matter of heroes and

---

middle of the eighth century, although two recent ones, both involving the more
positive story of the legendary religious tolerance and cultural admixtures of
caliphal Cordoba, are worth noting: *Journey to the End of the Millennium* by A. B.
Yehoshua and, in French, *Le calendrier de Cordue,* by Yves Ouahnon.

villains is largely left open-ended and the only exception to this
general human role is that of the handful of Castilian Christians
who appear in the story, who are almost invariably the villainous
and cartoonish heavies. But since this was in fact almost always offi-
cially and publicly the case, and since Ashour's few Christians here
are mostly public and not domestic figures, it is hard to quibble with
such a representation, although the extent to which ordinary Christians may not have shared the totalitarian program of the Church is
as vital to the genuine pathos of the history as the conversions to
Christianity by so many Muslims.[2]

But no matter: as with all genuine literature the ambiguities
seep out everywhere, and a part of the bittersweetness of this novel
certainly lies in the softly spoken understanding the reader has of
how many of these Muslims, and how much of their culture, will
indeed survive the crucible of this ghastly moment but transformed
into something quite different from what they were in Granada before 1492. What makes the novel gripping and enjoyable is that as it
progresses the characters are transformed by life in general—yes, of
course by the crises provoked, by the earth-shaking events of the
time, but no less—and sometimes far more—by the births of children and the deaths of fathers and mothers. And by the search for
love. In 1991, Salmon Rushdie published his own small but jewel-
like contribution to this body of imaginative literature, determined
to make us realize how close we all really are to 1492. In that story
Rushdie sums up peaks through the mouth of Columbus to sum up
these complex and often heart-breaking ties between our hearts and
history, the history that often seems to set a stage for us we have not
chosen and yet from which we cannot escape:" 'The search for

2. A forthcoming study, based on a detailed study of the extensive Inquisition
archives by Yale historian Stuart Schwartz and entitled "Each in His Own Law: Salvation, Repression and Popular Toleration in the Luso-Hispanic World,
1492–1700," will reveal the extent to which the harsh and devastatingly destructive
intolerance of 15th and 16th century Spain was neither understood nor shared by
many of the "Old Christians" of Spain.

money and patronage,' Columbus says in Rushdie's novel, " 'is not so different from the quest for love.' " And later: " 'The loss of money and patronage,' "Columbus says, " 'is as bitter as unrequited love.' " [3]

Ultimately, Ashour's Granada is as touching a historical novel as it is not because she has got the history right and is able to interweave its interesting details into her narrative although she does just that, and readers will profit from and perhaps be amused by her judicious and accurate revelations about everything from the original terms of the capitulation of Granada (which granted religious and cultural freedoms to the Muslims, but were soon revoked) to the first items and people brought from the New World and paraded through the roadways of Andalucia. Rather, it works because it is written from the heart, and about the heart, and the novelist does not thus condescend to her characters, who are no more heroic nor less frail because of the historical stage on which they played out their lives. And we understand that there is much life to follow at the end, that because *Granada* was not about the stone city of its title but about a flesh-and-blood family who lived there, that history lies in the hands of their children: some born and others not yet, some who will be expelled in 1608 with the rest of the "Moriscos" and go to Arab and Ottoman lands (but always keep their iconic keys to homes in cities like Valencia); others who will remain in Spain, as first and second and third generation New Christians, intermarried, and ultimately seamlessly interwoven into Spanish culture; and yet others will emigrate to the New World, as one from the pivotal generation here already has, one of the young men whose coming of age from early adolescence through mature manhood provides the backbone of the narrative. The success of this novel's marriage

3. "Christopher Columbus and Queen Isabella of Spain Consummate Their Relationship, Santa Fé, January 1492," was first published in the *New Yorker* of June 17, 1991. It was Rushdie's first published work of fiction after the fatwa forced him into exile.

of the public and the personal is such that we finish the book convinced that the children of these characters will not only continue
the family saga, but be the protagonists in the historical dramas yet
to come, dramas that one generation after another, lead to us.

MARIA ROSA MENOCAL

Translator's Acknowledgments

I wish to thank Radwa Ashour for her encouragement and support for my translation of *Granada,* as well as for her many suggestions and explications. Also, a profusion of gratitude to Ayman El-Desouky and Sinan Antoon, who graciously read the text over and over and made important contributions to the polished version. In addition, I wish to thank Shawkat Toorawa, Ariel Blumenthal, Jonathan Smolin, and Laila Parsons for their input, and Michael Beard and Marilyn Booth for their expertise and support. To Maria Rosa Menocal a special thanks for her magnificent foreword, and finally to Mary Selden Evans of Syracuse University Press a symphony of praises for her wisdom, understanding, counsel, and good humor.

W. G.

Granada

I

At the crack of dawn one day Abu Jaafar saw a naked woman walking down the hill and in his direction, as though she were coming deliberately to meet him. The closer she got to him the more convinced he became that she was neither impudent nor inebriated. She was a young woman of extraordinary beauty, slender and graceful, with breasts like small, smooth, perfectly shaped ivory vases. Her jet black hair cascaded over her shoulders, and a sadness made her wide eyes seem even wider on her intensely gaunt, pallid face.

The streets were still empty, the shops had not opened, and the light of day had not yet dissolved the violet haze of the early dawn. Abu Jaafar first thought that what he was seeing was a mere figment of his imagination. He then peered more closely, and he came to grips with his own utter amazement. He went toward the woman, took off his woolen cloak, and wrapped it around her body. He asked her her name and where she lived, but it seemed as though she could neither see nor hear him. He left her to continue on her way, and he watched her from behind as she walked on slowly, his eyes fixed on the jingling gold spangles that wrapped around her ankles caked with the mud of a road her two feet had been treading.

In spite of the wintry chill and the howling winds that shook the walnut trees lining both sides of the road, Abu Jaafar remained standing by the door of his shop until the sun released its pale yellow rays and exposed the street's prominent features.

Inside the shop he exchanged a few words with Naeem and then went to a corner where he sat quietly. The boy couldn't help but notice his patron's silence, and he responded by suppressing his usual noisiness, as he began the day's work with a desire to do a good job to please his patron and with a genuine concern for him, making Naeem sneak a peek at him every now and then.

"What's your name, my boy?"

The man was very tall and somewhat frightening, looking no different from all those older men who intimidated him, who would no sooner stop him on the street than he would leap away like a scared jackrabbit. He lifted his gaze and glanced up over his towering body until he came to the eyes, blue and peaceful. He didn't rush, and he answered in a soft voice: "Naeem."

"Where is your family, Naeem?"

"They went away, or they died. I don't know."

Abu Jaafar stretched out his enormous hand and took hold of the boy's hand, and the boy followed with the longest strides his two young feet allowed him to take in order to keep pace.

Abu Jaafar fed him, gave him shelter, and began to teach him all the tricks of his trade. He trained him in tanning and drying goat hides for binding. He taught him how to arrange the pages of a manuscript and bind them together. He allowed him to undertake every task save a couple he preferred to do himself. He instructed Naeem to follow him closely so that he could learn: to thread the twine into the awl, and slowly and carefully pass the awl and thread through the spine of the book, once, twice, a third and fourth time, back and forth until the stitching was tight; then he let him attach the spine to the cover and place the book under a press. Several days later, he would remove the book from underneath the press and Abu Jaafar would write the title and the name of the author, as well as the owner of the manuscript, in gold ink or something else that may have been requested. Finally, he would engrave the cover with intricate patterns.

Naeem became consumed by a desire to do all of that by himself, and when he persisted, Abu Jaafar handed him a piece of paper, smiling: "Here, write the opening chapter of the Quran on this." He felt as though he had backed himself into a corner because his penmanship was as crooked as a long and winding mountain pass.

"Are you feeling ill, Abu Jaafar?"

Abu Jaafar didn't respond, nor did he look in Naeem's direction. He remained with his head bent down and his eyes lost in distraction. The day went on and the phantom of the young woman remained fixed in his mind. He was disturbed and saddened by it, but it was not until the following day when he heard the news of the meeting at the Alhambra that a foreboding unease took possession of him. Rumors were circulating about Ibn Abi Ghassan's drowning in the River Genil. Could the naked woman then be a credible sign, he wondered, like a vision or an omen?

His pessimism grew steadily and entrenched itself deep in his heart when Naeem told him several days later the story of a woman whose naked corpse had been found drifting on the river.

"Was it the Darro or the Genil?"

"The Genil."

"Then there's no escape."

Naeem stared at him inquisitively, but Abu Jaafar remained silent, explaining nothing of what he had just said. The river's currents had swallowed up the last hope. The cord of the nation was severed and God's children have been orphaned.

For three nights neither Granada nor Albaicin slept.[1] The people talked incessantly not of the peace treaty but of the disappearance of Mousa Ibn Abi Ghassan. They were swallowed up by rumors that swept in waves from the River Genil to the Ainadamar watercourse,[2] from the Najd Gate to the Sahl Ibn Malik cemetery. The news seeped onto the streets and throughout every neighborhood, as well as into all the public gardens. The waters of the Genil

1. Albaicin is a suburb of Granada where the Muslims resided in the post-Reconquest. Its origin is most likely from the Arabic, *al-Bayyazin,* the falconers.

2. The Fuente Grande, known to the Muslims as Ainadamar, from the Arabic *'ayn al-dam',* the fountain of tears.

carried it from the outskirts of the city and brought it into the Darro where it crossed over to the west bank. From there it traveled to Sabika, Alhambra, and the Generalife. It reached the end of the east bank that connected to the old Casbah and Albaicin. It extended beyond the walls and gates of the city, past the towers and the fences of the vineyards, toward the Sierra Nevada from one side, and toward the Gibralfaro to the other.

Some claimed that Mousa Ibn Abi Ghassan had stormed out of the meeting at Alhambra resolved to fight the Castilians. He battled their troops single-handedly, but when they caught up with him and were on the verge of defeating him, he threw himself into the river. Others said that he was killed by the young King Muhammad who wanted to accomplish his goals without any conflict or opposition. The ill-fated *chiquito* handed over the country and sold whatever he could of it while Ibn Abi Ghassan lay in wait for him.

A third group believed that he neither drowned himself nor was killed, but rather that he escaped to the mountains to train men and prepare for battle. And yet a fourth group held the view that drowning or not drowning made no difference whatsoever, but that these were not his times, nor ours. So, why don't we either carry off what we can of our possessions and depart, they thought, or remain as Muslims, entrusting ourselves to God and the new rulers, and live out the remainder of our lives in peace.

How could this be? This question was like a sharp knife that made a deep incision in Abu Jaafar's soul, and like everyone else it made him wary just to think about it, let alone discuss it with others. He was pondering this question when the town crier passed by, announcing the articles of the new agreement. He walked out toward him until he stood right next to him. Abu Jaafar listened carefully to all the terms of the agreement, beginning with the decree that the king of Granada, his military officers, the judges and chamberlains, scholars and lawyers, as well as all other public officials, turn over the reins of power in a period not to exceed sixty days. Then the last term was read out, which decreed that King Ferdinand and Queen Isabella be granted the exclusive right to execute the terms of the treaty, and to pass this right on to their sons and grandsons and whomever succeeded them to the throne. When the town crier moved on to another place Abu Jaafar remained close behind.

The people of Granada always kept their ears to the ground and were prone to gathering as much information as possible. Whenever the town crier announced an item of news, or the imam at the mosque ascended the pulpit before the Friday prayer to expound upon a given subject, whether to explain or defend it, they listened out of a need for reassurance or for something to hold on to, and they were quick to fill the gaps left by any missing information from these public pronouncements. But this time, in spite of the fact that neither the town crier nor the imam announced anything concerning the Alhambra meeting, Abu Jaafar, like everyone else, knew what had transpired there:

Abu Qasim Ibn Abdel-Malik and Yusuf Ibn Kumasha, the two ministers appointed by the king to negotiate, entered the Grand Hall in the company of De Safra, the representative of the king of Aragon and the queen of Castile. All three carried copies of the treaty to read. The young king Abu 'Abdallah Muhammad sobbed,[3] lamenting the fact that he was ill-fated to be a king condemned to witness the fall of his realm. All the other ministers, the admirals and generals, and the religious leaders, wept in silence as they chanted over and over again, "There is no power or strength save in God," and "There is no escape from what God has decreed." Mousa Ibn Abi Ghassan objected vehemently to the agreement and demanded that those in attendance reject it outright. But when he found no one to support him, he stormed out of the castle in a fit of anger, mounted his horse, and disappeared. The attendees repeated, "There is no escape from what God has decreed," and assured themselves that the conditions of the treaty were the best that they could attain. As tears flowed from their eyes, they signed.

3. Abu 'Abdallah b. Muhammad, best known in the west as Boabdil, was the last Muslim ruler in Spain.

Abu Jaafar wondered how a king could commit himself to surrender his kingdom, and how the military and legal authorities of the land, along with all its lawful citizens, could acquiesce to hand over, in abject obedience, the Alhambra citadel, the fortress town and its towers, as well as the city gates of Granada and Albaicin, including the adjacent villages.

He walked behind the town crier who was surrounded by a dense mob of townspeople. People avoided looking at one another in the eye, and they tilted their heads to hide their broken reflections and trembling eyelids. They walked with their arms closely held to their sides. They moved their heavy feet slowly, in an atmosphere of silence eerily reinforced by the ringing voice of the town crier and the rustling of dry, yellow leaves.

When the town crier went away and the crowd dissipated, Abu Jaafar found himself walking alone in the cold of night, not heading toward any particular place, but just letting his two feet wander through the streets that they knew only too well. He was telling himself that this ill-fated king was not their first and wouldn't be their last, and that Abu Abdallah would go away and that no one else, ill-fated or not, would replace him except Christian kings. His insides convulsed at this thought and he quickly dismissed it from his mind, closing the door on it, and replacing it with concise facts and logical reasoning. Everything changes except the face of Almighty God. Hadn't Sultan Yusuf al-Mul concluded a more humiliating treaty with the Castilians, and hadn't Sultan Aysar then come along, abrogated it, and declared war on them? And hadn't Sultan Abu Hasan at first agreed to pay the poll tax, then reneged when he dispatched his enemies to inform the king and queen of Castile that our treasuries would only be minting swords these days? And that ill-fated pubescent, didn't he begin his rule by fighting them until he was captured? Who knows what will happen tomorrow? He's not the first of them, nor the last. They've all come and gone, may Granada remain safe and sound, with God's permission and will, he intoned.

Abu Jaafar was making every effort to calm his soul, which felt at that moment like a caged bird flapping its wings in fear of a sharp pointed knife. He was telling himself over and over again that Granada was safe and that it would survive. He jammed his mind with words, and extended his hand through the netting to his soul, stroking its wet feathers and its quivering body, soothing and caressing it, singing to it a soft lullaby to rock it to sleep.

The morning sun was changing direction above the streets until it eventually disappeared. Abu Jaafar continued his walk until he found himself at the bank of the River Genil. He stared into its waters and the phantom of the naked woman appeared as though coming out of the water toward him. He fixed his gaze more closely, and this time could only see the ripples of the water. Then she reappeared on the surface of the water, ivory-like, growing bigger in death, until she covered the entire surface of the river. He stood motionless and began to sweat profusely.

2

bu Mansour was sitting on the proprietor's bench in the bathhouse to the right of the front door. He mumbled a response to the two men's greetings, then pointed to the closet where they kept the clean folded towels. Saad took three towels and followed his master up three steps that lead to the western wing, where he helped him take off his clothes and cover up his nakedness with a loincloth he wrapped around his waist. He carefully folded his master's clothes and placed them in a large silk garment bag. Then he took off his own clothes except for his drawers and put them into an old sack. He handed both bundles to Abu Mansour who kept his head bowed down and said nothing.

Before entering the bath proper, the master went into the toilet while Saad sat waiting on one of the benches. There were only three other men in the central foyer. Two of them sat on a bench opposite Saad, while the third, a tall, lean man, paced back and forth, crossing the large foyer from the front door to the back door.

Saad was wondering what was wrong with Abu Mansour. He wanted to know if he was sick but didn't dare ask. It wasn't like him to sit at the entrance to the bathhouse like all the other bathhouse owners. He would rather have one of his employees sit there and take the customers' belongings while he would skitter about, shuffling hurriedly from one room to another, bringing soap to a client or a basin to another, or perhaps a loincloth or a towel to whomever asked for one. He would stop to tell an amusing story or crack a joke that would make everyone roar with laughter. He was a portly man in his fifties, or maybe even his forties. He had a ruddy complexion, finely chiseled features, and a smooth, sleek beard. He had a small head and a big paunch that jounced whenever he laughed. But today, he just sat there, sullen-faced, greeting no one and saying nothing.

"Who could be absolutely sure? Who?" Saad looked up and saw the tall thin man passing in front of him, pacing back and forth muttering these words to himself. As he walked he raised his shoulders so high that they almost reached his ears. One of the two men sitting down yelled out to him, "You're making us dizzy. Why don't you calm down and sit like everyone else?" But the man paid no attention and kept pacing and muttering to himself.

The inside room of the bathhouse was packed with clients. Some were seated on the tile bench next to the furnace sweating in the thick steam; others went into the pool to purify themselves before bathing. There were men lying down, on their stomachs and on their backs, submitting themselves to a servant or a bath attendant who busily groomed them, massaged them, or simply poured hot water over their heads. All of the men were engaged in some kind of conversation as their voices cut across both ends of the bath. Even those in the private rooms for hair-removal contributed to the banter from behind a curtain that shielded the others from their stark nakedness. Saad and his master sat cross-legged in their usual spot next to one of the water heaters. His master stretched out his arms while Saad poured water and lathered the washcloth, then he began to scrub his right hand and arm, then the underarm, before moving over to the left. Someone yelled out: "Abu Jaafar, may God be pleased with you! We don't have the privilege of choosing one thing or another. It's our fate! We're defeated, so how can we choose?"

Another bather interrupted. "I'm with you! The agreement is evil, there's no doubt about it. Our leader was in a difficult situation, and the resistance that Ibn Abi Ghassan wanted to launch was doomed from the start. So what could he do, and what can we do in the face of their awesome army and their new Italian artillery?"

"We can fight them. I swear by the God of the Kaaba,[1] we can fight them," responded Abu Jaafar.

Saad was following the conversation, straining to listen since he wasn't able to see who was speaking because he was seated facing his master, and all that was in his view was the wall and the water heater to his left.

"Why should we fight them? Aren't ten years of war enough? Do you want us to end up like the people of Malaga eating our own mules and the leaves off the trees?"

"After submission, they'll teach us a lesson we'll never forget. The treaty is nothing but a worthless piece of paper. If we surrender Granada to them, they'll force us to drop to our knees whenever a clerical procession passes by. They'll force us to live in separate quarters with only one gate, and they'll put the sword of expulsion to our throats. What will prevent them from doing all of this once they take control of our country?"

The master stretched out on his back while Saad worked on his knees. He massaged his upper body, stomach, and legs before the master turned over and Saad massaged his back.

"Surrender will prevent them from doing any further damage to us, and it will allow us to maintain some of our rights."

"How so?"

Other voices followed in repetition, in piercing tones that came close to screeching. The master pulled away his hand and sat upright.

"The treaty stipulates that we be treated honorably, and that our religion, customs, and traditions be respected, and that we be free to buy and sell, and that we preserve our rights to our property, our arms and horses, and that we have legal recourse to our judges in arbitrating matters of dispute. Even our prisoners shall be returned to us, pardoned and free."

"Merely ink on paper," retorted Abu Jaafar.

Saad went back to work grooming his master, and when he fin-

1. The Kaaba, a place of veneration at the Grand Mosque in Mecca.

ished he stretched out his hand to show him the dirt stains that came from his body, the living proof that Saad had done a thorough job in scrubbing him clean. Saad then took the basin and ladled out hot water and poured it over his master's head as he soaped and rinsed.

"If we reject the treaty and hold our ground, then help will come to us from the shores of North Africa, from Egypt, and even from the Ottoman Turks."

"Nothing of the sort will come!"

"Never! They won't leave us alone to defend ourselves."

"I agree with Abu Jaafar, and Ibn Abi Ghassan did not die as the gossip-mongers are claiming. The Castilians will not have their way. We will stand up to them while Ibn Abi Ghassan's men are breathing down their backs. The Egyptian, North African, and Ottoman fleets have them blockaded, and their only way out is to die."

The master motioned him to stop pouring the hot water on his head, and he continued to speak, enunciating every word with the utmost emphasis. "Granada has fallen, there's no doubt about it. Ibn Abi Ghassan was a fool who wanted us to plunge into a battle we couldn't sustain. Thank God he's dead! And now we can relax and he can rest in peace."

Saad was at a loss as to what happened next when his master suddenly jumped up and hurriedly dashed away. He looked around and in a flash caught sight of Abu Mansour with a thick stick in his hand and running amok. When had Abu Mansour come inside the bath, he wondered, and where did the stick come from? All he could think was, What happened? Abu Mansour was howling one threat after another.

"Ibn Abi Ghassan's riding mule is more honorable than you and a thousand like you put together, you dog, you son of a dog!"

The master's loincloth fell off as he ran away, terrified of the stick Abu Mansour was brandishing as he chased him. Abu Mansour then screamed out, "It's your mother who has fallen, not Granada, you raven of evil omen. Get out of my bathhouse or I'll kill you."

The bathers all jumped up and stood between Abu Mansour and the man he was about to strike. Men from inside the baths poured out naked as the day they were born, and those sitting or resting on the benches lost their towels in their forward rush to see what was happening. Saad stood there frozen in a state of shock, aware that he should go and help his master but unable to move a muscle, as though his feet were plastered to the floor.

His mind drifted. To wander aimlessly about in the daytime and greet the night sitting in the corner of a mosque reeling from the pangs of hunger that only sleep could relieve, wrapped in a coarse woolen cloak, what's new about that?

That was not the first time Saad found himself without any source of sustenance, as he thought about the days when his future appeared to him like a winter morning enveloped in a thick fog in which you could hardly see your own footsteps. Those days he used to ruminate over his past, the distant past when the branch grew freely, and the not-so-distant past when it was snapped off the tree, blown about by the stormy winds. And the more he tried to recall what had happened, the more the details came back to him, ones that had slipped his mind. He was astonished that he could forget, but more astonished that these memories came back to him with a sudden new clarity, and after thinking about it somewhat, he became certain that nothing was lost, that the human mind was a wondrous treasure chest, and that however deeply lodged in the head, it preserved things that couldn't be counted or weighed: the scent of the sea, his mother's face, pale shafts of sun that filtered through the green vine leaves moistened by drops of rain, threads of silk on his father's loom, his grandfather's hacking morning cough, the laugh of the little girl, the taste of a fresh green almond, a broken jar seeping olive oil, or a solitary rosary bead that had rolled behind the chest of drawers where he used to hide.

After three days of looking for work and sleeping at night in the mosque, Saad thought of asking Abu Mansour for help. "I left my master, or rather he fired me. I'm looking for work."

"Do you know the Paper Makers' Quarter?"

"Yes, I know it."

"Go there and ask for Abu Jaafar's shop. Tell him I'm the one who sent you. If he can't find you any work, come back to me."

Abu Jaafar spoke to Saad while he worked: "You should observe closely everything Naeem and I do. God willing, you'll learn quickly. Can you read and write?"

"No."

"That's another problem we'll have to deal with. Naeem, come over here. This is Saad who comes to us from Malaga. He's going to be working with you. You have to help him. I trust you're a good teacher?"

Naeem smiled, proud of the confidence his patron bestowed on him in assigning him such a task. However, Saad wasn't so happy, as he saw in Naeem a boy with a frail body and hazel eyes that glistened with sparks of shrewdness. Although no older than thirteen, Saad felt as though he were a man. Hadn't his body developed and his voice dropped, and the lines of his mustache grown in? What could this pale, mousy kid possibly teach him?

That evening Saad's feelings toward Naeem were reinforced and his annoyance with him increased. He was a chatterbox who went on endlessly about nothing and everything. He asked him about Malaga, about his father and mother, how he came to Granada all by himself, why he hadn't stayed with them, and where did he work before coming to Abu Jaafar. He never tired of asking questions, and Saad had no desire to reveal anything to him, so he responded with terse, evasive answers.

When Naeem realized he was getting nowhere with Saad, he began to talk about himself. He told him that he didn't know or remember his parents. In fact, the only person he remembers is the old woman who raised him, and when she died he had nothing but the streets, that is, until he met Abu Jaafar. "You know, Saad, I'm not afraid of roaming the streets at night, nor of stray dogs, nor of the head of the city police who struts about with his protruding belly like a sack of flour. Nor do I fear the evil spirits. What I do fear, though, is Abu Jaafar falling ill or something bad happening to him."

As Naeem spoke a look of sadness suddenly appeared on his face. Moments of silence passed before he continued to talk. "Abu Jaafar took me off the streets and brought me into his home. He asked his wife Umm Jaafar to bathe me. As soon as she poured the hot water over my head, I screamed at the top of my lungs and leaped away with every intention of leaving that house. But she was able to grab hold of me, and then she squatted on the floor and forced me to sit down. She wrapped her left arm around my chest and her two legs around my waist, and the only thing I could do was holler for help. The more I raised my voice, the more she scrubbed my body harder and harder, until I thought I was going to die right in front of her! She spent the whole day washing me."

"The whole day?"

"Well, that's what it seemed like at the time," laughed Naeem.

3

The muezzin had not yet called out the early morning prayer nor had the neighbor's rooster screeched its first crow when one of Alhambra's guards, whose services were recently terminated, came running out onto the streets, shouting out words that seemed to have no logical connection, some of them clear and others totally incomprehensible. Through his high-pitched screaming you could finally make out that he was saying that the Christian troops would be entering Alhambra today to receive its keys. Abu Jaafar woke up and counted the days, first in his head and then with his fingers, and added up thirty-seven. He sat up in bed. He heard the rooster's crow, once, twice, and then a third time. The muezzin then called out the prayer. The day began and the hours passed. The voice that awakened Abu Jaafar awakened Saad as well. He sat up despondently in the darkness of the shop, not knowing whether what he heard was a dream or real. He stood up, put on his shoes, wrapped himself in his cloak, and went out into the street.

Saad followed the winding alleys that lead toward the Gate of the Flour Merchants. As he passed it the red hill loomed before him, blurred by the purple haze of the early morning. The castles above it stood erect, protected by walls and towers. Perhaps it was all a nightmare. He reached the Judges' Bridge and crossed over to the other side of the river, then came back and crossed the bridge once again and headed in the direction of Albaicin. He stared into the river. The Darro flowed in God's protection, and the fig tree from which he ate fresh fruit only a few months ago was as it always was, still standing. Its branches had shed their leaves but were still intact. He looked up at the top of the road, which was still deserted. He headed toward Steamroller's Bridge and sat on a stone bench by the bank of the river. He waited. He saw the horizon from beyond the castles changing colors with the rosy hue of morning, a misty purple tinged with the blueness of early dawn. Then it lit up in full violet. The sun was about to rise, and when it did, it did so in utter silence, made more glorious by the chirping of the many species of birds. The day broke, and Alhambra came into full view in all its splendid detail: the sharply honed impenetrable walls; the lofty towers; the imposing palaces; the palm and cypress trees, luxuriant and majestic. He was about to turn back and make his way to the shop when he heard a sound in the distance. He pricked up his ears. He was sure he heard something. The sound was distant but it was getting closer. Soon, he was able to decipher the din of beating drums, the blowing of bugles, and the ringing of gunfire. Are they coming to take over Alhambra? Are they advancing from the direction of the east where they can't be seen? Is what the guard said true? He stood there petrified as his eyes followed the rays of the sun. The sound of the music was becoming more distinct, louder, and it kept pace with the rhythm of his beating heart. In spite of the bitter cold, a hot flash raced through his body.

As midmorning approached, Saad saw Castilian soldiers raising a large silver cross on top of the watchtower. When they succeeded in setting it firmly in place, they hoisted the Castilian flag and the banner of Santiago. They shouted out something in a strange language from which he could only make out the names of Ferdinand and Isabella. They repeated it three times, and then cannons roared in the air.

Waiting no longer, Saad took off like a crazy man up the Albaicin hill. When he reached the neighborhood he hollered as loud as he could from the street: "They've entered Alhambra! I saw them! I heard them! Citizens of Albaicin, I saw them, I heard them."

The streets were empty, not a soul, nor a donkey or bird in sight. The doors were sealed shut like coffins as he raced through

the streets shouting. When he found himself at the shop, he removed his cloak and shoes, and he sat down and burst into tears.

Saad's sobbing surprised Naeem who stood up, bewildered, not
knowing what to say or do. He moved about, stumbling, as he
looked for a pitcher of water to give his mate something to drink.

"What happened, Saad? Why are you crying?"

Saad couldn't stop his weeping, and the only thing that Naeem
could do was to turn back and look for the water. He filled a basin
and carried it over to his friend. He wiped his face gently, and then
he knelt down and began to wash his muddy feet that were bleeding
from the rocks and thistles.

Abu Jaafar spent the day in his bedroom, sitting and standing, pacing between the four walls. Had he been wrong, like all the citizens
of Albaicin, to help Abu Abdallah take control of the country? They
came to his assistance and engaged in skirmishes with the Granadans
on account of that miserable pubescent. At the time the young man
appeared to be neither a scoundrel nor an evil omen, but rather a ray
of hope who would save them from the abuses of his father, who
was up to his ears in vice. They sided with the son of La Horra,[1] and
slammed the gates of Albaicin in the face of his tyrant father who
pulled out from the walls of the city, defeated and dethroned. Did
they commit a serious error in siding with a prince who was
wronged, they being wronged themselves? Did they err in holding
a just prince to a promise? So what befell the young prince? Was it
his capture in the hands of the Castilians that destroyed him? Did
defeat defeat him, or is it merely preordained on the Preserved
Tablet?[2] Does God jot down on His tablet the defeat of His pious

1. The mother of Boabdil was commonly referred to as *al-Hurra,* the free
woman.

2. The preserved tablet, *al-lawh al-mahfuz,* is believed in Islam to be the ultimate and complete word of God.

servants? It's too late for help. It's too late. But it will come from our people in Egypt, Syria, and North Africa. They will come, by the command and will of God . . . But what if they don't?

Abu Jaafar looked out from a small opening in the wall to the sky. There's no earth without a heaven. O, Wisest of rulers, Lord of the highest skies, O Promise of truth, O God.

As daylight came to an end and everything grew quiet, night-time fell and settled in, and the people remained in their homes, depressed. Just as no one ventured out to work that day, no one took to his bed that night. Silence had imposed itself on the city, and silent it remained day and night. Yet no one slept, not even little Hasan who had been spanked by his mother for reasons he could not understand. He had gone out into the alley to play with his friends, but finding no one, he went to see the two little brothers who lived nearby. Their mother insisted they all play indoors. Unaware of his going out or of his absence, Hasan's mother panicked when she realized he was gone. She looked for him on all the streets and alleys of the quarter. When he finally came home she walloped him severely. The little boy cried and yelled out for help to his grandmother who rushed over and pulled him away from his mother as she scolded him hysterically. Hasan spent the rest of the day curled up in a corner of the house. He refused to play with his sister Saleema and sat sulking silently in his corner, wiping the tears from his eyes and the mucous from his nose with the sleeve of his shirt.

What had gotten into his mother? he wondered. Has she gone stark raving mad like the crazy man who lives over in the next lane and who makes the kids shudder in fear and run away? She had never laid a hand on him, even when he broke a vase or lost money. This time she gave him a good thrashing and for no apparent reason! When his grandmother pulled him away, his mother just stood there sobbing. He was afraid of her and for her at the same time. He was crying because she hit him and because she was crying herself. His grandmother wiped his eyes and gave him a piece of candy. "The Castilians came into Granada today. Your mother got scared.

She thought they kidnapped you to sell you in the market." Had Hasan heard such a thing at any other time he would have laughed at the very idea of selling children in the market like donkeys. Did she honestly think he was a donkey?

When his grandmother called him for supper he didn't respond, and when she didn't call him again, he retreated to his bed where he lay wide awake thinking about his mother's odd behavior, and his grandfather's as well. While his mother was sobbing and spanking him and he was yelling at the top of his lungs, Abu Jaafar was inside the house, but he didn't budge at all, as though he hadn't heard a sound. What was going on with his family today? he wondered.

Hasan never found the answer to his question, neither that night nor the many that followed. Even when he turned seven years old and his grandfather took him to a faqeeh for his schooling, the memory of that night remained a mystery to him. He learned that it had been a sad day indeed for all Granadans and that the Castilians took women, children, and men as well from the neighboring villages and sold them as slaves. But he still couldn't understand why his mother had spanked him so harshly, nor could he understand how one man could sell another man, or a child or a woman. Nor did he see anything especially frightening about the Castilian soldiers. They were just like any other men with nothing to distinguish them from the Arabs except for their fairer complexions and their spectacular uniforms, with their waistline jackets, form-fitting trousers, and feathered caps. They looked especially grand when they mounted their horses and trotted in parades with colorful banners, while some men beat drums and others blew bugles, and the streets were as festive as a holiday. So, what was all the sadness that surrounded their entrance into the city?

4

Had the people of Granada been bestowed with the gift of predicting the future, would the few years that followed the loss of their country appear as the ultimate extent of degradation and defeat? They lived the misery of each day, made no easier by what was decreed in the new Treaty of Capitulation, which was supposed to guarantee their right to worship and trade, and to live their lives as they saw fit. Nor was this misery at all alleviated by the fact that their new governor, Count Tendilla, ruled with a velvet glove and that the archbishop of Granada, De Talavera, exerted considerable effort, in spite of his advanced years, to make contact with them, even going so far as to learn Arabic and instruct his missionaries to follow suit. But occupation was nonetheless occupation, and the Granadans were burdened with even more worries that hovered over them like the huge silver cross that hung above the towers of Alhambra.

The secret matter of the treaty concluded by Abu Abdallah Muhammad and the king and queen of Castile and Aragon was soon exposed, and the news spread like wildfire far and wide. The young prince turned over the keys of Alhambra and was compensated thirty thousand Castilian pounds, along with the right to maintain in perpetuity ownership of his personal castles and farmlands, as well as all other family possessions. "The scoundrel got eternal rights to his own property and ran," people said.

They lived the misery of each day with the bitter discovery that they had been sold like chattel. They witnessed the flight of entire families among the nobility and elite, who, in a state of utter chaos and panic, sold everything they owned, and undoubtedly everything was bought. Houses, estates, orchards, precious manuscripts, and swords, heirlooms of their grandfathers and great grandfathers. "Buy, Abu Jaafar, the price is right and buying is profitable." But Abu Jaafar was as stubborn as a mule, and he didn't want to buy nor sell. He was furious at the sight of the departing ships that he viewed as nothing more than floating coffins.

The Granadans watched as their princes converted to Christianity. Saad and Nasr, the sons of Sultan Abu Hasan, now called themselves Duke Fernando de Granada and Duke Juan de Granada. Saad went even one step further by joining the Castilian army as an ordinary conscript. "Rest in peace in your grave, Abu Hasan," thought Abu Jaafar. "Sleep content, and may the breezes of Paradise blow over you. Your offspring have been leased in a rare business. They've certainly risen to the occasion!" The vizier, Yusuf Ibn Kumasha, who negotiated in the name of the nation and who prepared both the secret and public texts of the treaty, crowned his achievements by converting to Christianity and entering a monastery.

Abu Jaafar, now in his seventies, was becoming more taciturn as he shielded from those closest to him the inner turmoil he was suffering. He barely slept, and when he did it was never more than an hour or two. He would sit up and at the first crack of dawn leave the house and pace around the quarter until its doors were opened. At the moment when they did, he would leave.

He walked down to the bank of the Darro and strolled along the river, enjoying the Sabika and the fortresses and castles of Alhambra. He delighted in the many species of trees that sprouted up along the river, from the cypresses, palms, and pines at the foot of the hills across the river, to the fig, olive, pomegranate, walnut, and chestnut trees that graced the road that lead to Albaicin. He passed by and inspected each tree closely and then gazed at the river. When he came to the Grand Mosque, the river appeared in full view and picture-perfect. Then, looking over to the open square, he didn't fail to notice the relentless hustle and bustle of buying and selling and the familiar voices that called out their wares. He continued his walk and headed east until he reached the Jewish Quarter and the Najd Gate, then retraced his steps back to the marketplace, passing by the Alley of the Druggists, on to the Potters, the Glass Makers, and then to the covered market where he walked through every single passageway, running his fingers through the cottons, wools, and silks, both raw and embroidered, while the merchants were busy measuring and weighing, buying and selling, on the cuff or haggling. When he left the covered market and cut across Zacatin Street, he found himself once again at the Grand Mosque. He went in, performed his ritual ablutions, completed the four prostrations required of the midday prayer, and two extra ones in observance of the Prophet's custom, before returning to his shop in the Paper Makers' Quarter.

On another day he would either follow exactly the same route, or he would begin by paying a visit to his son and his parents at the Sahl Ibn Malik Cemetery. He would recite the opening chapter of the Quran, and then cross one end of the quarter to the other to visit the Potters' Cemetery and speak with a friend of his who was buried there. Abu Jaafar always kept a vigilant eye on Granada's buildings, its schools, mosques, hospices, shrines, and public gardens, as though he had been commissioned to draw detailed sketches of them. He would leave the house and come back without talking to a soul, and when it was absolutely necessary to do so, he said only what had to be said.

There wasn't much work in the shop since business became scarce with people emigrating, and those who remained couldn't afford the luxury of even thinking about binding expensive manuscripts. His wife blamed his silence on their financial difficulties and tried to help solve their problems, but every time she raised the subject, he cut her off.

"Sell the house at Ainadamar."

"It belongs to Hasan. I bequeathed it to his father, and now it's his to inherit."

"What about the manuscripts?"

"Those must remain for Hasan and Saleema. It's all I have left to give them."

"You could let Saad and Naeem go."

"They don't deserve that. Besides, shall I throw them out into the streets?"

"There's really no need to send the children to school."

"Saleema loves to learn, and Hasan has to!" Abu Jaafar acted as though the situation was under control and that nothing at all had changed.

"How will we manage, Abu Jaafar?"

"I've got little left of this life, so let me do as I please."

The anxieties that gnawed away at the hearts of the adults and sent many of them to an early grave had little effect on the young men who sprouted to maturity with hearts palpitating in the presence of young girls with kohl-lined eyes and safely concealed firm young breasts that toyed with their steaming imaginations.

Saad and Naeem laughed whenever they reminisced about the time they first met, when Saad would say that Naeem was arrogant for someone who had the size and color of a mouse, while Naeem complained that Abu Jaafar inflicted on him an insufferable, ill-tempered coworker. They were no longer merely colleagues who spent their young lives sharing a room in the same shop where they worked, but intimate friends who knew each other's life story as if it were their own. They were never apart, and the inhabitants of the Paper Makers' Quarter referred to them as "two fannies in one pair of drawers." [1] They were always seen together in their comings and goings, dressed in the same clothes that they shared, although Saad's clothes always seemed a bit too baggy for Naeem and Naeem's a tad tight for Saad. Saad was a year older than Naeem. He had an olive

1. This is the literal translation of an Arabic expression that is the functional equivalent of "two peas in a pod."

complexion and a smooth face with a sullen and stern look. He
grew a mustache that camouflaged his big nose and thick lips. His
big black eyes that used to arouse attention only a few years ago now
appeared less conspicuous as his eyebrows grew thicker. But that
was the most distinguished feature of his face, the depth of his black
eyes and a sullen, gaunt look that eclipsed his other features. He was
of medium height and build with broad shoulders. Naeem was
much thinner than his friend although they were practically the
same height. He had a complexion that bordered on the yellowish,
with finer features and silky, chestnut hair. There was a faint shadow
of blond fuzz above his upper lip that he longed to see fully grown,
but that hadn't yet. His soft features and his honey-colored eyes that
sparkled with a gleam of intelligence added sweetness and elegance
to his face.

Naeem still looked like a young boy although he was now fourteen. And besides, he was one who fell in love easily, head over heels,
living in a world of perpetual passion. He would see a girl whose
beauty captivated him and his heart would beat a mile a minute. His
face would beam, and like a madman he would inquire about her
name, family, and where she lived. His feet would drag him each day
to her neighborhood in the hopes of getting a glimpse of her. He
would repeat her name and write it on a small amulet he kept
around his neck for two, three, or four weeks, until another object
of his affection would take her place in his heart and in his amulet.

Saad laughed and made fun of Naeem, which angered him, and
they would end up quarreling practically all day long. But at night,
when they closed the door of the shop, Naeem longed to stop his
bickering and confront Saad: "You hurt my feelings!"

"Sorry, I was only kidding."

What started out as mutual teasing and ended up in playful banter always got them laughing, as they repeated their verbal jabs like
some exotic but familiar ritual that provoked an eruption of restrained speech that gushed forth in strong, loud spurts.

It fell to Saleema to convince her grandfather to let her and her brother go. Abu Jaafar insisted that it was a parade like any other, and that he didn't see any special reason why they should go.

"I beg you, Grandfather, please let us go."

"I don't see why I should," he responded.

But Saleema wouldn't give up and persisted throughout the following day, this time with the help of her grandmother who took the position that she saw no reason at all not to let them go if it meant so much to them and made them so excited. She pulled Abu Jaafar aside and whispered in his ear: "Abu Jaafar, they're just children. They shouldn't be mourning, and they're impatient. Let them go, at least for my sake."

Whenever Saleema got an idea in her head, she would become so obsessed with it that no one individual nor the whole family in unison could sway her from it. If she wanted something, she held her ground and persisted in asking, never flinching or backing down one bit, nor would she let anyone rest in peace until she got what she wanted. Her mother would say of her, "Saleema has the qualities of a gnat, constantly droning, and useless in the house!" Umm Jaafar would laugh and say that Saleema was like the queen of Sheba, who wanted to give orders and be obeyed and not take orders from anyone else. She even nicknamed her "Sheba." Yet despite all the joking, Umm Jaafar was concerned that her granddaughter didn't even know how to fry an egg, and unlike other girls of her age from the neighborhood, she didn't help her mother at all with the housework. Rather, it was her brother, two years her junior and more active and experienced than she, who was sent to the town's public ovens, carried the trays of fish and flat loaves of bread, who waited and paid the oven attendants and returned with the cooked food.

Abu Jaafar on the other hand wasn't concerned about any of this in the least. He was all too aware of the fact that the girl's laziness was completely compensated for by something else. Her mind was as sharp as a razor, and she never stopped poking around, observing, studying, and asking questions. She was only nine but had already learned by heart a third of the Quran and could recite it effortlessly and write in a clear and elegant hand. Her teacher marveled at how quickly she understood and readily grasped the complexities of Arabic grammar. As he watched her, it would touch his heart deeply to see how much his granddaughter, who had inherited his own blue eyes, had her father's bright, attentive look, his intelligence and vivaciousness.

These days Saleema was totally absorbed by what was constantly being said about the discovery of a new world.

"Why is it new?" she asked.

"Because it was recently discovered. Before now, we didn't know that it existed."

"But that doesn't make it new, Grandfather. When I first heard the expression I thought that God created it only recently, and I imagined its trees were little trees and that all the creatures in it were tiny newborns." She laughed at her own words, and then said, "How stupid of me!"

In the end Abu Jaafar gave in and allowed Saleema and Hasan to go to the parade but only on condition that Saad and Naeem accompany them. He warned Hasan, "Watch out for your sister. There may be Castilian boys who don't respect girls from good families. Be careful, and make sure you hold her hand. Don't take your eyes off of her for one second."

Two days later, the four of them set out to the town where the parade was to take place.

Although there was a cold breeze, the sky was clear, and the rays of the sun beamed on the river and warmed up the air, making it a pleasant spring morning. They chatted and chuckled with laughter, excited by the journey on which they were embarking and the wonderful parade that they couldn't wait to see. As they approached the parade site, the crowd grew dense and the roads swarmed with people. Even the balconies, window ledges, and rooftops that looked onto both sides of the streets were overflowing with spectators. Everyone seemed highly animated, talking, laughing, calling out to one another, or buying something for the children from the vendors who sold fresh almonds, dried figs, or honey-soaked cakes.

Then, suddenly, the crowd calmed down and the voices lowered, as necks began to stretch and eyes peered up ahead toward the top of the road. They could make out the rolling of the drums and the blowing of the bugles as the rifles and the bells rang out. These sounds magnified as they got closer, while the crowds drew to a near silence. People opened their eyes as wide as they could in the hopes of seeing as much as possible. The flag bearers appeared waving colorful flags, followed by the members of the band dressed in Castilian uniforms with their form-fitting trousers that came to the waist, their embroidered jackets, and caps. A man yelled out in Spanish, "Here he is! Look!" He was pointing to a horseman mounted on a magnificent white stallion trotting gracefully and rhythmically as though taken by its own beauty.

"Long live Christopher Columbus! Long live Christopher Columbus!"

The bearded horseman raised his black cap and with it waved to greet the crowds. He flashed a broad smile as though he were a king of kings. Saleema shouted, consumed by excitement, "They say that the land he discovered is full of gold and silver, and that he's now on his way to Barcelona to offer the king and queen the treasures he found."

"Why doesn't he keep the treasures for himself?" Hasan asked.

"They don't belong to him."

"Why not?" Hasan asked.

She answered, "The king and queen gave him the money he needed for the trip. It's as if they lent it to him to make the trip. Look, Saad, look!"

When the battalion of horsemen following the admiral passed, there appeared rows of men carrying large cages of magnificent birds of the most extraordinary colors. Some of the birds were as small as sparrows, others the size of parrots, and some were as large as geese. There were birds with gigantic talons the likes of which no one had ever seen. Some had exquisite crests that looked like crowns. Then next in the parade came men bearing glass chests through which you could see exotic creatures: huge spiders, giant snakes, and gruesome reptiles that made you frightened at the mere sight of them. The people followed the procession awestruck, riveted by something between excitement and fear of the strange new world that this grand knight had discovered.

And then, as though the organizers of the parade wanted the spectators to hold their breath, a group of men carrying all sorts of plants and vegetation marched, and soon the streets were adorned with palm leaves, not those of the familiar kinds, but branches of trees of unknown species. There were fruits in a brown shell that looked like wool, and some with peels as though they were cut from the trunk of a palm tree. Next came men carrying glass chests similar to those that passed by not too long before and through which you could see as plain as day what was inside, shimmering in the sunlight and dazzling to the eye. A woman shouted out, "It's gold, pure gold!" The shout was repeated as the people stood speechless, with hearts pounding anxiously and eyes widening to get a better look at the chests that encased the pure gold. Sand of gold, whole slabs of solid gold, large ingots no one could have ever possibly imagined in his or her wildest dreams.

"Long live Christopher Columbus," a woman cried out. This time the cry was repeated but not as enthusiastically as it had been before, perhaps because the surprise and excitement had sapped much of the people's bodily strength.

"It's not a new world," Saleema cried out to her companions, "it's just a different world, and that's all there is to it."

The parade's amazing attractions were not quite over. As the procession continued, the captives appeared, and whispers spread rapidly through the rows of spectators. "It's the natives, there they are, the inhabitants of the new world!" They walked along slowly, hands tied behind their backs while the guards surrounded them on both sides. They had delicate features and slender, fragile bodies. The men, like the women, had long, flowing jet-black hair that came down to the shoulders. Yet underneath the Castilian clothing they were made to wear, their differentness was all too obvious, not only in their physical features and the look in their eyes, but also in the colored feathers that stuck out of the bands they wore around their heads. Although strange indeed, they were not at all repulsive to look at. On the contrary, they were attractive in their refined faces and their graceful physiques, or perhaps in something else about them. Many of the Spaniards were laughing. Saleema turned to Saad and asked, "What are they laughing about?"

"I don't know." The laughter also took Saad by surprise. At first it baffled him, and then it made him angry.

"Saad, do you see that girl?" Naeem asked.

"Which one?"

"The prisoner who's wearing the white robe?" Naeem pointed to a young woman thin as a rail who had stumbled and fallen down, but when one of the guards rushed forward and tried to help her get up, she pushed him away with her shoulder and regained her balance, standing up by herself although her hands were chained, and continued to walk.

"I wonder what her name is?"

"How should I know?"

"If only I knew her name!"

The procession went forth immersed in a cacophony of rattling tambourines and beating drums, while the whistling of flutes mixed with the roar of discharging artillery and the boisterous guffaws of the masses. But the four youngsters were dumbfounded by the fact that all the cheer that was bursting in their hearts had mysteriously disappeared. They hadn't noticed that it slipped away and was now replaced with a melancholy that seemed to overtake the entire parade. They watched in silence the cuffed hands behind the backs of the captives, the slow, deliberate pace, the bowed heads, and those sudden, furtive looks that stared them right in the eye whenever a captive looked at them and they at him.

"Why don't we go home?" Saleema suggested.

"Let's go. Where's Naeem?"

They stood there for a while and waited for him to come back. But the longer they waited, the more anxious they became. Saad wanted to go and look for him but felt constrained by the promise he made to Abu Jaafar not to leave the children alone, not even for a blink of the eye. They waited some more and then Saad decided that they should go back.

"Let's go back to Albaicin. Hopefully Naeem will have already gotten there before us." Saad didn't reveal to them, however, his intention to come back and look for his friend. On the way home, Hasan and Saleema kept assuring themselves that Naeem had gone back into town, and Saad was quick to agree with them that was most likely what had happened. But deep down he didn't believe a word of it, and his heart grew heavy with worry.

Silently they walked through the mountain passes as the sun went down and the colors of the hills faded, giving way to the impending night. Saad was thinking about the procession of captives that had come and gone. He wondered whether they attacked them by land and sea the way they did to the people of Malaga. Did they starve them to the point of forcing them to eat their own horses? Or did they raze their homes and pounce on them before taking them away as prisoners?

At the beginning of the summer, the warm weather follows the copious rains that bring to the land the scent of fresh wet grass. The grown-ups say, "The Malaga Palace has fallen and the Castilians are coming." The grown-ups say, "They arrived and pitched camp outside the walls of the city. They dug trenches and they built towers and wooden bridges. They set up Italian artillery posts. King Ferdinand arrived, and then Queen Isabella came from Cordova." His father says that Hamid al-Thaghri, who led a heroic defense of the town of Ronda, was asked immediately after its fall to become leader of the garrison at the fortress of Gibralfaro, which overlooks Malaga. His father says that al-Thaghri came down from the fortress with his troops, removed the governor of Malaga who intended to surrender it, and set up a blockade around the city. That's the only thing that the grown-ups talk about. They hear the words and sometimes they understand, and at other times they don't. In either case, they repeat what they hear in playful imitation.

Racing through the neighborhoods, playing hide-and-go-seek behind the trees, and stealing sour grapes from the neighbors' vineyards all came to an end with the onslaught of the new pastime: they give each other roles and then get into disputes and wage battles with one another. Everyone wants to be al-Thaghri or, at least, one of his soldiers, and then, in the end, settle for the part of King Ferdinand or one of his senior officers, or perhaps a knight. They have everything they need, for there is an abundance of things to choose from, either from home or in the streets. Someone sneaks out a clay vessel and uses it as Ferdinand's crown by turning it upside down and placing it on top of the head; by becoming taller he turns into a king. Or the branches of the trees are made into ready-made swords, while small pebbles turn into gold dinars and stones become precious gems. An old garment is wrapped around one child's head, thus becoming an awesome turban, transforming him into a prosperous and powerful merchant.

With the clay vessel towering above the others, King Ferdinand summons three of his knights and commands them to go to Malaga. "Tell them to surrender the city." The knights bow before him, kiss his small hand, and turn around and head out to convey his message to the other side. "King Ferdinand orders you to surrender." The turbaned heads draw close and huddle in consultation. The merchant speaks: "If we don't surrender, he will destroy us."

The others reply, "No surrender."

It falls to Darwish, the leader of the town, to settle the matter: "We will surrender!"

Al-Thaghri appears mounted on his make-believe horse. He raises his sword to Darwish and strikes him. He falls to the ground and dies. The others run away. With his tree branch weapon drawn, al-Thaghri proclaims, "Tell the king that Sidi Zghal did not entrust us with the command of this fortress only to surrender it. We will defend our city!"

The king's emissary replies, "But His Majesty has sent you this gift," stretching out a handful of stones and pebbles. "He will give you all of this, plus a castle and even more money, if you surrender."

Al-Thaghri returns the handful of gifts to the royal emissary and says confidently, "I want nothing from you."

Whereupon war breaks out. They all take part in attacking with their wooden swords. The battlefield extends into the entire vineyard as they pair off in different directions, battling one another until they collapse in exhaustion.

These were the daily games in the first weeks of the siege before the provisions dwindled and people dropped dead of starvation, and their empty stomachs prevented them from running and playing. Even the sour grapes, which they delighted in stealing and whose sharp pungency they once savored, were now repugnant to them as their acidity tore away at their insides.

His father refuses to slaughter his horse. His mother sobs: "The children will starve to death."

He yells back, fully aware of his own lying: "Who said I'm starving? I swear to Almighty God I am not starving." Yet he cries in hunger and in fear for the horse.

His father refuses to slaughter the horse. His mother picks vine leaves, boils them in water, and feeds the children. She pounds palm fronds until they turn mealy, like flour. She kneads it with water, flattens it out, . . .they eat.

The fading dusk light did not obscure Saad's face from Saleema, yet she couldn't understand his nervous fidgeting nor the restrained anxiety that manifested itself on his twitching face. At the same time she felt a profound sadness deeply embedded within him but was at a loss as to why it was there. When she noticed the tear stealthily trickling from the corner of his eye, she held out her hand and took hold of his.

Saad had succeeded in bringing Hasan and Saleema home safely and then headed toward the shop. I'll wait for him there awhile, he thought, and if he doesn't return, I'll go back to the parade site and look for him. Then he noticed the light of the lantern creeping in from underneath the door of the shop, and he knew that Naeem had finally come home.

"What happened? Where were you?"

Naeem mumbled something underneath his breath and looked as though he were upset, then he answered sheepishly: "I marched in the parade."

"Why would you do something like that, and why didn't you

tell us?" Saad was shouting at the top of his lungs, and all too aware that he would pounce on Naeem at any moment if he didn't get a satisfactory explanation for his conduct.

"What happened?"

"Calm down, Saad. I can't answer unless you calm down. I'm just as upset and depressed, and I'm at my wit's end."

"What happened?"

Naeem stood up and started to prepare something for supper. They ate in silence, without a word. When they finished Naeem spoke.

"I've fallen in love with the young girl."

"What young girl?"

"The one in the parade, the one in the white robe."

"And, so?"

"She's stolen my heart, and I'm frightened, and I don't even know her name. I ran after the procession and tried to catch up with her. I began to make noises to attract her attention. She looked in my direction, and I felt she noticed me too, but the guards pushed me away. I fell down. She was watching, and she smiled. Then the guards moved her to the other side of the procession so I couldn't see her. I marched along keeping pace in the hopes of seeing her again, but I didn't. Now what can I do?"

"Blow out the lantern and go to sleep!"

Saleema came to the shop looking for Abu Jaafar, but he wasn't there. "Tell him when he comes that Grandmother . . ." Saad didn't hear a word she said. It happened faster than a flash of lightning. He averted his eyes, unable to look at the face he saw a thousand times but could only see when the blindness fell from his eyes. When he glanced up and the butterflies gathered in his stomach, he looked down again. That night, Saad couldn't fall asleep. He lay awake, tossing and turning as though he were consumed with fever. The next few days he stopped going to Abu Jaafar's house and asked

Naeem to go instead whenever the need arose. He concocted one excuse after the other. Whenever the urge to divulge his secret to Naeem overcame him, he became tongue-tied. The more he tried to cure whatever was gnawing at his heart, the stronger it kindled with the flames of passion.

Two months later he told his friend everything. Naeem jumped for joy when he heard Saad utter the words, "I'm in love," but when Saad continued, "with Abu Jaafar's granddaughter, Saleema," Naeem's joy turned into reticence and he found himself at a loss for words. After a few moments he said, "Love her for awhile, and then love someone else." What Naeem was saying was totally in tune with what Saad was thinking. What would Abu Jaafar say if he knew? Would he say, "I entrusted Saad with the safety of my family, and now he has betrayed my trust." Would he accept if Saad asked for her hand in marriage? Wouldn't he say that he has no money nor family, and he only wants to marry his granddaughter to secure wealth and position for himself.

Naeem repeated, "Love her for now, a week or two, but then look for someone else to fall in love with. I was worried about you, brother. I said to myself, Saad's locked himself away from women, but now the lock has been opened."

After several moments of silence, Naeem asked, "How is it that you came to fall in love with her?"

"I don't know."

"I'm concerned about you. I want to compare your love for women with mine. Tell me everything, all the details of how it came about, this love of yours for her."

Hasan and Saleema received the usual pampering of being raised in a grandfather's house, if not more, especially since they were the children of their dearly beloved father whose life was cut short before his time. Abu Jaafar not only provided them with everything they wanted, but he also pinned all his hopes and dreams on them. He brought Saleema a private tutor to give her lessons in reading and writing, and when Hasan turned seven, he enrolled him in the class of the most prestigious faqeeh in town. He would say to Hasan, "Granada has fallen, Hasan, but who knows, some day it may return to you, even by way of your own sword, or perhaps you will write its story and record its glories for all time. It's not my intention that you become a paper maker like myself, my boy. I see you rather as a great writer, like Ibn al-Khateeb,[2] and your name will be synonymous with Granada and memorialized along with it in every book."

Saleema was only nine years old the day Saad looked into her eyes and turned away in shame. She definitely noticed it, and it caused her to wonder. What she saw confused her since Saad's presence in the household was as familiar and natural as that of Hasan, Naeem, her grandfather, and even her tutor. But his look that day and her feelings about it were both strange and new to her, and she didn't know how to deal with them. The matter preyed on her mind for several days, and she pretended to forget it, until eventually she did. Saleema was not conscious of her femininity the way other girls her age were, girls whose families were already making arrangements for their betrothals. Abu Jaafar, who never revealed his innermost thoughts to anyone, harbored a fervent hope that Saleema would become like Aysha bint Ahmad, the pride and joy of Cordovan ladies and gentlemen alike, who surpassed them all in intellect, erudition, and culture. He was not concerned about her marriage, nor did he ever raise the subject with her. Her mother felt the same way, but for entirely selfish reasons. Her intense attachment to her daughter made her shiver even at the thought of being separated from her, living far away with a strange man in a strange house.

Friends and acquaintances of Abu Jaafar warned him about what it would cost to educate both his grandchildren, calling it a senseless waste of money. These are not times for Islamic scholars and judges, nor for Arabic manuscripts, for that matter. Spanish is the language of the future, and there will be no financial rewards for knowing Arabic, they would say. Abu Jaafar would listen to them

---

2. Lisan al-Din Ibn al-Khatib (1313–74), vizier at the Nasrid Court, was an eminent bellettrist and historian, but was later accused of heresy, exiled to Fes, and murdered while in prison.

and not say a word. But he never gave a thought to depriving the two little ones of an education, not only because he was adamant about realizing his dreams, but because he was resolutely convinced that refusing to educate them was tantamount to surrendering to a defeat that Almighty God may not decree in the end. His dreams had not abandoned him, so why would he abandon his dreams? He liked to imagine that everything that was happening was only a fleeting nightmare, and that it was impossible that God would abandon His servants and forget them as though they never worshipped Him nor built His abode with their hearts bursting with love for Him. He imagined days to come in which the Castilians would withdraw to the north and leave Granada to live in peace, in the security of the Arabic language, and in the comfort of the muezzin's call to prayer. He knew that he would most likely not live long enough to see all of that. He told himself that his soul one day would be seen circling the skies of the city in the form of a white dove, gliding in the air, flapping its wings from the towers of Alhambra to the minaret of the Great Mosque, landing in its courtyard to pick up the scraps of bread the young pupils leave for him. Then it would take flight and hover over the city and follow a path, and land at the end of the day on a window's edge in a house in Albaicin that used to be his own, and that is now occupied by Hasan the Granadan, the writer, who burns both ends of the candle as he dips his plume into the inkwell and writes.

The two grandchildren sustained Abu Jaafar's dreams by excelling in their studies. Saleema succeeded in memorizing vast amounts of poetry that full-bearded scholars failed to do. Hasan developed an exquisite calligraphy and his letters looked like perfectly carved moldings from a mosque, and the page that came from his hand was a joy to all who laid eyes on it. The children's teachers regarded their intelligence as a sign of great promise. Abu Jaafar showered them with generous salaries even if it forced him to cut down on other expenses, like a scarf or a pair of shoes he needed to buy to replace a worn-out pair.

5

The man arrived in Granada during the month of July in the year 1499.

War or no war, occupation or joyous occasion, the hills in summertime hold their matrimonial feasts and spread throughout the land their all encompassing greenery, scented with the sweetest aromas, and embroidered with colorful wildflowers, especially the anemones that eclipse them all with their scandalous and teasing red. Summer in Granada brings forth fruit-filled olive trees and the flirtatious apricots appear and disappear behind the lush green leaves. The reticent pomegranates slowly gather their sweetness before being peeled away at the hands of those who will devour them. Arbors and trellises, walnut, almond, and chestnut trees shade the roads as spouting waters merrily cascade from the mountain tops onto the valleys.

That summer, the man came to the city. His head was shaven except for a ring of curly hair that encircled his fleshy, shiny bald crown. His face was stern, bordering on a sickly yellowness. His forehead was wide and his two beady eyes stared out with an inspector's penetration. He had a hooked nose and two tight, thin lips, the upper of which was slightly fuller than the lower. His torso was excessively lean, and when he spread out his arms from underneath his flowing black robe, he appeared like a frightening giant bat.

The people asked themselves who he was and where he came from. It wasn't long before they learned to pronounce his name, Francisco Ximenes de Cisneros. He was the archbishop of Toledo who came to them, so they say, from the city of Alcala where he had founded a university. He was a scholar and a faqeeh, a Castilian faqeeh, who came to meet the faqeehs of the Arabs. He reached out to them, treated them with respect, and showered them with gifts.

The town crier announced to the people that Hamid al-Thaghri was going to be released, and that whoever desired to see him in person was free to proceed on the following day to the Church of San Salvador. Abu Mansour was indignant and asked disdainfully, "How can we enter the courtyard of the mosque they turned into a church?"

Saad replied, "The place is ours even though they changed its name. Besides, we're going not for their sake, but to see a man who is of great concern to all of us. We are his flesh and blood, so is it right that al-Thaghri come out of his long imprisonment only to be alone and deprived of the company of his people? We will carry him on our shoulders from the mosque square, as befitting both him and ourselves."

Abu Jaafar didn't utter a word.

On the following day the three of them went to the Albaicin Mosque, which was now called the Church of San Salvador. A great number from the Arab community came out. Some of them were from Malaga, those fortunate enough to have made their way to Granada, men and women alike, who had known al-Thaghri and whose souls had clung to every word he said and every decision he made. The others were citizens of Granada and the surrounding villages who followed the exploits of al-Thaghri, a man who held a warm place in their hearts, that is, next to the place they set aside for Ali,[1] the one who won them over with his feats of heroism and acts of justice.

The people assembled in the courtyard of the mosque and sat cross-legged, pressed together, shoulder to shoulder, waiting in breathless anticipation. Then, Cardinal Cisneros appeared in his long black cassock and, with slow deliberate steps, headed toward the east portico where a large, luxurious throne was placed and

---

1. Ali Ibn Abi Talib, cousin and son-in-law of the Prophet Muhammad, is universally revered by Muslims.

upon which he sat. He stared out at the people and they at him. He clapped his hands, and four guards came out escorting an extremely emaciated man dressed in tattered clothing. His hands and feet were bound, and he walked with a bowed head and shuffling feet.

The crowds began to whisper. "Is that Hamid al-Thaghri? Is it possible? Could that really be him?"

"It's him," shouted a man from Malaga who had fought alongside him. From row to row the people passed the word that Abu Ali the Malagan recognized him. Some asked who had recognized him. They repeated, "Abu Ali the Malagan."

With his unusually long and pointed fingers, the cardinal motioned to the guards to untie the prisoner. Then the cardinal spoke. "Now, Hamid, tell the people what you saw."

Hamid stared out at the crowd, lowered his head, then stole another quick, unsettling look. The crowd seemed to be holding its collective breath. Hamid spoke:

"Yesterday . . ."

One of the guards shouted at him to speak louder. Hamid cleared his throat, straightened himself up, and raised his voice. "Yesterday, while I was in my cell, I fell asleep." He stuttered, coughed, and then continued. "While I was sleeping yesterday, a voice called out to me and told me that God wants me . . ."

He stopped. Several silent moments passed in which it appeared that the man had nothing further to say. He closed his eyes and said: "He wants you to become a Christian. This is His will."

A dead silence fell over the crowd as though the square, teeming with hundreds of people, was totally deserted. The guards took al-Thaghri away, and the masses of Arabs were jolted by the sudden piping of the organ and the hymns that echoed loudly throughout the courtyard of the mosque. Saad spoke up: "Let's go, Abu Jaafar. Come, Abu Mansour, let's go home." He turned toward Abu Jaafar and was shaken by the tears gushing out of his eyes as though he were a little boy. He put his arm around him and repeated, "Let's go, Grandfather." Abu Jaafar shook his head and beckoned with his fingers to Saad who understood immediately that he wanted to stay.

The guards returned with al-Thaghri whose hands and feet

were now free of the chains. They had washed his face, combed his hair, and dressed him in a silk robe. Al-Thaghri walked toward the cardinal with slow, heavy steps as though his feet were still in chains. He knelt at the feet of Cisneros who took the small decanter of baptismal water from one of the deacons. He dipped his fingers into the water and sprinkled the drops over al-Thaghri's forehead as he recited a prayer. Hamid al-Thaghri had chosen for his Christian name Gonzales Fernandez Zegri.

The people had not yet recovered from what had happened, nor had anyone dared to even recall the details or dwell on the painful events when the news traveled in whispers that the Castilians were breaking into all the mosques and schools, and that they were collecting all the books and bringing them to an unknown destination.

For a week, the Paper Makers' Quarter witnessed unusual activity. The shops closed during the daytime and were kept open all night as a cover-up. Two or three hours after evening prayers the quarter came alive and went to work. Abu Mansour and three of his young employees stood guard over the quarter from a position behind the bathhouse, while Naeem and two others kept watch from the other side.

Behind the doors that were kept slightly opened was the soft glow of candlelight. In every shop you could see the shadows moving back and forth in the flickering light. Cupboards full of books were opened on both sides as the hands moved in and out of them with great care and caution. Large sacks were stuffed, and straw baskets and cartons were filled to the brim. There was the shadow of someone filling a sack and carrying it off, or of someone stuffing a basket, or perhaps two men hoisting together a heavy crate over their shoulders and vanishing into the night. The dark, gloomy street came to life with voiceless phantoms, some sinuous and hunchbacked, others straight as reeds, looking as though they were capped with a strange and mysterious crown on the top of their heads. Some took bizarre shapes like elevated thrones with walking legs. The whole quarter was animated with these silent phantoms whose torsos conjoined with the loads they were carrying, as they communicated with their arms and legs, appearing like eerie phantasmic creatures that come to life only in the black of night and fade away at the crack of dawn.

Abu Jaafar had agreed with his colleagues in the Paper Makers' Quarter that he would move his books to their houses only under cover of night, and that in the daytime he would take them to their permanent hiding place. He would load them on donkey carts or on the backs of mules camouflaged as household goods and utensils, pretending to be moving house. They all agreed that this should be carried out in stages, quietly and cautiously, in a way that wouldn't draw any attention. They agreed that the books would be distributed evenly in a number of places, in mountain caves, under the ruins of abandoned houses, and in the vaults of their own homes.

Several days later Abu Jaafar rented two carts and loaded them with his books and those of some of his friends. He mounted his wife and Saleema on one mule, Hasan and Umm Hasan on another, and he himself mounted a third. They rode in the direction of Ainadamar. Abu Jaafar wanted to make it known to whomever passed them by that he could no longer bear to live in Albaicin, nor tolerate the onslaught of the Christian missionaries who invaded the quarter like a swarm of locusts. They arrived at the house at Ainadamar and unloaded the goods. They paid the drivers and moved the books to the vault. Umm Jaafar turned her attention to the windows as she and Umm Hasan made a courageous attempt to coax Saleema into helping them clean the house as though they had every intention of staying for good. Saleema spent nearly an hour helping out but soon crafted the excuse that she heard her grandfather calling her from the vault. She then left them and went down below. Umm Jaafar smiled, knowing full well that her granddaughter was not inclined at all toward housework. Her mother, on the other hand, also knowing the same thing, only sighed and secretly feared for her daughter.

Hardly two weeks passed when Abu Jaafar hired another three mules and a cart and returned the family to Albaicin. Once again,

Abu Jaafar let it be known to anyone who would listen what he wanted them to believe. "I had every intention to live out the remainder of my days at Ainadamar, but I just couldn't do it. I can't survive away from Albaicin. I was born there, and God knows I will die there as well."

Just as Umm Hasan was opening the door, Naeem came rushing in panting: "Where's Abu Jaafar?"

"What's gotten into you, boy? No 'good morning'?"

Naeem acted like a madman as he called out to Abu Jaafar as loud as he could. Abu Jaafar came as quickly as his many years would allow.

"They're piling up all the books they can get their hands on at Bibarambla Gate," he shouted. They're going to burn all the books!"

Abu Jaafar put on his shoes and hurried out of the house behind Naeem. Saleema came out to see what all the uproar was about, and her mother repeated to her only what she was able to catch. Saleema rushed back to her chest and came back in a few short moments ready to go out.

"Where are you going?"

"I'm going with Grandfather," she said, not waiting to hear her mother's response, as she darted past the door as fast as an arrow. The only thing her mother could do was to call out to Hasan to go and follow his sister.

They all assembled at the bank of the Darro. The river flowed in a mad rush in the same direction as the hordes of people—those who knew or didn't know, some silent and others boisterous. When they reached the Tanners' Bridge, the river bent in the direction of the Genil, and the throngs of people made their way toward Bibarambla Gate. At the main square of Bibarambla, they saw many carts drawn by oxen, mules, and donkeys. Each cart would pull into the center of the square, and when the driver pulled on the reins the animal slowed down. The wheels screeched to a halt and the cart came to a full stop. Three guards who had been sitting on top of the piles of confiscated books loaded on the cart stood up and stretched out for a moment to rid themselves of the numbness that had set in during the ride. Then they went to work. Their backs arched and their heads disappeared and reappeared as their torsos straightened out and their hands worked together in lifting the loads. Again and again, bodies bent and straightened, hands grabbed and let go, in unison and with efficient speed, as the books dropped to the ground, piling on top of one another, some closed, others opened, as fragments and pages flew apart, tumbling like autumn leaves through the air before they hit ground, reaching their final resting place. The people followed with their eyes as the many copies of the Quran fell to the ground, both large and small, as the leather binding, embellished with exquisite engravings and magnificent script, came apart. They watched their precious manuscripts falling to pieces, ancient ones and those newly inscribed, as well as hundreds of folios that bore the same words, whether composed in prose, line after line, or set in verse, with their two columns neatly balancing every page.

The guards continued their task as several more carts pulled up, one after the other, each one making its way to the center of the square. The screeching of the wheels mixed with the thump of the books as they crashed to the ground, while the people shouted in horror and the guards warned them with their weapons not to come close to the books. Abu Jaafar watched this specter, then turned his eyes away. He looked back again and muttered something that nobody could understand. He was completely oblivious to Saleema's hand that was pulling his, as her nails were digging into him. He was oblivious to her and deaf to what she was saying, even as she raised her voice, asking time and again. "They won't burn the books, Grandfather, will they? They can't do that!" Saad and Hasan stood dumbfounded as Naeem sobbed and wiped his nose with his sleeve. Carts rolled in from every direction, from Albaicin and the hospital, from Alhambra and the Jewish Quarter, from the university and the Grand Mosque. Saleema was distraught by this horrible spectacle, and she told her grandfather she didn't want to look any longer. She pulled her hand away from his and ran away. Abu Jaafar remained motionless, drowning in the inner turmoil of his most private thoughts. Could it be that God was abandoning His pious servants? Could He allow His book to be burnt? Abu Jaafar raised his eyes to the sky searching and waiting for an answer, when he suddenly became conscious of the moans of the crowd as the smoke thickened the skies.

The soldiers hastily dispersed in different directions to avoid the spreading flames. The fire quickly consumed the books, charring the edges and desiccating the pages, as the paper curled up on itself as though it was trying to protect itself, but to no avail. The fire devoured everything that fell in its way, and gobbled up every line, every page, book after book. It crackled and sizzled so intensely that it seared your eyes and suffocated you with its thick, black smoke. Abu Jaafar stared, horrified, as his mind screamed out in silence: this is not a forest set ablaze by fire that devoured its greenery and seared its branches and trunks; this was not a forest whose seeds were carried off by the winds or drenched by the heaven's rains, growing wild and on its own. This was not Granada's Vega, a field that the farmers cultivated year after year, with wheat, figs, olives, lemons, and oranges, and when it suddenly catches fire before their very eyes they respond, "There is no power or strength save in God," and then roll up their sleeves and go back to tilling the soil until they're blessed with a new harvest. It was not a forest or a cultivated land. Abu Jaafar knew it, but he could only see a land and forest besieged by vultures hovering over their heads, swooping down to pluck men's hearts out of their chests.

Abu Jaafar turned around and went home to Albaicin. On the way he watched the people walking alongside him, but the only thing he could see was the blazing fire. He was coughing and wiping the sweat from his brow. As he walked on the only thing he realized was that the door to God, which he had lived his life believing in, its existence and proximity, was now shut like a solid wall. He stopped in the middle of the road, besieged by a long, un-controllable fit of coughing that nearly choked him to death.

When he turned away from the Darro and headed up toward the hill, the inclining mountainous pass appeared ominous and in-surmountable. His legs were barely able to carry him, and he felt as though he were carrying a thick tree stump not humanly possible to bear. He managed to go up a bit further, stopped, and continued his climb. His legs wobbled and he fell flat on his face. A trickle of blood flowed out of his nose and he injured his knee. But he didn't seem to notice and got up and continued his ascent until he reached the main square of the Albaicin Mosque, now the Church of San Salvador. He sat on a stone bench motionless until sunset. That night, before retiring to his bed, Abu Jaafar said to his wife: "I'm going to die naked and alone, because God has no existence." And he died.

The men washed the tall, naked body, recited the shahada prayer over it before covering it with the burial shroud. They lifted the coffin over their shoulders, recited some more prayers, then took him to his final resting place.

Abu Mansour, Saad, and Naeem went down into the tomb and with outstretched arms took hold of Abu Jaafar's body, slowly and gently. They laid him to rest and then came up and covered his grave with soil.

That afternoon Abu Jaafar's home was swarmed with the neighborhood women who came to join in the mourning cere-monies with the women of the household. They cried together and rivaled one another with stories and anecdotes of the many fine qualities of the deceased. They beseeched God for the patience to endure His decree that given by anyone else would not be so lauded. Saleema was the only one who didn't shed a tear nor utter a word to any of the mourners. The women may say that everyone's time must come, but was this Abu Jaafar's time, or was it the book burning that really killed him?

When the last of the mourners departed and night crept in slowly, when everyone in the house went to sleep, Saleema lay awake staring into the darkness, thinking. She was just as upset as her grandfather by the burning of the books. Naeem had wept bitterly, and Saad and Hasan both looked pale and frightened, but why was it that it was her grandfather who died, suddenly, and without a warning sign, without a previous illness? She had barely reached four when her own father died, but he had been sick and in pain. She used to ask:

"Why is he moaning?"

"Because he's sick."

"When is he going to get better?"

"When God permits it."

But what God permitted was something else, and they took him to his grave.

"Where has he gone?"

"He died."

"What does 'die' mean?"

"That God chose him to be next to Him in heaven."

She pictured in her mind that God had especially chosen her father to sit right next to Him on a big throne in a heaven more beautiful than all the gardens of Ainadamar, with fountains and water trickling through the towering trees and the brilliantly colorful flowers. She wondered if she should ask God to chose her as well to go to live with Him in that beautiful place or to stay with her grandparents, her mother, and brother. Or should she pray to Him to take all of them together? Then she would think about her playmates and decided it may be best to stay where she was.

One day a little more than a year after her father died, Saleema found a small lizard in the courtyard. She went toward it and when she noticed that it didn't try to escape from her she picked it up by the tail. It was cold and dead. She brought it to her grandmother: "This lizard is dead, right?" Her grandmother shrieked in disgust and yelled at her to throw it away and go and wash her hands. But Saleema just stood there.

"When lizards die, do they go to heaven?"

Her grandmother muttered something under her breath without answering.

But the question lingered in her mind until more questions began to fill her head: what's the use of having lizards, bats, and scorpions? And why did God create these species only to have them die later on?

Months later little Saleema asked her grandfather if scorpions and lizards go to heaven just as people do. Her mother pulled her away and scolded her for bothering him with such silly questions, and told her to go outside and play with her friends. But she got no further than the outside door as she stood thinking how absurd it was for dead scorpions and snakes to go to heaven and frighten and bother people. So she ran back to her grandfather.

"Grandfather, do lizards go to heaven or hell when they die?"

"To hell."

"But what did they do to make them go to hell?"

"Because they cause harm to people, they go to hell."

She left the house and went out into the neighborhood not entirely convinced of what she had just heard. It's strange to think that scorpions go to heaven, but even stranger that they go to hell. Didn't God create them with their harmful sting? They didn't choose to be born that way, so why should God punish them for something they didn't choose?

Saleema went back to thinking about her grandfather, about the blazing fire and the piles of smoldering books at Bibarambla Square. She dozed off but soon awoke in a state of fright. She felt a blaze of fire rush through her body, and as she opened her eyes she realized that her whole body was shivering and her teeth were chattering. They covered her with lots of blankets, and in her feverish trance she felt as though she were about to join her grandfather.

The day Saleema recovered from her fever, Umm Hasan wept in sorrow because she was convinced that the illness had impaired her daughter's reasoning and made her lose her mind when she suddenly leaped out of bed, washed her face, put on her clothes, and announced to her mother that she was going to Ainadamar.

"Yes, I am going to Ainadamar, and if you want to come with me, that's fine. If not, I'll go by myself."

They all tried to talk her out of going, but when they didn't succeed, they went along with her, thinking that if they made her happy then perhaps she would regain her peace of mind and powers to reason. They rented a cart and went to their country house. No sooner had they reached the front door than Saleema jumped off the cart and went immediately down to the vault. She wiped away the dust as best she could and began to rearrange the books. Then she took out the paper, pens, and bottle of ink she brought with her and made a list of all the books and manuscripts, writing down first the name of the author and then the title. She moved to the next line with the second book and wrote until she reached the bottom of the page. She filled ten pages with each page containing seven titles except for the last, which had only six. When she was finished, she sat Hasan down in front of her and dictated the whole list to him.

"What's this for?"

"I want two copies of this list."

6

In the main square in the center of town, where both the old and new casbahs intersect with the roads that lead to Albaicin, a young girl carrying a basket was walking along the street. She had left home to do an errand or perhaps visit an aunt. On her way, either to or from home, God only knows, she walked along minding her own business while the veil on her head failed to conceal her long braids, and her loose fitting gown revealed her slender figure.

She noticed two Castilian men approaching. She lowered her eyes and continued to walk in an attempt to pass them or let them pass her. She glanced up quickly and noticed that they were watching her. She pretended not to notice and quickened her pace. When she looked up again it became clear to her that they were following her. She gasped for air and froze in bewilderment. After several moments she decided to run in the opposite direction. They ran after her until they caught up with her.

"What do you want?"

"What's your name?"

She was unable to run away this time. One of them put his arm around her while the other took hold of her braid and twirled it like rope around his fist. She cried out for help, and the two started to hit her. She yelled with all her might until four young men, hearing her screams, rushed toward her. Though the Castilians saw them they continued to slap and kick the girl so violently that she fell to the ground unconscious.

"That's Velasco de Barrionuevo, the police commissioner."

"And who's the other one?"

"That's Salicio, the cardinal's servant."

The fact that the four youths knew the Castilians made them all the more furious, and soon a brawl erupted, with fists, heads, and feet pounding each other. While two of the youths remained to punish the Castilian assailants, the other two carried the girl to the nearest house, not knowing whether she was dead or alive. Back on the street, one of the youths shouted that the bastard Salicio was getting away. His friend ran after him and they both quickly disappeared. The one who had stayed took such a punch from Barrionuevo that he slipped and lost his balance, allowing the Castilian to escape. He ran after him and just at the moment when he was about to grab hold of him at the entrance of the quarter, someone appeared at a window and threw a rock, hitting Barrionuevo on the head and killing him instantly.

Within hours the news spread like wildfire throughout Albaicin, and with it the pent-up feelings of anger were unleashed. "What shall we do?" "Lock the gates of the quarter." The men spread out in every direction and locked the gates with their massive iron bolts. Behind the gates and walls they set up barricades of wood, iron, and even their own bodies. They blocked off all the gates except the one from which a group of young men left to go to the cardinal's palace near Alhambra. From the Bunoud Gate a throng of people gushed out toward the old casbah and crossed the Darro in a state of extreme agitation. The profound sadness that had weighed heavily on their shoulders, heads, and hearts now carried them. They mounted their dejected spirits like a stallion, with their backs straightened, and their heads held high. Their eyes glimmered and their feet compelled its spurs as this dejection turned stallion broke away, unbridled, and exploded like a canon.

The people of Albaicin stayed awake that night in the security of God's divine light that illuminated their path with a full moon ablaze in the sky. In the houses the women lit the stoves and ovens. They turned the hand mills and kneaded the dough, sprinkling it with drops of water and pinches of salt. They rubbed, rolled, spread it out, and baked it. They layered the bread into baskets that the children hoisted on the heads and marched in step behind the delicious aromas toward the men standing guard behind the barricades.

The blacksmiths also passed the night working away. They fanned the bellows, hammered, welded, and forged, repairing what time had eroded, resolved to repair it all on that particular night. They brought out their grandfathers' swords, daggers, and knives, and wiping off the dust, they cleaned and polished all that was still usable. They sent the rest to the ironsmiths to repair a broken handle or a warped blade. The entire quarter of Albaicin stayed awake as though it were the night before the first day of Ramadan when all the streets come alive with children running and shouting and the grown-ups animated in conversation, busily working as the candles and lanterns shimmer in the houses and the eyes of the people glisten as the day gives way to the night. That particular night, just before daybreak, the town crier came out and announced that the Albaicin Mosque was open to all those who wished to perform the dawn prayers, and that whosoever wished to participate in leading the community in running its affairs would be wise to make his way there to pray.

They didn't wait for the call to prayers. Everybody appeared, religious scholars, teachers, merchants, craftsmen, old-time soldiers, and hairless young boys. They congregated at the square adjacent to the mosque. They talked amongst themselves, some standing or strolling about, others sitting on the ground. Then the muezzin's voice rang out with a strong resonance, and the multitude entered the mosque. After they formed lines, the imam stood in front and they began their prayers. The imam wasn't one of the usual prayer leaders of the mosque, not one of those senior jurists who packed their bags and fled the city only a few days after the treaty was signed. This time the imam was an elderly carpenter known to only a handful of the congregation. Upon completion of the prayers, he addressed the crowd.

"I was asked to lead the prayers here at Albaicin Mosque after God restored it to us."

Choking with tears, he cleared his throat and continued: "This is a great honor for me, one I wish I truly deserved. O, people of Granada and Albaicin, this is our city, for better or worse. We must resolve today to work together and put our affairs in order, with sound planning and judicious counsel. For failing to do so will lead us to drink from the cup of bitterness and live a life of agony until the day we die. So, what shall it be?"

Several moments of silence passed before the people stood up and formed a tight-knit circle so that each one could see everyone else as well as the imam. They huddled in conversation from the time the dawn prayers finished until the noon prayers began. Back home Umm Hasan was pacing frantically like a caged animal, while Umm Jaafar tried to calm her with no success.

"He went out to perform the dawn prayers and he's late. He usually comes right back, and if he's late its not more than an hour or two. Where could he have gone?"

All sorts of images ran through her head. She supposed that one thing happened and then suddenly thought of something else as being more likely. She wondered if he ran off to join the young men behind the barricades. If this was in fact what happened, then how could she bring him back? Should she go and look for him at the Fahs al-Lawz Gate to the north, or the Qashtar Gate toward the south? She wondered whether to go east to the Wadi al-Ulia Gate or to the Elvira Gate in the west. Had her son lost his head and left from the Bunoud Gate with the others and gone to form a blockade around the cardinal's residence? She sobbed uncontrollably and repeated over and over again that her heart was telling her something bad had happened to him, and that a mother's heart never lies. Neither Umm Jaafar nor Saleema could say anything reassuring to stop her from crying.

When Hasan finally came home, his rosy cheeks, beaming smile, and animated motions mirrored the joy he felt. His mother leaped up and greeted him as though he had just returned from a long journey. He was totally oblivious to her teary face and the emotional excitement of her greeting. In a loud, resonating voice,

he announced, "Today, at the Albaicin Mosque, a government inde-
pendent of Castile was formed, and we elected forty men to take
charge of our affairs and of all of Albaicin."

Umm Hasan was so distracted with worry over her son's absence and her relief of his safe return that she barely comprehended
what Hasan was telling her. Umm Jaafar, on the other hand, understood only too well as her face grew pale and agitated, mustering
only enough strength to say, "May God give you good fortune, my
son, and make you victorious. For He is capable of all things."
Saleema was the only one who reacted to the news with enthusiasm
as she sat skittishly on the edge of her seat, insisting that her brother
sit and tell her every single detail of what happened at the mosque,
probing as though she were one of the men. In the middle of his
story, Naeem rushed in and told him that the men who formed the
blockade around the cardinal's residence had returned. The two
men dashed out, heedless of Saleema's questions and deaf to Umm
Hasan's futile pleas to Hasan not to leave.

At the Bunoud Gate the crowd formed a circle around the returning men to hear what happened and to ask questions.

"We pelted his house with stones and hurled a slew of insults."

"Why didn't you break into the residence?"

"Believe me, we tried. But the gates were impenetrable and the
house is like a fortress."

"How about the windows?"

"We managed to smash the glass out of all of them, and the
pieces came crashing down right before our eyes."

"And that dog didn't show his face?"

"Never! He stayed inside like a bat in his cave, so we decided to
surround the palace until hunger and thirst forced him to come
out."

"So, what happened and why did you come back?"

"The Castilian army surrounded us. They far outnumbered us,
and they were armed and we weren't. Then we huddled in consultation. Should we take them on and fight, putting ourselves in
God's hands and die as martyrs, or is there an alternative? When

Count Tendilla appeared on his magnificent, ashen-colored stallion, he dismounted and shouted in a loud, forceful voice, 'Who represents you? It is only your leader I will address.'

"No one among us responded, since we all came together, and there was neither a leader nor a follower amongst us. When he repeated the question, four of the men stepped forward and approached him. They listened to what he had to say, and they came back. They told us he asked them to lift the blockade from the cardinal's residence at once. He said, 'I personally will go to Albaicin tomorrow and speak with your comrades, and I will put an end to this problem.'

"We told him we would hold our ground until he departed, and that if our leaders responded favorably, and if he acceded to their demands, then we would lift the blockade from the cardinal's residence. The four men conveyed our message to him and came back with his reply: 'Either you lift the blockade first, or else we will remove you by force. You're nothing but a little gang of unarmed men. And here you see our troops, horsemen, and foot soldiers, armed to the teeth.'

"We consulted with one another and decided to end the blockade. Did we make a mistake?"

It was Saad who had accompanied the young men to the cardinal's residence and it was he who asked this question, "Did we make a mistake?" Nobody dared answer even though their eyes responded with bewildered glances.

At that moment the children who had climbed the walls and towers erupted in shouts when they spotted a battalion of the Castilian cavalry approaching the gates of the city. The air grew tense and everyone turned to thoughts of what he had to do. Some of them fortified the barricades, and some rolled out the weapons. Others, like Naeem, climbed the walls carrying stones and insults that they would hurl at those bastard sons who wanted to attack the quarter. Stones and curses came flying in every direction, and the knights who were able to protect themselves from them and arrive safely to the gates found them bolted shut. Drawing together on their horses and forming a circle, they withdrew amidst the shrill clamor that mixed shouts of anger, cries of joy, insults, spitting, and praise and thanks to God.

Another restless night passed in Albaicin, oscillating between slumber and sleeplessness, between hard work and a grueling silence. The forty men elected to put Albaicin's affairs in order never had the chance to shut an eye, much less even think about it. They spent the night deliberating over what they would say to Count Tendilla if he came to negotiate as he had promised, or what they would do if the Castilian army attempted an assault on the quarter. They also had to manage the affairs of a hundred thousand citizens of Albaicin, and in the event of a siege that could last several weeks or months, would there be enough flour and grain to feed them? Since the road to the Darro was cut off, would the wells discharge sufficient water? Would it be necessary to ration basic staples, or to smuggle out messages to those hiding in the mountains? How could they send messages requesting help to the North Africans and Egyptians, or to the Ottoman sultan Bayzid? In the event of an attack on the quarter and the outburst of fighting, would they open the northeast gates to let the women, children, and elderly escape and seek refuge in some faraway place, or would wisdom dictate that they remain behind the barricades under the protection of their menfolk entrenched behind the gates?

On the following day Count Tendilla arrived as promised and met with the members of the newly elected government. "Your uprising against the king and queen is an act of rebellion that will be seriously punished," he warned.

"The conditions of the treaty that the king and queen both signed and to which they committed themselves have been violated. You force us to convert to Christianity against our will, burn our books, and molest our women," they retorted.

"Calm down, and return to your work, and we will consider your grievances."

"Expel Ximenes from Granada, for it is he who ordered our

books to be burned and forced al-Thaghri to convert after months of torture. He is the source of all our misery. Our condition is that he must leave."

"If you don't open the gates, we will storm Albaicin by force."

"Get rid of Ximenes and abide by the treaty, and the gates will be opened."

Tendilla mounted his horse and departed, followed by his cavalry guards. A sense of relief mixed with a tinge of pride filled the crowd, for the gates of Albaicin remained closed, the barricades were still standing, and they were capable of persevering, of holding their ground without compromise.

The negotiations lasted a number of days during which Count Tendilla came back and forth several times. Then he appeared with Archbishop Talavera, the first to pass through Bunoud Gate smiling his familiar smile. Tendilla followed, and removing his skullcap and waving it in the air, the crowd began to whisper among themselves, "He wants peace." A little boy ran over and picked up the count's red cap and lifted it up to him. The count smiled and the little boy smiled back. The governor of Granada and the archbishop spoke with the forty officials as well as some of the leading merchants and jurists.

"Let us live in peace," said the count. "Let this crisis pass. What you have done is not an act of rebellion against the Crown of Castile. You wanted only the implementation of the treaty, and as a concession we give you our assurances that we will abide by it."

"From whom do we get such assurances?"

"From me, personally," responded the archbishop.

"In what way?" they asked.

"There must be trust between us," said Tendilla. He stood silent for a moment, then continued. "I will have my wife and children live here in Albaicin amongst you. Will this suffice as a guarantee? Then it's settled. On this very day my family will move here to live with you, and today the gates will be opened, you will put down your weapons, and you will return to your work."

The count, his bodyguards, the archbishop and his servants departed, and the crowd remained intact, stunned and speechless. Eventually, the news spread rapidly, and the women who hadn't left their homes learned about it even as they kept busy feeding their babies and washing the clothes. Should they believe the count or what their own hearts were telling them? And why didn't their newly elected government say anything? Could it be possible that Tendilla would sacrifice his own wife and children? The man must be trustworthy, yet their hearts were needlessly aflutter with doubt.

The treaty was ratified, and the doors of the abandoned palace next to the Albaicin Mosque were swung open to let in the fresh air and sunshine. The huge, spacious rooms witnessed a frantic hustle in preparation for the arrival of the count's family. Yet, in spite of it all, the gleam had been extinguished from the people's eyes and the grimaces on their faces expressed the tension they felt as they made no effort to hide or remove the gloom permeating their souls. The young men began to take down the barricades and remove the huge bolts off the gates. The high-pitched squeaking of the bolts sent a shiver to their souls, and the droning sound of the opening gates only added to their inner turmoil.

Every hour seemed heavy and every day depressing, and they were at a loss to understand why they felt this way, even though the crisis had passed and the archbishop, whom they held in high esteem, guaranteed that they be treated with kindness and respect. They didn't know whence those ravens of ill-omen, which cawed in the skies and tainted the air with their blackish color, came. Their hearts were obstinate in their misgivings, but the residents of Albaicin mistrusted their own hearts. But time proved their hearts right. The Castilians demanded vengeance for Barrionuevo's death, and the judge complied by handing over his killer. But not satisfied with the one, they returned and arrested three more. The gallows were erected and the bodies of four young men were left hanging. Everyone knew that the next strike would be against the forty elected officials, and soon thereafter the rumor circulated that they had headed for the hills. Some condemned their escape while others defended them.

"Should they have sat around and waited for the noose to be tied around their necks?"

A small number of people you could count on one hand saw this as an auspicious sign, and they began counting the days.

7

After Abu Jaafar died, Saad went to work at Abu Mansour's bathhouse. Naeem found work with a cobbler who taught him the trade. He learned quickly, and the first thing he did was make a pair of shoes for Saad. When Saad asked him why he didn't make a pair for himself, he evaded the question at first, but then decided to come forth. "I couldn't make another pair without my boss noticing the leather and nails missing."

The two friends met up every day, as was their habit, and sat either by the bathhouse or outside the cobbler's shop after closing time. Sometimes they would take a stroll throughout the quarter, just chatting.

Saad spoke endlessly about his love for Saleema and his desire to ask for her hand in marriage. But he was afraid of being rejected. Naeem listened to him without ever breathing a word of his feelings of anxiety that grew by the day. At first he would make fun of Saad, and Saad responded in kind. God created Naeem with a tender heart that swayed like a branch with every passing breeze. Then he laid eyes on the captive girl in the parade and she stole his heart. But where had she gone, God only knew! She disappeared and left only her phantom to haunt his days and nights.[1] He would curse her and the day he first set eyes on her, and he swore that he would fall in love with the first girl who caught his eye. But through all the young girls who passed before him, he could only see the phantom,

1. The phantom of the lover is a popular motif in classical Arabic poetry, and also was believed to exist by pre-Islamic Arabians.

as clearly in dreams as in wakefulness. But poor Saad was a late
bloomer, and when he fell in love it struck a heavy blow. Whenever
he found himself in Saleema's presence he froze like a statue. But
now, with Naeem nineteen and Saad twenty, they couldn't afford to
remain like this much longer, or else they'd both end up growing
old and rejected, even by snickering young girls.

"Put your trust in God, Saad, and ask Abu Mansour to arrange
your engagement to her."

When Saad broached the subject with Abu Mansour, the old
man reacted skeptically.

"Do you think these are times suitable for getting married and
raising families? I swear by God of the Kaaba that every night I tell
myself, if only you hadn't gotten married! If you hadn't had a wife
to provide for and take care of, you would be free of your subju-
gation, free to plunge a dagger into the heart of a Castilian, or
plunge yourself into the river to relieve your mind and calm your
soul."

The following week Abu Mansour came to Saad while he was
cleaning the bathhouse. "I went to Abu Jaafar's house and spoke
with Hasan. He'll give me his answer in two days."

Saad stood petrified with broom in hand, and when what he
had just heard sank in, the broom fell to the floor. He rushed forward and kissed Abu Mansour on the forehead and shoulders and
dashed out like a madman toward the cobbler's shop. Naeem was
leaning over the anvil attaching a leather sole to a sandal with a small
hammer. He was too absorbed in what he was doing to notice Saad
coming. He was startled when he heard his friend's voice and the
hammer fell out of his hand and struck his thumb.

"When did you come, and what's going on?" he shouted.

"Abu Mansour has interceded on my behalf and asked for
Saleema's hand!"

Naeem jumped up and, in his excitement, once again dropped
the hammer, this time on his foot. He yelled out in pain but his joy
at the news made him laugh. "I will dance so much at your wedding
that people will remember it when they're old and gray!"

After Abu Mansour left the house, Hasan wondered if Abu Jaafar would approve of this marriage had he been alive. He anticipated his mother's negative reaction, protesting that Saad was too poor and deprived, owning only the shirt on his back and his daily bread. He also imagined his grandfather retorting that they, too, were in similar dire circumstances, and that Saad was a decent young man who would take good care of Saleema, so on what basis could he refuse Saad's request? And Saleema? Hasan paused a moment as though caught off guard. Saleema was unpredictable. She could rejoice at the idea of the marriage proposal and she was equally capable of flatly and adamantly refusing, with no one in any position to change her mind. He could never figure her out. She was the only young girl he knew well, and he often asked himself was it just her, or did she have the incomprehensible nature of all young girls.

The first person he confided in was his grandmother. "If she agrees," she answered, "then it will be with God's blessing. These are difficult times, and Saad is good and decent. We won't have to worry about waking up one morning and discovering that he turned his back on us and went to serve the Castilians."

"But would Grandfather have given his consent?"

"God only knows, my son."

That evening Hasan and his grandmother sat down with Saleema and Umm Hasan.

"Today Abu Mansour came to see me, and he asked me for Saleema's hand in marriage to Saad."

"Saad?" asked Umm Hasan with a tone of surprise mixed with a tinge of disapproval.

"What do you say, Mother?" asked Hasan.

"Why does he want Saleema? He's from Malaga, so let him go and find a girl from a family from his own city to marry."

"What kind of talk is this, Mother? What's wrong with Saad?"

"What's wrong with him is his poverty, and the fact that he

doesn't have a family we know and who can reassure us, not to mention . . ."

"There's nothing wrong with that," Hasan said, interrupting his mother.

"What's also wrong is that he doesn't own a house where he can live with his bride."

Umm Jaafar laughed, "That's a fault that should suit you nicely, Zaynab. The girl would never leave this house, but would stay and live here with her husband."

"Your grandfather would never have approved," insisted Umm Hasan.

"Grandfather loved Saad as much as he loved me, and he even told me once that if Saad ever asked for permission to marry Saleema, then I should agree."

"Did he really tell you that?"

"Yes, he did."

"But Saleema would never agree to that!"

At that point Saleema entered the discussion and spoke without any hesitation. "Who said so? I would never find a husband like Saad."

That night the three women, who all shared the same bedroom, didn't sleep a wink. But not one of them dared say a word as they kept their thoughts and comments to themselves. Umm Jaafar knew only too well that her husband never said any such thing to Hasan, and that he was never in a hurry to marry off his granddaughter. It was as though he harbored a secret wish that she complete her education without any constraint or interruption, and that he knew deep down she wasn't a girl inclined to marriage and raising a family. Hasan, for his part, is quite fond of Saad and knows him intimately, she thought, and he wants to strengthen his ties to him by marrying his sister to him. Therefore, Hasan's positive response didn't surprise her in the least, nor did his mother's reluctance, for even if a prince mounted on a white stallion came to her daughter from the shores of North Africa, she would find fault with him, that he was a prince, or that his castle was on the other side of the sea.

She simply couldn't bear the idea of being separated from her two children, and would never be truly at ease unless both of them remained right before her very eyes.

Umm Jaafar sighed as she tossed and turned that night. The children grow up, and those who pass away never come back. May you rest in peace, Abu Jaafar, she prayed to herself. She held on tightly to his image lest it be replaced by that of the other, one more dear to her, from whose loss many years ago she never recovered. She couldn't bring herself to utter her son's name after his departure, let alone conjure his image in her mind.

Saleema also tossed and turned that night. She lay wide awake, asking herself what made her respond so readily. The thought of marrying Saad never occurred to her before, nor of marrying anyone else for that matter. She was startled by his proposal, which she hadn't expected or understood. But now she had to think about how to deal with this situation, how to think about it before giving her final answer, one way or the other. Becoming the wife of a man whom she would have to obey, serve, and bear his children . . . why? When her mother began to list all of Saad's faults, she was taken aback, just as much as she had been by the proposal itself. And when she said, "I would never find a husband like Saad," she hadn't even been thinking about a husband, so why did she respond the way she did? But now it was important that she think this through carefully. The sky wouldn't fall to the earth if she announced tomorrow that she didn't want to marry Saad or anyone else. But it if weren't for her mother's comments that provoked her, she may very well have said so.

Umm Hasan was just as baffled and worried as Saleema. She lay in bed thinking she was asleep, but soon realized she was in fact wide awake. Fragments of images flashed through her mind, as memories and thoughts flickered like broken light, appearing as though her life was being rearranged in a straight line, composed of bits and pieces: her husband's bearded face, husky voice, and piercing blue eyes; the tilt of his head and his long, thick eyelashes as she placed Saleema in his arms the day she was born; the tender touch of

his hand on her belly while she was pregnant with Hasan; her sobbing voice after his passing; a shabby and emaciated Saad the day she
first set eyes on him, and Abu Jaafar describing him as a poor, un-
fortunate boy from Malaga who had lost his entire family.

Hasan finally gave his consent to the marriage, but when Abu
Mansour relayed the good news to him, Saad felt ill at ease. A shiver
ran through his body and a sense of foreboding bordering on sadness unexpectedly overpowered him. He went on working in silence, then decided to take a stroll throughout the quarter to clear
his mind and try to understand what was bothering him. Didn't he
want Saleema? Not only did he want her but the persistence with
which he pursued her made his proposal and Hasan's response seem
like matters of life and death. But now the response had arrived,
bearing a joy for which his soul has been yearning for a long time,
and he was miserable! He missed his father and mother, his little sister, and the sea and the vineyards. And he was at a loss to understand
how destiny brought him knocking at the door of his betrothed,
alone and naked.

Saad sat under a chestnut tree and closed his eyes. He saw the
boy he once was, running through the rugged thickets, leaving behind him a house inhabited by his mother, father, grandmother, and
sister, a house deserted in a city demolished by a blockade, starvation, and the constant bombardment of the Spanish canons. He
runs from all of that to God only knows where. In the daytime he's
able to keep busy despite the forlornness. But at night, the vision of
the bleak rocky mountains of Malaga, the austere splendor of their
peaks, gorges, and valleys, is transformed into frightening monsters
whose ominous presence nearly stops his heart from beating. He
doesn't dare look to his right lest he see those terrifying animals as-
suming different shapes, the slithering bodies of cobras, the hump-
backs of camels, and the heads of owls. They appear to him as ogres,
and when they approach him they almost touch him or grab hold of
him. The colossal coppery moon that is suspended over his head
makes him all the more petrified. The air around him is an enemy
that wants to take possession of him. He screams as he runs, panic-

stricken, and he hears the echoes of his own voice and swallows the next scream. He whispers to himself, "Your father told you, 'Saad, be a man! Don't be afraid, because men are never afraid. Be brave, Saad. These are mountains made of rock that you've seen in the plain of day. They're desolate and they can't harm you!' " His teeth chatter and his body shivers, sweating profusely. He sits down and crouches, quivering, resting his head on his knees tightly compressed together as he wraps his arms around his torso. Fatigue overwhelms him and he falls asleep in that sitting position until the morning sun awakes him and assuages, somewhat, the fears of the previous night.

Saad stood up exhausted and slowly made his way back to the bathhouse where he found Naeem sitting on the floor by the door, legs crossed, waiting for his return.

"Where were you?"

He didn't respond.

"Did they say 'no'?"

"They said 'yes.' "

Naeem was baffled as he looked at his friend's face that said one thing while his tongue was saying something else. He wondered what was going on.

"Did they give their consent, or not?"

"They agreed."

"Then what's come over you?"

"I don't know!"

"Have you fallen in love with someone else?"

"Naeem, this is no time for joking."

"Who's joking?"

They took a walk. Saad was absolutely silent and Naeem saw no reason to say anything. He didn't understand his friend, but he had grown accustomed in the many years of their friendship to accepting these situations that he not only failed to understand but that seemed to him as though Saad had bolted all doors shut and locked himself in like a hermit, not opening up to anyone who came knocking, not even Naeem. He was surprised at how he would want to go out on his own, saying that he couldn't breathe, and that he needed to get some air. What air was he talking about? Naeem wondered, when the snow had covered all the roads and the cold air had frozen everything. But he always went as if he didn't hear a word Naeem said. Naeem learned how to leave his friend alone, be it for a day or several days at a stretch, and he would wait until Saad came back to him and opened the doors, laying out before him a bridge of affection and communion as if nothing ever happened.

What would be an appropriate gift for Saleema? Saad paced up and down the Square of the Grand Mosque that was bursting at the seams with buyers and sellers. He looked at bars of fancy soap and bottles of perfume, straw mats and intricately woven baskets, lamps and candlesticks, and wooden boxes carved with different designs. He thought about a beautiful box inlaid with mother-of-pearl and ivory, with two tiers of drawers. He considered another one, smaller than the first, studded with tiny nails whose circular heads formed parallel and crisscrossing patterns. The vendor greeted him cordially and coaxed him into making a purchase. Saad returned the warm greeting, thanked him and left. He passed by the shops that sold harnesses, bridles, and stirrups, and walking along he looked at the pots and utensils, made out of clay, tin, and glass, in all shapes, sizes, and colors. Then he stopped in front of a shop whose owner had laid out in carefully arranged rows his utensils, pots, and jars on a wool carpet, matching its colors with the colors of his goods, making his shop, along with its festive commotion, by far the most attractive sight to behold. The vendor lifted up a brilliant blue vessel made of lapis lazuli adorned with a shiny black ring of Kufic script.[2]

"It dazzles the eyes. A magnificent gift, don't you think?" he asked.

2. Kufic script is a style of Arabic calligraphy used especially for ornamentation.

Saad thanked him and meandered on toward the jewelers' lane where he inspected the displays of gold and silver trinkets. He was stunned by the sight of all the precious gems. He stood for a long time in front of a necklace of connected gold rings with a pendant made from a precious stone as blue as the deep blue sea. "Now, that's a gift befitting Saleema with her blue eyes," he thought to himself. When he noticed that the owner was watching him, Saad moved away to avoid an embarrassing situation, since he was in no position to be buying a piece of jewelry such as this.

He headed toward the junk dealers' market before going into the tinsmiths' quarter. He passed by the silk vendors where they laid out their wares of raw, interlaced, and woven silks. One of the vendors shouted out to Saad, "Pure silk! They come from as far away as Genoa to buy it, and it's in high demand in Cairo and Damascus."

"Do you have any silk from Malaga?"

The vendor flashed a sorrowful smile. "What kind of question is that? Where are we going to get silk from Malaga? Have any of us been able to go back?"

Saad walked on not saying a word. What could possibly be said besides an apology for the heart that suddenly asks for something it cannot have? To hold in his hands a piece of silk woven by his father and with the scent of the sea and of his mother. How strange the heart is!

He strolled on through the tinsmiths' quarter and veered toward a small side street that lead to another, and then another. He looked at all the shops that sold fabric for men's clothing, women's garments, scarfs, headwear, sandals and shoes. He decided to leave and head back toward the Square of the Grand Mosque until he reached the food and sweets vendors. He saw displays of dried figs, walnuts, and almonds piled high in big straw baskets.

What would be an appropriate gift for Saleema? he thought, as he continued his walk.

He thought long and hard as he made his way toward the open space next to the souk. He walked around it until he reached the livestock market. He glanced at the horses, mules, donkeys, sheep, and goats, and just as he was about to turn back and head home, he saw what he was looking for. Was it the blink of her eye or the shutter of her eyelid that brought him to a halt, or merely a glance of distraction between fear and composure?

Her skin was so smooth and white, with a reddish yellow tinge, and her tiny body was held by four delicate paws. "Can I hold her?" He lifted her up and felt her quivering in his arms. "I'll take her," he said to the vendor as he handed him the money and left.

The gazelle Saad bought for Saleema and carried to Abu Jaafar's house aroused in Umm Jaafar a fit of laughter that brought tears to her eyes. Umm Hasan took one look at her and repeated what she thought all along, that he was crazy. Saleema, for her part, was taken aback. She went over to the gazelle and stretched out her hand to pat her. When the gazelle quivered, so did Saleema, and she pulled back her hand. She stared at her intensely and noticed how its wide, black eyes flickered in fear. "She's afraid," she said. Then she stretched out her hand once again, only this time very slowly, and although the gazelle didn't quiver this time, Saleema could sense a reaction as she stroked her gently. She went and got a small bowl of milk and sat down next to her as she drank. Saleema spent the rest of the day occupied with the gazelle, leaving her side only to fetch her some food or water. That night she quarreled with her mother, who insisted that the animal be tied up in the outer courtyard. However, Saleema persisted that she stay with her in her room. Umm Hasan protested: "Does that make sense? Do beasts belong in bedrooms?"

"First of all, she's not a beast," Saleema retorted. "Besides, she could catch cold or be attacked by a wild bird."

Neither Umm Hasan nor Saleema were willing to give in, and it was only when Umm Jaafar intervened and suggested that the gazelle stay on the veranda that the squabble came to an end. "On condition that you clean up after it in the morning," she added.

Both Saleema and her mother agreed and everyone went to bed. When Saleema was sure that her mother had fallen asleep, she piled up her mattress and crept softly out of the room.

"Where are you going?" asked her grandmother.

"I'm going to sleep on the veranda. The heat is stifling me. Good night, Grandmother."

"Good night," replied Umm Jaafar, giggling to herself.

A week before the wedding, the scent of celebration permeated the house of Abu Jaafar. The aromas of savory pastries fried in olive oil followed Naeem and Hasan to friends and neighbors' houses as each one delivered leather-skinned vessels stacked with honey-soaked cakes, bringing them from one house to another and coming back only to start over again. Umm Jaafar, Umm Hasan, and a third relative worked from dawn, sifting the flour, kneading and leavening the dough, and shaping it into little triangles. Then they fried them in large copper pans that sat on the stove from dusk to dawn. They placed the sheets of dough into the scalding oil, and, when they turned into a golden crisp, they removed them, drained them of the excess oil, and layered them in stacks.

Two days before the wedding, three mule-teamed carriages were seen leaving the house carrying Saleema, her mother, and grandmother to the Hana Bathhouse. Several women from the neighborhood and their small children, as well as a few girls Saleema's age, joined the bridal procession. They brought baskets neatly packed with fresh towels and clean clothes, washcloths and loofahs, water scoops and soap. They also brought small jars and vessels of henna, musk, as well as almond and olive oils.

The roasted sheep Umm Jaafar had prepared the night before was placed in a huge, tightly sealed copper pot, and two of the muleteers helped carry it onto the carriage. The neighbors brought the drums and tambourines, and to celebrate the festive occasion they prepared delicious pastries soaked in honey and stuffed with cheese and aniseed or crushed walnuts. They also brought the sweet fruit ciders they brew and set aside in bottles for such special occasions.

When the bridal party entered the bathhouse, the youngsters

shouted, the women ululated, and everyone wished each other good fortune and prosperous marriages. They set down their bundles and went to take off their clothes. They wrapped towels around their waists and shoulders, some covering the breasts and others not bothering at all. As they moved into the baths, the voice of one of the women rose above the din as she recalled the day Umm Hasan gave birth to Saleema fourteen years ago.

"I held her in my arms and I caressed her against my breast, and I said to you, Umm Hasan, 'May God grant me a life long enough to bathe her on her wedding day!' Do you remember?"

She didn't, but answered, "Of course, I remember."

The woman sat Saleema down in front of her and untied her braids, and with a scoop she dipped into the hot water and poured it over her head. As the other women began to ululate once again, one of them took the tambourine and started to sing the customary wedding songs that were frequently interrupted by exclamations of wishes for a long life and healthy offspring. The children danced in excitement despite their mothers' warnings against breaking an arm or a leg on the slippery floors.

When the neighbor finished scrubbing, depilating, and perfuming Saleema's body and lathering and rinsing her hair, she asked her to stand up in order to inspect her work. She removed the towel that was wrapped around Saleema's waist, and Saleema found herself as naked as the day she was born in front of all the women. She blushed, and in her confusion she started to grab the towel to cover herself, but not wanting to appear childish she stood motionless, embarrassed but too proud to show it.

"May the Creator be praised," one of the women cheered. "I swear to God, your groom is indeed a fortunate man."

Drops of water and beads of sweat trickled down Saleema's neck that was covered by her thick, wavy black hair. Her olive-skinned body glistened from the scrubbing of the loofah and the hot water. Her breasts were young and firm, her waist slender, her buttocks ample, and her legs perfectly chiseled. "May He who gave you shape be praised," exclaimed one woman as another pulled her toward her to remove her pubic hair. The singing continued as some of the women washed their own children, or busied themselves washing one another. A few of them participated in the more exhausting ritual that was taking place in the stall out of view of the others. Umm Jaafar and Umm Hasan decided to take their baths after the lunch. Umm Hasan prepared the henna in a bowl large enough for everyone, while Umm Jaafar prepared to serve the lunch. As usual, she fretted about not having enough food to feed the crowd, and Umm Hasan reminded her this was not the first feast she had ever prepared. "There's no food more delicious or more plentiful than what you serve," she said praisingly. But Umm Jaafar would only rest assured after all the women had eaten, and the food had been scrumptious, and there had been more than enough for everyone to have her fill. She watched the women as they ate, walking around and through them and the children, prodding this one or that one to a second or third helping. She herself didn't touch the food and was only satisfied when her guests were sated and she was certain that her duty as a hostess had been fulfilled in the most perfect manner.

After lunch the women rested awhile before returning to the tubs to finish their baths. Umm Jaafar declared resoundingly, "I will bathe Saleema." She soaped her head three times, lathered her body over and over again before rinsing her with hot water. Then she dried her off, greased her hair with almond oil, and rubbed musk and olive oil over her body. While her hands were occupied, her face radiated and then suddenly changed expression. Her eyes gleamed one moment and were bathed in tears the next, as her thoughts moved from the little bundle of flesh she carried as a newborn infant to this magnificent young woman, the precious daughter of her precious son. She could see Abu Jaafar and she held on to the image like a little girl frightened by the phantom of someone she could never stare at without feeling her soul abandoning her. Her spirit withdrew, and she felt as though she were going to die.

"Why aren't you singing, Umm Jaafar?"

"I'm singing. I'll sing," she replied as she joined in with a quivering voice.

"Pass me the henna, Umm Hasan."

"I'll henna her hair," shouted one of the neighbors.

She went over to the large bowl and scooped out a handful of the smooth, moist mixture. "Stand up, Saleema." Saleema stood up and the woman sat down next to her on crossed legs. She took a small bit of the henna with the tip of her right index finger and meticulously drew a squiggly line above her ankle. Then she took more henna and continued her pattern until she formed a beautiful design in the shape of flowered branches in a deep dark red that embellished her anklebone and the top of her foot. "Sit down, Saleema." Saleema obeyed and the woman applied the henna to her heels and the bottom of her feet. Then she set to work on her palms. All the women followed suit by taking a bit of the henna, while the older ones took more to dye their hair.

Saleema remained seated without moving a muscle as her arms and legs were stretched out to let the henna dry. She glanced all around her and thought about herself and how little she understood of all of this. She wished she could be with her gazelle, to pat her head or watch her sprint and prance about in the privacy and confinement of their house.

The wedding night was boisterous and generated more than the usual excitement for such occasions. The news of the uprisings and the success of the rebels at Alpujarra[3] in attacking the Castilians and regaining control over some of the fortresses along the coast had unlocked the doors of hope that were now wide open. They might be able to reach Murcia from where the uprising could spread and thus reclaim Granada; or, reinforcements could come from Egypt or

3. Alpujarra or *al-Basharrat* in Arabic, a mountainous region east of Granada, was the site of fierce Arab resistance to the Spanish Reconquest.

North Africa, and the freedom fighters and exiles coming aboard the ships could unite with their brothers who were fighting on land.

The incessant talk of the uprising became the people's daily wine of which they imbibed ravenously, making them giddy with delight. They never tired of repeating the details or listening to the same stories over and over again as though they were strummings on a lute or the chanting of love poems that gave increasing pleasure the more they were heard.

The Castilians had sent their cavalry up the mountain road with their heads swelling with arrogance and confidence as if victory were already in hand. All they needed to do, they thought, was strike their heels on the sides of their horses that would neigh thunderously and dash to the prize at the top of the mountain. But a torrent of rocks came pelting from above and onto their heads. They fell with their horses and tumbled down the deep ravine, calling for help with no one to help them. The people all laughed with joy as one recited Quranic verses with a smile that never left his lips: "Have you not seen how your Lord dealt with the people of the elephant? Did He not make their plan go wrong, and sent hordes of chargers flying against them, while you were pelting them with stones of porphyritic lava, and turn them into pastured fields of corn?" [4]

The devious Count Tendilla had launched a military campaign on the mountain. As he sat smugly in his castle, awaiting the news of the attack on the villages, the waterfalls were drowning his horsemen with the water from the canals that the rebels opened from the top of the mountain, as though the flood was unleashed against them from God who sent them neither a Noah nor an Ark.

Their hearty and boisterous guffaws mixed with the women's singing and the rolling of drums. Hasan and Naeem helped Umm Jaafar and Umm Hasan set up the patio for the male guests and lay

---

4. Quran 105:1–5. This chapter, "The Elephants," recounts the Battle of Abraha in 571 when the Christian viceroy of Sana' marched against Mecca with elephants and a large army to destroy the Kaaba. See Ahmed Aly's translation, Princeton, 1993.

down carpets for them to sit on. Then they accompanied Saad to the bathhouse with Abu Mansour who insisted on bathing the groom himself. "This is the bath of all baths, my boy," he said as he scrubbed the back of his neck and back, laughing and embracing life and people as though the uprising of Alpujarra had brought him back to his old affable and pleasant self.

On the wedding night Abu Mansour danced to the rhythms of the lute and kept beat to the applause of the guests. He shook his shoulders and stretched out his arms, then he stiffened his back and swayed his body while flexing the muscles of his belly. He laughed and all the guests laughed with him. He danced with wild anima-tion and his face flushed in ecstasy as though he were the groom. He then grabbed Saad and made him dance, but in utter embarrassment the groom was unable to keep up with the old man nor could he compete with his fine movements and subtle gesticulations. He stumbled as he danced and he felt the blood rushing to his head like a young girl forced to dance in front of a group of men.

Saad sat down, so too did Abu Mansour, and a group of men jumped to their feet to join in the singing and dancing. Some of them hoisted sticks in the air, and as one man raised the stick hori-zontally over his head, his partner would cross it with a strike of his stick in the middle. Or one would swing a stick around in circles while another would leap high in the air over it. They danced in such a frenzy until their bodies were drenched in sweat.

Naeem jumped up all of a sudden and asked that they clear the floor for him. "I want to dance alone," he announced, winking to Saad as a reminder of what he had promised him ages ago. He stretched out his arms as far as they would go and straightened his back. He tapped his toes on the ground and lifted his left foot, and in rapid motions he spun around several times and lifted himself off the ground as the contours of his spinning body were blurred as he spun. Then suddenly he stopped, and the crowd cheered and ap-plauded wildly at his astonishing prelude. With slow, delicate, and deliberate movements he started up again, and as in a solo recital he gyrated back and forth to the rhythmic beat of the applause. His arms lifted, his back straightened, and his body swayed very slightly, as though he weren't moving at all. Then he tapped his foot on the ground, lowered his arms to the side without touching his body, and his chest protruded like the arch of a tightly strung bow, and suddenly he pumped his legs and thighs over and over again, as the eyes of the crowd followed his movements and their breaths panted to the beat. It was as though there was eloquence in his dancing, and magic in its eloquence.

8

Before Saad and Saleema awoke, Umm Jaafar and Umm Hasan had prepared everything. They heated the water for their baths, kneaded the dough and made fresh bread, and left two plump chickens simmering in a savory sauce over a fire for the newlyweds' lunch. There was also an array of deserts that Umm Jaafar had prepared before the wedding, not to mention the many different sweets some of the neighbors sent over the night before.

As soon as Saleema came out of her room, Umm Jaafar shot her a quick and inspecting glance. Her face was flushed a rosy red and her features revealed no particular expression. Umm Jaafar's heart beat easily, said "Good Morning" to her granddaughter, and gave her a kiss before going back to her chores. The next two days confirmed what Umm Jaafar had observed. She commented that the peaceful and glowing couple looked like a pair of lovebirds. Even Umm Hasan smiled and joked to Saleema, "Had I known that marriage would make you this content, I would have married you off as soon as you learned to talk."

But things started to change soon thereafter. It was Umm Jaafar who first noticed Saleema's pale complexion and puffy eyes as though she had been crying. It's natural for newlyweds to disagree, she thought, but so soon after the wedding? She confided to Umm Hasan about what was bothering her, and they thought long and hard about what possibly could be wrong. Either they had a quarrel, or perhaps he put demands on her that were just too difficult, or maybe he was unable to fulfill her needs in some way. If she hadn't known Saad, she would have guessed that he insulted her or mistreated her the way some husbands do early in the marriage in order to assert their authority and assure absolute obedience from their wives. But Saad seemed as perplexed as Saleema. His face grew gaunt, and he avoided looking them straight in the eye whenever he spoke. In her need to know, Umm Hasan asked Saleema what was the matter.

"There's nothing wrong!"

"Did Saad mistreat you?"

"Saad?"

"Did he quarrel with you?"

"What are you talking about, Mother? Of course he didn't quarrel with me."

Umm Jaafar and Umm Hasan took turns fretting over what needed to be done. They toyed with the idea of bringing the matter to Hasan's attention but decided against it. After giving it careful thought, they devised a plan both of them would carry out. When the couple closed the door to their bedroom, Umm Jaafar would stand guard behind it and listen in on what's going on between them until her eyes and ears grew heavy with drowsiness. Then Umm Hasan would relieve her and take her place standing guard.

As agreed the two women executed their plan and spent the first night, each one taking her turn with ears glued to the newlyweds' door, straining every muscle in her body to hear what was going on. When Umm Jaafar awoke the following morning, she got up quickly and went out to join her daughter-in-law who was still standing outside Saad and Saleema's bedroom door, and the two women crept away slowly and quietly to exchange information on what they were able to gather during their watches. As the older of the two, Umm Jaafar spoke first and began to recount her sequence of events.

"I stood as long as my feet held out, but nothing at all happened."

"What do you mean, nothing at all happened?"

"They didn't quarrel. I didn't hear Saad raise his voice or reprimand her in any way, nor did I hear her snap the way she always does whenever somebody scolds her."

"They were totally silent?"

"Not exactly. They were whispering as though one of them was revealing a secret to the other. That's what it seemed like to me although I wasn't able to make out what they were saying. And I couldn't tell if it was because the door was too thick or because my ears are too feeble."

"You didn't hear any other noise?"

"Not at all, as though he never approached her the way a husband approaches his wife."

"I didn't hear anything of that sort either," responded Umm Hasan, as an expression of bewilderment came over her face. "I said to myself, what happened must have happened at the beginning of the night and Umm Jaafar must have heard it. But now they've made up, passing the night whispering gently in each other's ear. This is something I cannot keep silent about!"

Umm Hasan decided to bring up the matter to her son in the hope that he would deal with this young man whom he married off to his sister. Despite Umm Jaafar's attempts to stop her, she made up her mind and headed straight to his bedroom. She sat down at the foot of his bed and waited for him to wake up to tell him what she had come to be certain of after a night's vigil. But when she finished telling him everything, he scolded her and told her that what she was saying was no better than the idle gossip of crazy old women. "Why don't you leave Saad and Saleema alone to start their life the way they see fit?" he added. But his words of rebuke only left her seething in anger.

Had someone told Saleema two days before Saad's wedding gift arrived that she would have a gazelle that she would love as much as her mother, grandmother, and brother, she would have laughed in his face and thought him insane. But she was taken totally by surprise at how much this little creature crept into her heart and lodged herself securely in it as though it had always been her natural habitat. Every night she tied her on the eastern portico and no sooner would morning break than she would unleash her, and she and Saad would feed her, play with her, and take turns holding her. When Saad went to work, she would do those chores her mother insisted she do, quickly and carelessly, rushing through them to leave herself free time to spend with the gazelle or to read. She would take a book and go out to the courtyard, sit cross-legged on a carpet, read for awhile, and then lift up her eyes to watch the gazelle prancing about or standing still. Sometimes she would come on her own and stretch herself out at Saleema's feet while she read, holding the book with one hand and gently stroking the submissive gazelle with the other.

The night Saleema said "I'll never find a husband like Saad," she lay wide awake, unable to understand why she had responded so readily. Now, as she was going over in her mind what happened that night, she smiled at the very thought of that sentence that had caused her so much confusion. For it was now clear that divine inspiration had come to her when she agreed to marry Saad, and in this short time together, she had fallen in love.

On that first night Saad approached her gently and timidly, and she in turn responded to him without understanding what it was that allowed her to do so. When their bodies joined as one, a tranquility the likes of which she had never known enveloped them. It was a tranquility that released in her an overflow of affection, meekness, and tenderness she had never experienced before.

On the third night Saad told her stories of the sea and of anchored ships that set sail and returned. He spoke of Malaga, which lies between the sea and the mountains. On top of the mountains there is a castle and a fortress. The fortress has high walls, and it is magnificent to behold. And although its magnificence doesn't compare with that of Alhambra, it is more awesome and glorious because it sparks in your soul strange feelings of fear and security at the same time. Malaga is a big city with many buildings, gardens, and verdant mountain pastures cultivated with fig, olive, and orange trees, as well as grape vines and palm trees. He asked her if she ever saw a rainfall over the vineyards. The dark rain clouds in the sky block out all but the slightest bit of sunshine that penetrates the vines and pierces through their lush verdure, producing brilliant flashes of yellow made even more radiant by the raindrops, which then appear as the morning dew. He told her about this one field that sat next to his house, and that even though they didn't own it, it was theirs alone to feast their eyes on.

"My father's name was Muhammad Abdel-Azeez al-Hareeri whose family came from a long line of silk weavers. He was a tall man with a dark, olive complexion and finely chiseled features. He had thick, curly hair like mine and jet black piercing eyes that added to his towering presence. My grandfather lived with us, too. He looked a lot like my father although old age made him look short and frail. He spent much time in prayer, and he always had prayer beads twirled around his fingers even when he wasn't praying. He shouted at us whenever we made too much noise, but I wasn't afraid of him. I don't know why I wasn't.

"My mother's name was Aysha. She was a fair-skinned, plump, and jolly woman. She laughed a lot and her face always lit up when she did. Every year my father would weave her an exquisite piece of silk and with it she made a dress she'd wear on the fifteenth night of the month of Shaaban, the first night of Ramadan, and the night of Laylat al-Qadr.[1] She also wore it on the two grand feasts[2] and whenever she was invited to a wedding. What I remember most is a blue silk dress and a black caftan with white embroidery.

"My sister Nafeesa was four years younger than I. My mother

---

1. The 27th of the month of Ramadan is the night on which, according to Quran: 97, the Quran was revealed to the Prophet Muhammad.

2. The first is *Eid al-Fitr* (the feast of the breaking of the fast), which marks the end of Ramadan, and the second is *Eid al-Adha* (the feast of the sacrifice), which falls forty days after the end of Ramadan when Muslims commemorate Abraham's acceptance to sacrifice his son to God.

loved to say how no sooner did she wean me than she suckled Nafeesa. I remember holding her and rocking her to sleep. I can even remember the first steps she took as she toddled in the foyer, and how I used to give her piggyback rides and run beside her as she raced through the vineyard laughing."

Saad's face was pale and drawn and Saleema did everything she could to keep from crying. They had lost all track of time and didn't notice that the sun had risen. Nor could the early dawn call to prayer remind them of the time since the Castilians now forbade it. Saad stood up to change his clothes and get ready for work. He had no desire to go on with his story, but Saleema persisted.

For the next three nights he recounted all the details of the siege of Malaga and its inevitable defeat after the horrendous cannon fire from both land and sea. "The Castilians besieged the city, first by shooting ignited arrows and then with cannons that could kill you with their screeching sounds before their shells even hit the ground. Then their troops attacked the city and installed bells and crucifixes in the mosques. And over the citadel, all the city gates and every public building their flags were hoisted.

"Several days after the Catholic monarchs issued the orders to distribute rations of wheat to the people, my grandfather passed away, hungry and defeated. Starvation also took my little sister Nafeesa, or perhaps it was fear that killed her. My mother wept and lamented, 'What good will the wheat do us now?' But in the end she did go and return with our allotted ration. She kneaded the flour, baked bread, and said, 'Eat!' And so I did.

"At first they told us that the residents would be able to contribute collectively to the ransom from their money, jewelry, and other possessions, in the amount of thirty gold doubloons per head, including children and infants. It was reported that there were fifteen thousand residents in Malaga, so how could they come up with the exorbitant amounts that the Castilians were demanding? They dispatched a delegation to Granada and they even sought help from North Africa.

"The Castilians rounded up as many citizens as they could lay their hands on, and proclaiming that the amount of ransom collected was not complete, they announced that every citizen of Malaga was to be treated as a servant to the king and queen of Castile and Aragon to do with them as they pleased. The royal couple agreed to exchange a third of them for Spanish soldiers held captive in Morocco. Another third was condemned to a life of hard labor to compensate for the expenses incurred by the Castilian treasury to finance the war. The remaining third, most of whom were women, were parceled out as gifts to the Pope, European nobility, the Royal Court notables, and the military commanders. My mother was among this last third.

"I was screaming when they came to take her away. I wept and struck the sides of my face repeatedly. A Castilian soldier took pity on me and patted me on the head, trying to reassure me that everything would be all right. He told me about his children who were my age. I was eight at the time. He said, 'Stay with me, and no one will lay a finger on you. I'll take you home and raise you with my own children.' I stayed with him for one month in Malaga, and when we set out to go where he lived, that is, me and this man who's name was Jose Blanco, I escaped on the way."

Saleema sat next to Saad as he was telling her all of this. Her back was slightly arched, her head tilted, and her hands resting on her stomach. A quiver rushed through her body, her head throbbed, and her insides contracted in cramps. She jumped up from the bed and rushed out of the room and went to the bathroom. When she got to the door and opened it, she bumped into her mother, and they both let out a scream at the same time. Then Saleema continued her way to the bathroom and vomited. Her grandmother brewed some mint leaves and made her a hot, steaming infusion. It was noontime. Her mother watched her closely and said, "I think you're better now. You don't look as pale. Don't you feel better?"

"What were you doing behind the door, Mother?" Saleema asked as she looked her mother straight in the eye.

9

Hasan's eyes first fell on her in the tavern. She had a pair of castanets wrapped around the tips of her fingers and she was gyrating to the rhythms of three musicians. One of them was an older man who had a leather strap wrapped around his right shoulder that cut across his chest and went down to his waist, and that held a large, round drum he beat with two small wooden sticks. The two younger men were playing woodwinds that made their cheeks puffy and their faces ruddy.

The loud but melodious music with its quick and catchy rhythms was what first caught his attention. But when he looked more closely, his eyes focused on the girl. He estimated she was no more than thirteen years old. She was small and thin and her body had not yet ripened to full maturity. Her face was a golden brown and her hair black and wavy. She had pleasant but ordinary features like many of the girls he'd seen in the souks. What was it about her that made him take notice? There was something in her eyes or her face, or maybe the combination of the two, that opened up a door for you, and you would pass from darkness to light. Or maybe you exit from the darkness of your prison and walk into freedom from confinement, and you take delight in that because you were never aware of the existence of that door that was always inaccessible to you. What was happening? he wondered. Was she one of those gypsy girls who cast spells on men and fill their minds with strange notions?

He couldn't take his eyes off of her for the longest time, but when he did, he realized that his soul had already attached itself to her. He left the tavern but her phantom never left his side. He knew that she was dark skinned. He was certain of that, as he was of her black hair and black eyes. But from where did the colors come from? Was it the color of her dress, the same color as the henna on her palms? Was it the color of the green tattoo underneath her lower lip, or was it her dress that was green? Did the clinking of the castanets and the rhythm of the music ignite his imagination with a fire that blazed in bluish flames?

The phantom clung to him, and he whispered to himself that if he went back into the tavern and saw her again, the colors would disappear and he would return to normal. He went back in and then out, several times. He watched her, then turned his eyes away until he saw them carrying away their instruments and leaving the tavern. Just at that moment he made his way toward the older man. "My name is Hasan. I was raised in my grandfather's house. His name was Abu Jaafar the Paper Maker, may God have mercy on his soul. I work as a calligrapher and I'm being trained to write contracts." He didn't stutter or hesitate for a split second. He continued, "If this girl is your daughter, then permit me to marry her."

The man's eyelashes fluttered, then he held out his hand to shake Hasan's. "Bring your family to our house, and, God willing, all will turn out for the best."

And so went Hasan, along with his grandmother, his mother, Saleema and Saad. The house wasn't as impoverished as he'd expected. It was an old house, the kind that passed through generations. It had a fountain in the middle of the courtyard that was surrounded on three sides by arches that led into the main rooms. The women all went off into one room, and the men congregated in another, one furnished with antique carpets and throw rugs that still had their beautiful patterns even though their colors had lost much of their original brilliance. The walls were not bare but richly adorned with an antique sword in its sheath, an inscription, a pair of silver-encrusted daggers, a piece of parchment with a Quranic verse written in Kufic script, and an old banner.

Hasan and Saad sat opposite the older man and two others close to him in age. The older man told them that one was his brother and the other his cousin. There were also the two younger musicians whom Hasan figured out were the older man's sons.

They were offered oranges and dried figs, as well as dates and raisins. Hasan said a silent prayer asking God to untie his tied tongue, but his prayer went unanswered, and Saad did all the talking. They spoke openly and freely, and so too did Saad. Then they came to an agreement and recited the opening chapter of the Quran as was the custom for such an occasion.

When they arrived back home Umm Hasan reproached her son. "You never told me that the man and his sons were musicians in a tavern!"

Hasan's face grew sullen and his grandmother responded quickly. "The man has nothing to be ashamed of. He used to be a professional singer who performed at religious feasts and festivals, and sang about our beloved Prophet and his miracles, and about the brave feats of his cousin, Sidi Ali. Then those demons invaded our country and forbade these ceremonies. What was the poor man to do? Steal, or worse, sing the praises of the Christian monarchs?"

"I don't know what you see in her," protested Umm Hasan. "Her skin is so dark and greenish, and she's as thin as a rail. The neighbors' daughter is much prettier than she. Why don't you let me go and ask her hand for you instead?"

Hasan darted a reprehending glance at his mother and said, "We already recited the opening chapter of the Quran, Mother. And what happened there is the word of honor amongst gentlemen. Besides, she's the one I want."

Umm Hasan had a pained look on her face. "God give me strength to bear should you marry the daughter of a drummer!"

Hasan's face dropped and once again Umm Jaafar quickly intervened in an attempt to put an end to the conversation. "What's gotten into you, Zaynab? The girl is very pleasant and sweet, and she's still just a girl who hasn't fully matured. You, yourself, were thinner than she when you got married. Congratulations, Hasan. May your new bride bring good fortune to you and this whole house. All our best wishes!"

A week later Hasan signed the marriage contract that his tutor drew up for him:

In the name of God the most Compassionate, the most Merciful. Prayers on the Prophet Muhammad, on his family, his followers and companions, and all his loved ones. This marriage contract has been concluded, by the Grace and Blessings of God, and in accordance with His holy law, between Hasan, son of Ali and grandson of Abu Jaafar, the Paper Maker, and Maryama, the daughter of Abu Ibrahim, for the sum of five gold doubloons, as well as the house bequeathed to the husband by his father, may God have mercy on his soul, located at Ainadamar on the outskirts of Granada, including the olive groves and vineyards surrounding the premises, extending to the estate of Muhammad Shatibi to the south, the house of Umm Saad bint El-Masoud to the north, the property of Ridwan Abu Khaleel to the east, and the mountains on the west.

In accordance with the aforementioned, this contract is enacted.

Maryama had a large chest that she owned ever since she could remember and first started to recognize things by their names. Her mother always said that it belonged to her alone, and that she would take it with her to her husband's house the day she got married. The chest had belonged to her grandmother and was passed down to her through many generations. It was a rectangular-shaped wooden trunk engraved with birds and flowers and ornate tangles of delicate foliage. It had the colors of orange, pale yellow, and shades of pistachio and mint green. The engravings included a sequence of miniature pairs of identical birds facing one another but separated by a single rose. Each miniature was enframed in a garland of leaves. At the point where the arch of the wing touched the tip of the tail another miniature began, and the tail of each bird nearly touched the tail of the previous one. As the arch of the back ascended, it branched out and away from the arch of the other bird, and it ended where the head faces the opposite direction where you would find its rose and its twin bird. In the inverted triangle that separated the two miniatures, branches, leaves, and small clusters of flowers abounded. The composition was repeated in a weave of colors and set against an olive-green background grown darker and deeper with age.

The chest was so big that until only a few years ago Maryama could fit her whole body inside it. She used to pester her mother to let her sit in the chest, and only occasionally would the mother allow her to do so. There she sat along with the few other things in it: a porcelain jar of water from the Zamzam well her grandfather brought back from the Hejaz when he made his pilgrimage to Mecca; a black, brocaded velvet blanket; a pair of brown wooden clogs inlaid with tiny squares and triangles of shiny mother-of-pearl; two small kohl bottles, one of pure gold in the shape of a peacock, and the other silver, with a tiny, round applicator engraved in a floral design; a small ivory case; and a rare gemstone of a dark pinkish color.

At five years old Maryama would sit inside the chest and hold the objects gently, as her mother cautioned her to do. Sitting in the chest was as pleasant an occasion as a feast day that only came after long periods of waiting, and that only she alone was allowed to do. She would go to great lengths to tell her neighborhood friends whatever popped into her head about the contents of the chest, and they would believe her because they could never see what was inside, since it was always locked with an old heavy metal latch.

After Hasan proposed to Maryama and read the opening verse of the Quran with her father, her bridal trousseau was added to the chest: three new dresses, a pair of leather slippers, a striped scarf and veil, two blouses, four pairs of knickers, a pair of heavy stockings, and a woolen cloak. Her mother folded them and placed them neatly inside with the other things. She also placed in it a small Quran in a green leather binding with the words "Holy Quran" inscribed on the cover and set in an octagonal star surrounded by a floral design that looked like a rectangular gold necklace, creating a subtle frame of two golden lines in which the green of the binding contrasted nicely with the border of engraved hexagons.

A cart drawn by a team of sturdy mules transported the trunk, Maryama, her family, and a few of their neighbors across Granada and over to Albaicin where a beaming and glowing Hasan awaited his new bride. When she did arrive, everyone flashed smiles of joy and called out their best wishes for a happy life together. But no one from the household nor any of the neighbors shouted a single ululation on account of Abu Mansour's objection that Saad conveyed to Hasan. Hasan agreed and passed it on to his mother, sister, and grandmother who then informed all the women of the neighborhood.

"Saad," asked Abu Mansour, "are you going to hold a wedding in Abu Jaafar's house while the villages of Alpujarra burn and their inhabitants are slaughtered by the hundreds every day?"

Saad lowered his head at a loss for what to say.

"Will the joyous sounds of celebration ring out from Abu Jaafar's house as the freedom fighters in Alpujarra mourn their dead?" Abu Mansour was long past the point of anger. He now merely sat in front of his bathhouse with a downcast expression, speaking only occasionally, and letting his assistants tend to the bathhouse chores.

"You're a sensible and decent fellow, Saad, so do what you think is right."

He went into the bathhouse for a few moments before coming out, as if he couldn't stand to be in a place that was closed off by a roof and four walls.

When Hasan told his mother and grandmother what Abu Mansour had said, it was his mother who responded. "What would the girl's family say, a wedding without music and singing?"

"Her family and neighbors as well as our own neighbors will be coming. How shall we greet them and celebrate with them?" his grandmother added.

"Slaughter the sheep and prepare all the food fit for such an occasion, but no need for ululations and singing," answered Hasan.

The two women were not happy with Hasan's decision, but they passed the word around the neighborhood nonetheless. Some of the neighbors agreed with Abu Mansour while others felt that if there weren't to be any kind of celebrations to warm their hearts and souls, they would all die of grief. But finally, Umm Jaafar spoke up and had her say. "We will celebrate the marriage and we'll all come together and share in Hasan's joy. We won't ululate or sing, but we will be happy." She stood up and turned her back as she spoke these words so that the neighborhood women wouldn't see the tears trickling down her cheeks she couldn't control no matter how hard she tried.

Only Abu Ibrahim knew that his daughter's wedding would be an unforgettable event throughout Granada and Albaicin. When Hasan told him what Abu Mansour had said he nodded in agreement. "He's right, but I wish it were you or I who had said it first." At that very moment he made up his mind, cursing the Castilians to hell with their laws and orders, to sing at his daughter's wedding feast, knowing in his heart of hearts that in so doing something magic would come out of it.

On the day of the wedding, the men sat in the outer courtyard of Abu Jaafar's house as Saad, Naeem, and Maryama's brothers passed around platters of food and distributed small flasks of an almond drink Umm Jaafar had prepared. When the guests finished the meal and the young men took away the leftover food, Abu Ibrahim stood up.

"Come here, Hasan. I want you to sit next to me." Then, raising his voice, he addressed the crowd:

"May I have your attention for just one moment? I'd like to present this gift to my daughter's husband."

The men grew silent and looked over toward Abu Ibrahim who had absolutely nothing in his hands. They wondered what the present could be. Abu Ibrahim flashed a broad smile. "Before we begin," he shouted, "let's pray to the memory of the Prophet." A deafening silence fell over the courtyard as the men craned their necks to get a good look at this most unusual and unexpected offering of a gift. He raised his voice and began to chant:

How gallant a band of men riding their noble camels to the
*   presence of the Merciful Lord,*
They passed their time remembering the traces of the beloved
*   and came to the realization of the mysteries of the Quran.*
They inherited the Hashemite Prophet, chosen as the most
*   honorable of the Adnani Arabs,*
*   they mounted the Buraq of Love in the sanctuary of Hope,*
*   and traveled by night*
*   to the Jerusalem of Light and Proof.*
Their bodies were a sky at whose door they rang, and its doors
*   were opened,*
*   and two eyes appeared to them,*
*   one eye whose port smiled when it saw its sons in Paradise,*
*   to its left another eye whose tears trickled down when it saw*
*   them*
*   in the blaze of fire.*

The guests were startled and confused, like plowmen stunned by a sudden torrent of rain after long years of drought. They wondered what brought on the uncontrollable shivers running through their bodies and the sudden pallor of their faces. Abu Ibrahim went on with his litany to the Benevolent Prophet, the "light of our eyes," "God's chosen one," the "exalted one," "the most noble and honorable of Arabs." The wedding guests sat dumbstruck, not knowing whether they had fallen into the snare of nostalgia or if a demon from amongst the supporters of the Castilians had descended upon them disguised as an angel of heaven. But how could this be in the house of Abu Jaafar?

Abu Ibrahim then chanted the story of King Muhalhal Ibn El-Fayyad with Khalid Ibn El-Waleed. He sang about the Prophet and how one day he was praying with the people when he began to cry as he told them that an enemy was coming to wage battle against them, a massive army of a hundred thousand horsemen, fifty thousand foot soldiers, and forty thousand slave mercenaries.

"What do you say? Muhammad asked them."

Abu Ibrahim said, "The Companions answered:

" *'O, Muhammad! We are your sharp sword, your far-reaching spear, your crushing rock, your wounding arrow, your racing war horse. We will stand by your side until death.'*

"*Then the Prophet of God, peace be upon him, sent for Khalid.*

" *'O, Khalid, what keeps you from us? My brother, did you not hear Bilal's call to prayer from the Grand Mosque? May God show you mercy!*

"*Khalid began to cry, and this moved the Prophet deeply. Then Khalid spoke:*

" *'O, Messenger of God, for three days now a fire has not kindled in my house. I must play with my three sons and three daughters until they go to sleep to distract them from the hunger that threatens to consume them.'"*

The women who stuck their heads out timidly from the doors were oblivious to their feet rustling them off, one step, two, three at a time, before holding ground. They stopped at the lattice-wood arcade that surrounded the courtyard. The trunks of the trees were strong and sturdy, and the branches swayed back and forth creating stretches of shade under which the men sat cross-legged.

"*Among all his disciples the Prophet chose Khalid Ibn El-Waleed to carry his message to Muhalhal. 'My brother, Khalid, if you climb a mountain, mention God's name. If you forge a stream, say God is great! And if darkness casts its shadow over your heart, then recite from the Quran, since it is the cure for the grief-stricken heart. If you reach these people, do not be alarmed and fear them not!'*

"*When Khalid departed from the gates of the city, he sped away and never stopped for one moment, night or day, until he reached deserted, hostile terrain. The one who enters it is lost, and the one who leaves is reborn. It was a land devoid of water and cultivation. His horse fell from severe hunger and thirst. Khalid cried out to his stallion:*

" *'O, my companion, are you going to abandon me and leave this world?' The stallion looked at him with sad eyes and Khalid patted him on the head and belly. He took his clothes and put them in his pouch and lifted*

his saddle over his shoulders. He bid the stallion farewell and went off. He walked for two miles, but feeling sorry for his horse, he returned. He found his horse with eyes closed and in the throes of death. Once again, he cried out: 'O, Angel of Death, don't you know that I'm carrying a message from the prophet of God? Leave my horse be and depart! Stand up, my beloved horse!' No sooner had these words reached his lips than the angel of death disappeared and the horse stood up on all fours, tapped the ground with its hooves, and started to move. Khalid walked behind as they continued their way until they came to a steep mountain. They ascended slowly and cautiously until they reached the top. They looked down and saw a big valley with many trees and rivers flowing through it. Then they made their way down, again, ever so slowly. When they reached the bottom, Khalid said, 'O, my horse, eat, for this is sustenance from God.' After the horse ate and drank, it regained its strength and neighed a powerful neigh.

" *'Watch over me, my companion, for I must rest awhile.' He removed his coat of mail and placed his sword close to his chest. In a swoon of fatigue, he fell asleep. But when he felt the vibrations of the horse's tapping on the ground, Khalid awoke. Alarmed, he put his feet into the stirrups, mounted his horse, and balanced himself securely onto the saddle . . . He saw a thousand horsemen advancing toward him . . . giving their horses free rein as they brandished their swords in the air.*"

Abu Ibrahim sang on about the encounter between the knight and the horsemen, how the sharp swords glistened and the colors of their clothing turned a dark, crimson red as the horses neighed in the tumultuous confusion of battle.

"*But they surrounded Khalid and captured him and tied him in ropes. The king said, 'Take his horse, slaughter and skin it. Then put him into the skin and tie him to a tree. Prepare the firewood, and tomorrow we'll roast him, thus burning the heart of Abu Qasim,[1] and one of the pillars of the Hejaz.'*

"*Such was the condition in which Khalid remained. When night fell, he raised his eyes to the heavens and looked at the stars. When the world closed its eyes and no one and nothing stirred except the Creator who never sleeps, a breeze from the west blew in his direction, and he began to chant . . .* "

1. "Abu Qasim" is a nickname of the Prophet Muhammad.

Abu Ibrahim raised his voice and sang his sad song while the crowd listened in rapture, never taking their eyes off of him. They wondered where such a voice had come from. Was he not mortal like themselves, one who walks through the marketplace and feeds his children like every man? So what was it about this voice that stirred their souls in such a way? Their roving eyes tried to conjure images for this voice. Their faces, like the waters of the river that flow in ripples, were shiny mirrors that reflected at once the sunlight and their own reflected images.

"It was Ali who heard the voice and who came to save Khalid. It was the young Ali who took up his sword, Dhul-Fiqar, and mounted his stallion, Sarhan, and raced on to Khalid's rescue. He followed the sounds of his cries for help until he found him. He shook the tree from which he was hanging.

" *'Who is it that shakes my gallows?'*

" *'O Khalid, God stands by the destitute.'*

"Ali plucked out the tree from its roots and Khalid came tumbling down into his arms without hitting the ground. Ali pulled out a dagger he was carrying and cut the rope that bound him. He carried him over to the river and washed off the scraps of skin and blood of his slaughtered horse. Ali then took one of his robes and tore his head scarf in half and gave them to Khalid. When God blessed them with an awakening to a benevolent morning, Ali and Khalid reached the top of the mountain as the day had broken and the sun shone bright. All of creation was astir and the accursed enemy was on the march, as the horses, the military command, and the infantry and cavalry followed King Muhalhal in procession. Then Ali spurred his horse and sprinted toward them as though he were an eagle descending from heaven. When the insignia of his Hashemite lineage was revealed, Muhalhal addressed him:

" *'O Ali, not everything white is the purely driven snow, nor everything black is coal. Whatever appears green isn't necessarily sweet basil, nor is every horse fit for battle.'*

" *'O Ali, I am King Muhalhal Ibn El-Fayyad. No woman has ever given birth to the likes of me. If you wish to save yourself from a fate worse than death, then I will give you what will save you.'*

" *'What do you want, accursed enemy of God?' asked Ali.*

" 'Dismount from your horse, kiss my stirrups, and pay me great homage before my men.'

"Ali dashed toward his horse shouting, 'O, my horse, May God give you the strength and power to move quickly.' He balanced himself securely on its back and switched his sword from the right hand to the left. With both arms he swung his sword just beneath the armpit of the enemy of God and plucked him from the saddle like a tiny bird in the clutches of an eagle. He threw him to the ground and dealt him a fatal blow with his sword.

"At that moment Ali went back to Khalid crying out his thanks to God. Then, like a pair of ferocious lions, they went on the attack, each from one side, as the infidel enemy fell in droves. The sun was still shining that day when the last of the enemy ceased to stand."

A long, resounding, robust ululation exploded from inside the house. The men looked in its direction and the women turned their heads. It was Umm Jaafar, standing in the interior courtyard, who was making that joyous trilling sound.

10

As sure as the days were passing Naeem grew certain that he was struck by an evil eye, one so potent that its effect would last a long time. How else, then, could he explain how his heart could be stolen by a young girl whose name he didn't know, or from where she came and where she lived, that he might go and knock on her door and ask for her hand in marriage? A year or two, perhaps three years went by and he couldn't look at any girl without seeing her face, whether in the light of day or the dark of night. He was tortured by this void in his life to the point of feeling anger toward his absent lover and rage at himself. He swore by everything sacred that he would marry, and so he chose the first radiant face that passed through the neighborhood.

On that day he inquired about her and made up his mind. Then he went with Saad to her father's house, and when the father gave his consent they recited the opening chapter of the Quran, and Naeem was the first to congratulate himself on his new bride and the end of this bout of misfortune. Then the father of the bride came to him and said, "The Castilians are making life more difficult for us and imposing great financial burdens on us. My brother in Fez tells me to go there, for work is plentiful and life is prosperous." Naeem responded, "No need to worry! I will take good care of your daughter and treat her with respect. May you have a safe journey, and when God solves things here, come back!"

"Why don't you travel with us, so that God's blessings will be complete," he added.

Naeem declined the offer to leave Granada, and the man took his daughter and departed.

Naeem confided in Umm Jaafar about his feelings of anxiety.

"I'll find you a bride more beautiful than her."

"More beautiful, more ugly, I don't care! I just want a nice girl to be my wife. I feel old and useless, Umm Jaafar, and the years pass me by and I'll find myself an old man with no wife or children."

"Leave the matter to me," laughs Umm Jaafar. "I'll marry you off to a young girl as radiant as the full moon."

Umm Jaafar set out in search for the right bride for Naeem. She found one and told him all about her, her height, size, face, hair, personality, and temperament. Naeem paid a call on the girl's father, accompanied by Saad and Hasan. A day before the signing of the marriage contract, the mother of the bride came to visit Umm Jaafar and with tear-soaked eyes told her that her husband had decided to convert to Christianity after the Castilians announced an edict banning contacts between the Muslims of Granada and the inhabitants of the other Castilian cities.

"He's a muleteer and we all live off of the loads he transports from one place to another. Now we must all convert, I mean the entire family. If Naeem wants to marry our daughter, he too must convert."

Umm Jaafar relayed the bad news to Naeem.

"The truth of the matter is that she was crying, and even though I scolded her for her husband's decision, my heart went out to her. She left after I told her that Naeem would never do such a thing even if they put a knife to his throat. Isn't that so, Naeem?"

"Of course, Umm Jaafar."

At that very moment Naeem realized that he was ill-fated and that misfortune would be sure to follow him until his back grew humped and his teeth fell out.

"It's true that you're late getting married, but you're still only twenty."

"I'm twenty-two, Umm Jaafar."

He held back telling her that he had become the target of an evil eye, and that when he was thirteen he fell in love with a different girl every week. With a sigh of sorrow, he thought. He wondered who it was who cast the evil spell on him. If only he knew, he would beg that person to redirect his aim toward the Castilians and strike them a fatal blow. Now that Saad had gotten married, their daily encounters had dwindled to a solitary once a week. He was busy with his wife, and now she's expecting their first child. Tomorrow there'll be children and he will be all the more preoccupied. Hasan, too, is married and his wife keeps him busy as well. But what about him? He only has the sandals that he works on all day long to occupy him, and at night he wanders about the streets or sits outside the door of his shop, brooding over the evil eye that has befallen him.

Naeem was sitting outside his shop, depressed, when he suddenly saw Saad coming toward him. It wasn't the usual day of the week when they met. He sprang to his feet and shouted out a joyous greeting to his friend. He dashed into the shop and emerged with a bunch of grapes, five ripe figs, and a fistful of fresh almonds. He set them down in front of Saad as he beamed with pride. "I bought them just today. It was as if my heart was telling me that you'd be coming to visit. Here, help yourself."

As he stared into Saad's face Naeem sensed that something was wrong. "What's come over you?"

"Saleema's giving birth in two months."

"I know!"

"I may have made a mistake in marrying her."

Naeem's eyes widened in amazement. With a subtle smirk on his face, he asked, "Have you been tapping into Abu Mansour's wine?"

"I have not been drinking!"

"Did you quarrel with Saleema?"

"Not at all."

"Well, then what happened?"

"What's the use of getting married when a man can't take proper care of his family?"

"Did Umm Hasan say anything to offend you?"

"They came today and closed down Abu Mansour's bathhouse. In fact, they closed down all the bathhouses in Albaicin."

Naeem froze in shock, his mouth agape, unable to comprehend what Saad was saying.

"Are you sure of this?"

"I'm telling you, they closed it down. Some soldiers came and they threw everyone out and closed it down. They said from this day forward anyone who opened a bathhouse or worked in one would suffer the severest of punishments."

"Why is that?"

A scornful, bitter smiled flashed across Saad's face. "They say that bathhouses are unsanitary, and that it's an evil Arab custom with no useful purpose."

"So then where should people bathe?"

"Why should they bathe? Do their Castilian lords bathe?"

"And what does all of this have to do with Saleema? Did you quarrel over the bathhouse closing down?"

"O, Naeem, please! I didn't fight with Saleema, nor she with me. It's just that I'm now without a job. Isn't it enough that I live in Hasan's house? Must I now tell him to take care of me, my wife, and the child we're expecting?"

"Hasan's a brother to you, and so am I. You'll find another job."

Several moments of dead silence passed before Naeem broke it and spoke as though he were talking to himself. "Sons of bitches, they closed down the bathhouses. So where are we to bathe now?"

They grew silent once again, both lost in their innermost thoughts. Then Naeem picked a grape from the bunch and popped it into his mouth and spoke. "Tomorrow, come by my place at the crack of dawn. I'll teach you some of the things I do here. After three or four days, you'll learn everything you need to know, and I'll ask my boss to give you a job. He'll be furious to learn that they closed down the bathhouses, and his heart will go out to you and he'll give you a job. Of course, he'll ask if you have any experience in shoe making. Just tell him that you worked for a cobbler for several years before working at Abu Mansour's bathhouse. He'll ask you where and when. Tell him in Malaga. And when he asks you to show him how to do something, do what I taught you. What do you think of that?"

When Saad left, Naeem sat pondering the strange matter of closing the bathhouses. To wage battle against your enemy is understandable, but what is the wisdom of closing a bathhouse or coercing someone to change his religion? Those Castilians are indeed a strange people and apparently deranged. But what causes them to be so irrational? Did not their mothers give birth to them like normal, healthy human beings? How can their minds be so corrupted and their behavior so erratic? Naeem thought about all of this but was at a loss to find a logical explanation. Maybe it was the intense cold of the north that froze part of their brains, stopping the blood from flowing there, making them die or go insane. Or perhaps it was their excessive consumption of pork that made them dim-witted. Yet despite the closing of the bathhouse and Saad losing his job, Naeem couldn't help but feel happy at the prospect of them working together at the shop. He was a little embarrassed to think of the utter joy he would feel if the two friends went back to working together, meeting every day and talking nonstop, as they used to do.

As soon as he settled into bed, Naeem fell into a deep sleep until a knocking at his door at the crack of dawn awoke him. He opened it, and there stood Saad who had come as they agreed the night before.

"My boss doesn't get here until late morning, so there's plenty of time. So, tell me what's new before we start to work?"

Saad smiled as he stared at Naeem who just then realized that his friend had left him late last night, so how could there possibly be any news? Justifying his question he added, "I mean, did you run into anyone last night after you left? Did Umm Hasan make one of her annoying comments? Did you dream of something unusual last night or did you have a restful sleep? There's always news to tell!"

Saad laughed and so did Naeem, and then they started to work.

❦

Umm Hasan couldn't control herself from expressing her annoyance with her daughter-in-law. "Women arrange good marriages for their sons, and the daughters-in-law come and lift the burden from them. But this Maryama is a good-for-nothing dimwit!"

"She's still a little girl, Zaynab," pleaded Umm Jaafar. "Teach her and she'll learn."

"How can I teach her when she never comes and stands with me in the kitchen when I'm cooking? She never rushes to come over and pull the broom out of my hand when she sees me bent over sweeping out the house."

Umm Jaafar laughed heartily as she pointed out how Saleema is no different, and that Maryama, although younger, at least responds when someone asks her to do something. But Saleema always makes a big fuss and concocts an excuse about something else she's doing and complains that she can't be doing two things at the same time. "They're both still very young and not up to carrying all the responsibility. They'll learn in time, especially when they have children."

Unappeased, Umm Hasan continued her tirade against Maryama without ever mentioning Saleema, and Umm Jaafar only laughed and passed it off as a mother-in-law never satisfied with the woman who marries her son, even if she were as sweet as pie. "I guess all mothers-in-law are alike, except for me!"

Umm Hasan defended herself and added that she's never seen a woman whose husband wakes up and goes to work while his wife is still sleeping, and who whiles away the entire day lounging about in bed and prattling foolishly like a child.

Umm Jaafar held her ground: "Your daughter is no different! It's as though you've given birth to both of them at the same time. Why do you blame the one and not the other?"

Umm Hasan wasn't comparing Maryama to Saleema, but rather to herself. She was convinced that her son wasn't lucky enough to marry a girl clever and efficient around the house. Even though Umm Jaafar defended her by saying she's young, and that the young do learn, that they follow the example of their elders, imitate them, and benefit from their knowledge, Umm Hasan insisted that this Maryama is clumsy and stupid and doesn't want to learn a thing. She was exactly her age when she got married, but she was eager to gain the trust and admiration of her mother-in-law. She followed her around like her shadow, observed her, imitated her, and worked hard at sweeping and dusting, washing the clothes, and polishing the pots and utensils until they shone like mirrors. She stood next to her mother-in-law in the kitchen or sat next to her, never taking her eyes off of her as she observed closely how to prepare couscous, lamb stew with citrus fruit, chicken soup with dumplings, and meat and spinach pies. Even though she learned many different recipes from her own mother and aunts, she was nonetheless eager to learn new things, and it wasn't long before Umm Jaafar grew to depend on her to prepare many dishes. She was exactly Maryama's age when she mastered the arts of jerking meat, disemboweling a newly slaughtered sheep, salting fish, and pickling olives, lemons, and eggplants. She learned quickly how to make different kinds of pies, with cheese, date or fig jam and syrup, and all the things that a house full of family and guests never did without.

A few days ago she noticed that the powdered soap they used to wash their hands after eating was running out, and she called out to Maryama and asked her to make some more. She didn't ask her to stuff a sheep, or to light a fire and knead dough and make bread. She simply asked her to make some hand soap, nothing more or less. Maryama responded, "Tell me how it's done, and I'll do it."

Umm Hasan was stunned at how stupid the girl was, but she decided to be patient. "You mix the lotus fruit with some dried thyme, rose petals, and a bit of dried lemon peel. Then add some sandalwood dust and a handful of nutmeg. That's all there's to it."

Maryama went into the kitchen but came out a dozen times to ask questions: where's the dried thyme, or the little mill to grind whatever needed grinding? She even came out to ask about the amounts. When Umm Hasan finally went into the kitchen to see the soap her daughter-in-law was preparing, her faced contorted in anger and disgust. She was on the verge of dumping it all when Umm Jaafar came in and begged her not to hurt the girl's feelings. What would happen if she asked her to prepare a meal of couscous? She probably would have come up with a big glob of sticky semolina and raw meat! She couldn't for the life of her understand what Hasan saw in that girl. She wasn't pretty, talented, or skilled at anything besides prattling with Saleema!

Saleema's relationship with Maryama deepened by the day, compounded by the fact that Saleema was older than her sister-in-law by three years, thus giving her the role of the older sister. Maryama was sweet and pleasant, and she was perfectly happy in her role of younger sister. She felt great respect, if not pure awe, for Saleema's ability to open a book, stare into it, and decode the meanings of its mysterious words. She even was kind enough to talk to her about what was in it. And when Saleema suggested to her that she teach her how to read, Maryama's feelings turned to pure affection.

"Do you think I'll be good at it?"

"Why wouldn't you be good at it?"

Umm Hasan piped in: "My God, this is all we need!"

Now, added to their long talks and endless chatting were their daily lessons where Maryama would hold her slate and Saleema would sit in front of her and dictate letters and words, and then correct what Maryama had written.

Thus, while Umm Jaafar and Umm Hasan prepared the meals, cleaned the house, and did the laundry, the two girls sat in their places without moving a finger. Even when they weren't chatting or having a lesson, the two always sat next to each other, Saleema reading a book and Maryama knitting swaddling clothes for the babies they both were expecting.

Naeem spoke with his employer. "My friend is an excellent shoemaker. He learned the craft in Malaga. Then he came to Granada and worked with a well-known cobbler, but when he found out his new patron was a sympathizer of the Castilians, he let it be known to Abu Mansour. Well, you know Abu Mansour's position on this matter, and so he invited him to leave the scoundrel and come and work at the bathhouse."

"That poor man, Abu Mansour! They closed down his bathhouse."

"I must tell you, sir, that I'm afraid my friend might go to the cobbler in the next neighborhood, and they'll give us some fierce competition."

His boss stood silent for a moment, and Naeem saw no other recourse than to cut right to the matter.

"Say, why don't you ask Saad to come and work with us?"

"I'm in no position to pay wages to two workers. Besides, there's not enough work for that."

That sly fox! Naeem thought to himself. Everyone in the neighborhood knew what a penny-pincher he was and how much gold he was able to hoard. Some even claim that he keeps his money stashed at home in three large vessels. Should he convince him there's too much work and it can't be done with one employee alone?

"But I swear to you, boss, there's a lot of work, thank God! And if we're two, we can get twice as much done."

"But I can't afford to pay two wages!"

Thinking there was no use pursuing this line of argument, Naeem changed his strategy. "Allow me to speak truthfully. I won't beat around the bush since you're my patron who's treated me with respect and never refused me anything.

"Truthfully?"

"The truth is that I made a marriage proposal."

"Did you find yourself a bride?"

"I haven't found one yet, but I've hired a matchmaker. I also found a job that pays more money, and that will allow me to save what I need to take care of a family. But I said to myself that this is not the conduct of a gentleman, to leave a job suddenly, just like that, and abandon your boss. So I went to my friend and asked him to come back to his former profession."

"Then you want to quit working with me?"

"God forbid, sir! It's just that I am compelled to accept another job I don't want, but I need the wages."

"Is this friend of yours trustworthy? Can I depend on him?"

"Far more than me, sir."

"Then let me see him."

"Shall I go and fetch him?" Naeem asked as he sprinted to his feet.

"Not now. Finish what you're working on, and then you can go and bring him."

When he finished his work, he darted out and headed toward Abu Jaafar's house. He ran through the side streets taking shortcuts until he reached their quarter. He then realized that he hadn't thought about what he was going to say to Saad when he asks him about the job he was leaving the cobbler's shop for. He needed to fabricate a convincing story that wouldn't arouse any suspicion on his friend's part. Naeem backtracked and walked on slowly, thinking of a solution to his latest dilemma.

II

I n the dark of night Abu Mansour stole away to his bathhouse, and when he arrived he paused for a few moments before taking out the key from his pocket. He inserted it into the keyhole and turned it twice, slowly. He pushed in the door and entered. Although he shut the door behind him gently, it made a loud squeaking sound that he was sure all of Albaicin heard. Despite the pitch-black darkness, Abu Mansour didn't need to grope his way but rather proceeded five steps to the left and walked up three stairs. He stretched out his arm, took down the lantern, lit it, and put it back in its place. Then he went over and lit two smaller lamps, first on one side and then two more on the other.

He went over to the bench and sat down. He tilted his head backward slightly and closed his eyes as though he were giving himself over to sleep. He had no need at all to open his eyes or light the lanterns to decipher the details of the place, but he nevertheless opened them wide and began to inspect. There was the square carpeted courtyard as well as the four high arches that connected to a circular dome with drawings of leaves and branches in shades of a deep, rich olive green. And on the triangles that separate one arch from the other were drawings of Cordova with its Grand Mosque, its gardens and palaces. Abu Mansour stared at the pictures, then lifted his head and looked up at the dome. His eyes fell on the surface that held up the dome, counting the windows around it that he knew to be twelve. He counted them. Then his eyes moved over to the two cabinets facing one another before ascending three steps

where they fell upon the three benches covered with rugs and carpets. On the wall behind the benches, there were pairs of niches,
some holding lanterns and others for the folded towels that emitted
the scent of dried lavender trussed into tiny cloth sacks pressed in
between the folds.

Abu Mansour lifted his arms and leaned them against the back
of the bench. He closed his eyes and saw his father yelling angrily
and slapping him across the face, and himself running out of the
house with the intention of never returning to that family that im-
prisons its sons, generation after generation, in a cage built by the
madness of an old grandfather. The story of the grandfather, who,
in actuality, was the father of his grandfather's grandfather, was a
family heirloom passed down from grandmother to grandfather, father, mother, aunt, and uncle, amassing detail upon tireless and endless detail as though it summarized all of existence.

The great-grandfather who emigrated from Cordova after its
fall more than two hundred years ago, leaving behind his house and
his bathhouse, arrived in Granada with nothing more than his wife
and children, a little money in his pocket, and one solitary persistent
desire that he wanted nothing more than to fulfill. What he
dreamed by night and accomplished by day and all that he did in between was focused on this one desire: to build a bathhouse more
grand than the one he once owned. So he left his wife and children
and traveled to Syria to see for himself if what they say is true, that
the bathhouses of Syria are more beautiful than those of Cordova.
He made the journey, he looked around and compared. He came
back two years later. The ship let him off at Malaga from where he
returned in a procession of five donkeys. He rode one, the Dama-
scene architect he brought back with him rode another, and he
loaded the three remaining with all the things he bought to make a
bathhouse from Damascus, Cairo, and Alexandria. When he came
into the house to see his wife and unload his cargo, she burst into
tears, not only because he forgot to bring her a piece of fine Dama-
scene silk, but because he brought back nothing for his daughter's
wedding present, and because he came back with nothing for his

son who awaited dutifully the father's return to announce his own engagement.

Afeef began to build his bathhouse. He spent two whole years, day and night, supervising the construction. In the winter months he wrapped himself in an old woolen cloak, and in the summer he would only wear a light Tunisian jersey. In the bitter cold or scorching heat, he remained with the architect, the builders, and carpenters. They'd finish one door and he would shout in disappointment, "Do you call that a door? To me its's just a slab of wood!" They'd react in bewilderment as they stepped back to inspect their delicately and meticulously carved workmanship. But Afeef dreamed of all the beautiful doors he saw in Cairo, Syria, and Cordova. "I'll provide the wood and pay you whatever you want. But for God's sake, you have to make a new door!"

The door, the pond, the marble fountain, the floral engravings on the dome, the chest, the bench, and the pendant lamp, all these things robbed Afeef of his time and money. He could always borrow the money, but how could he borrow time? Only one week after the completion of the bathhouse, Afeef passed away, leaving his wife and seven children heavily indebted to family, friends, and neighbors. But his children and grandchildren worked in the bathhouse, and God provided them with a decent living. They worked very hard and the Zayn Bathhouse of Afeef the Cordovan was a sight to behold and a comfort to the body, and with it the family settled the grandfather's debts.

Abu Mansour stood up and went over to the chest he used as a safety deposit box where customers put their bundles of clothing and money. It was a long rectangular chest that rested on four wooden legs several inches from the ground. It was made of walnut wood carved with floral designs that intersected and crisscrossed, inlaid with pieces of ivory in square and triangular patterns whose bright creamy white contrasted sharply with the old dark wood.

Abu Mansour inserted the key into the metal lock and lifted the top of the chest. There was a small Quran inside as well as a handkerchief folded over some dried lavender flowers that diffused its overwhelming scent into his nose and chest.

"I don't want to work in the bathhouse."

"What do you want? To run around with musicians and get drunk and sing?"

"That's better than working in a bathhouse!"

His father slapped him on the face. Young people can be hard, they can be foolish, and they can be blind. Only now he understood what his father had feared. It wasn't just a bathhouse but a family history, and he was the only one left to preserve it. He felt the tears swelling in his eyes. His father died while he kept company with musicians playing his lute. When he found out, he returned to his mother. She gave him the key. He opened the bathhouse and refurbished it. He was eighteen years old.

Forty years he's been holding onto this key that his father once carried, and before him his father and his father's father, opening that door that the carpenters worked on so laboriously to carve that plain slab of wood into a medley of geometric patterns and incisions that you immediately recognize as though you were seeing your own reflection in a mirror.

Abu Mansour got up and sauntered toward the central foyer in the middle of which was an octagonal pink stone pool with a marble spout in the shape of a flower from which the water gushed out. It was he who added the pool and remodeled the wash rooms on the sides. He was also the one who bought the lantern made of leaded glass.

Abu Mansour left the central foyer and went to the inner bath where everything was as it had always been. The heating bench divided the area south to north. There were water basins on both sides, the small pool and the large pool, five marble sinks, and a floor tiled with rose-colored marble with blackened trim. This was the great-grandfather's vision and what the builders did to realize it.

Abu Mansour saw all of this with eyes wandering in close inspection. The lamps that hung from the arches on opposite sides emitted their refracting light onto the dark walls. He lay down on the heating bench, which was now cold. The stoker hadn't come and the fire hadn't been lit. He stretched out his arms and closed his eyes. A year's worth of sleep overtook him. In his sleep he saw himself as a boy with nothing more that a faint shadow of a mustache over his upper lip. He was sitting cross-legged in front of the furnace room basking in its warmth, clutching his lute and strumming its strings as he hummed a few melodies. His solitude was broken by an older man with a powerful build and taller than usual. "Get up, boy!"

He stood up, put his lute aside, and undressed the older man. He dipped the Meccan water scoop into hot water from the basin and poured it over him. Then he washed his body and lathered his hair and beard. He scrubbed and rinsed it. He clipped his fingernails and toenails and washed them thoroughly. As he was bathing him, his heart pounded in fear and shivers ran through his body. When he finished he asked the old man in a stuttering voice, "Are you my grandfather, Afeef?"

The old man looked him straight in the eye, and his fear grew more intense. There was a gleam in his eye and a piercing stare.

"Yes. I am your grandfather, Muhy al-Deen. How is it that you didn't recognize me?"

He flustered and dropped the brass scoop, creating a loud clanking noise as it hit the floor.

The old man stood up and leaned over and picked up the scoop from the floor. He filled it with water and ordered him to sit down.

"Did you wash my feet?" he asked.

"I washed them."

"Then it's your turn."

The old man leaned down toward the boy's feet and started to wash them gently. As he did this, water gushed from his eyes and soaked his beard, and his tears mixed with the water from the Meccan scoop from which he was pouring.

12

Despite the hardships of managing daily life, especially under the humiliating pressures of occupation, life in the home of Abu Jaafar was relatively comfortable. The house was open and imbued with the spirit of its inhabitants. Umm Jaafar was the pillar of strength that raised its roof high, filling it with the aromas of the bread she made, the lavender flowers she dried, and the oil she pressed from the olives from Ainadamar. She filled it with her carefree, hearty laughter as she watched her children, happy and healthy despite everything. Hasan was in love with Maryama whose belly swelled with the child she was expecting. Saleema was growing up, unruly and distracted, in the shadow of Saad who was sympathetic despite the sadness in his eyes that overpowered him every so often and carried him off to a faraway place where no one could reach him. In her heart of hearts, Umm Jaafar intoned, "Thanks be to God," in the hope that God would continue to bestow His blessings on them and bring her grandchildren to fill the house with the raucous noise of life.

Saleema was in her seventh month the day she came rushing in to her grandmother, gasping for air. Her grandmother scolded her for her reckless behavior before she even told her what was wrong. But Saleema paid no attention to her grandmother's scolding. She seemed more terrified than angry, saying over and over again that she couldn't understand what made her lie on the floor without moving a muscle. Umm Jaafar followed Saleema out to the courtyard where the gazelle was lying on her side, her body stiff and her eyes like glass.

"She's dead, probably since yesterday."

"It's not true," Saleema shouted at her grandmother as she stared at her severely.

But the gazelle was dead and there was nothing anyone could do except take her away and leave her to the vultures and scavengers.

How could she have died and why? These questions preoccupied Saleema so much that she forgot her own sadness, which disappeared behind a curtain of questions seething with indignation and denial. Was it God who killed her? What could the High and Almighty possibly want with a gazelle that was like a star in the firmament that caressed the heart and delighted the soul? But God is not a tyrant, so perhaps it was the devil! But who was the devil and who created him and unleashed him onto God's creatures? Her grandmother says that death is a reality and the fate of all living things. Her grandfather Abu Jaafar died, but he was an old man. The longer one lives the shorter his life gets, and when a body grows old it ages. A fruit ripens and then it turns rotten, and when a fabric gets old it wears out. But this gazelle was neither old nor feeble. She was beautiful and her eyes flashed with life as she pranced about. So who could have snatched her life away? A scorpion? Or something like a scorpion in the body that discharges its yellow venom and spreads death in a new, shimmering web?

"How did my father die, Grandmother?"

The question stunned Umm Jaafar as the image of the healthy son flashed in her mind with the sounds of his cheerful laughter, while suddenly he slips into illness and his face grows pale, his eyes swell, and his tongue languid. His head shakes in painful discomfort as he gasps desperately for air, while life slips away in a rasping, rattling trill. The look in his eyes tries to hold on to life, but is unable, and a sad rebuke with a tinge of hope stares out.

"He got sick, and then he died."

"I know that, but what sickness killed him?"

Umm Jaafar could not bear to contemplate the image of her son, and she stood up and left Saleema.

❦

Maryama gave birth to her first child, a daughter, and joy filled the household as everyone obsessed over the new mother and child. Then Saleema gave birth to a son, and both the joy and the obsessing grew twofold. But the soul of the baby boy Saleema gave birth to departed only two weeks into life, and Umm Jaafar realized that the death of the gazelle was a sign, an omen, and that the ways of God are inscrutable. The household was turned upside down, from the joy of birth to the sorrow of death. Their hearts were broken, having experienced the glad tidings of a new life and the sudden bitter reality of loss, as both resided, shoulder to shoulder, in the same house.

Only Saleema was beyond sadness and joy, consumed by burning questions: Was God so evil that He wished them destruction? Or does Saad give her what doesn't last, the splendor of his gift dissipating into a pain that pierces and torments the soul? Her delivery had been difficult. It nearly ripped open and destroyed her body, stretching it beyond its capacity until the infant was pulled out and she heard his feeble scream. She held him in her arms and examined him closely. She touched his skin gently and kissed his cheek. She sensed his taste on her lips and her breasts were overflowing with milk. She placed her nipple into his mouth, and her insides moved like the earth sprouting a new seedling. It wasn't joy that filled her heart, since joy always runs its course. It was something that pervaded her body and soul, an odd mixture of awe, joy, fear, amazement, and a thousand other things, the way life comes together with its hills, rivers, skies, the daylight sun, and the moon and the stars on high. It all came together and was concentrated where this tiny mouth was sucking on her nipple and the breast that embraces, shows tenderness, and provides milk; God only knows from where and how it came, like a miraculous spring gushing from the depths of the earth or a cloud in the sky perpetually pouring rain.

Two weeks Saleema spent with her newborn, hearing and seeing nothing but his overwhelming presence that both consumed and enriched her as she needed nothing from anyone or anything else. Then God took him away. Why?

Saad, who resigned himself bitterly to the loss of his son, grew more and more depressed each day. To no avail would he knock on Saleema's door and then withdraw into himself, rejected and dejected, outside her walls. She wouldn't talk to him or get near him, as she was averse to any union, physical or emotional. Yet he went on with life, talking to Naeem about his worries and his fear of the future.

No matter how big or depressing life's disasters seemed, along came another one more intense and ferocious, making what seemed so horrific yesterday mild in comparison today, reducing it to a matter of insignificance that shrunk into a tiny corner of the heart.

The Catholic kings issued their decree of forced conversion on everyone. The orders were posted and made public for all to see. The people of Granada and Albaicin had the choice of converting to Christianity or banishment from the kingdom.

Hasan said that departure was the only solution, and that he would sell the house at Ainadamar and the house they were inhabiting in Albaicin, and they would all go to Fez.

"Or does anybody have another suggestion?" he asked.

Umm Jaafar said that she would not leave since she didn't have much longer to live. "I'll never leave my house nor will I leave Abu Jaafar alone to wait for me in vain. I want to stay and lay green leafy branches by his grave until God permits me to join him."

"Then will you convert, Grandmother?"

"I'll never convert!"

"Then what are we going to do? What do you think, Saad?"

Saad sat silently, thinking about Malaga, which was now so far away. When the boat carries him off to the shores of Morocco, Albaicin will seem distant and Malaga even farther. "Departure is difficult, but . . ."

"Then, we go."

"We go."

"We won't go," shouted Maryama. "Only God knows what's in people's hearts, and the heart lives only in its body. I know who I am, Maryama, and this is my daughter, Ruqaya. Would it make much of a difference if the rulers of this country forced me to take the name 'Maria' and my daughter 'Anna'? I'll never leave because the tongue doesn't disown its own language and the face its features."

They all looked at her in astonishment, wondering from where this young girl Maryama got all this wisdom. It was as though she had opened a window and the light came rushing in and illuminated the dark room. They decided to stay. The decision was difficult but carrying it out was even harder.

The women of the neighborhood stood in large groups to receive the baptismal drops of water collectively. The priest muttered some words that none of them understood. They stood motionless, watching him without making a sound. Their faces were deep and raging, like a hostile ocean on the surface of which small boats rock back and forth, battered by the high waves causing loss and dread. They gasped desperately for air as they are about to sink, but they did not sink. The big wave broke only to be replaced by another wave, more ferocious, and another gasp for air, more desperate, as though the soul were submitting itself to Azrael, the angel of death, while screaming, "I do not want."

It wasn't the simple matter of a name on a piece of paper replacing another name, as Maryama had thought, but a whole new life of accusations and mortal sins: the circumcision of young boys, contracting marriages according to Islamic law, celebrating the wedding feast with drums and songs, waiting for the new moon before and after Ramadan, chanting the prayers on the holy night of Laylat al-Qadr, the five daily prayers, Ramadan fasting, keeping Friday a holy day, using henna to dye young girls' palms and older women's hair. All of these were now crimes, and the gates of prison were wide open for sinners and the piles of wood were readied to be ignited under those who committed them. It all seemed like the wheel of Satan rolling along and the soul unable to keep pace with its terrifying speed.

"It is forbidden for the newly converted to wear Arab clothing. It is prohibited for any tailor to weave this unlawful garb, and for women to wear their traditional veils."

"A new convert may not sell his possessions to anyone of Arab origin, like himself."

"It is absolutely forbidden for anyone of Arab origin to sell his possessions. And those who violate the order will have their wealth confiscated and will be subject to a severe penalty."

"Those Arabs from Granada and its surrounding villages who possess books and manuscripts must submit them all, or else they will be tried and imprisoned. Those exposed for possessing an Arabic book after the date will have all of their possessions confiscated."

"It is unlawful to own or carry weapons, and this decree includes swords and daggers."

"Islamic inheritance laws are no longer in effect. Estates will no longer be divided among the heirs, but will be passed down according to the current traditions of the kingdom of Castile."

"It is forbidden to abet, protect, or give shelter to Muslim terrorists who come in ships from the Moroccan coasts to invade the shores of the kingdom. It is also unlawful to establish contacts or to cooperate in any fashion with the rebels hiding out in the mountains. Violation of this law will result in certain death."

"Whosoever shall depart from Granada and return shall have no legal rights to his former possessions, and he will be arrested and sold as a slave in public auction."

A wheel that exhausts the soul turns, and the young ones, in spite of it all, grow up. After Ruqaya, Maryama was blessed with five more children, the last of whom was a boy whom they named Hisham. Saleema however was not so fortunate, but how could she be, given that she withdrew from Saad and immersed herself in reading books, mixing herbs, and concocting blends, ointments, and potions. At first it was only the books that held her attention, and she would stay up all night pouring over them, underlining the important passages, and writing notes in the margins. Then she took great interest in asking women savants for the ancient remedies they used to cure different kinds of pain. She began to purchase pots, jars, vessels, and vials, and she mixed herbs both fresh and dry, making infusions, powders, and salves that she boiled, froze, and distilled. The women of the neighborhood came seeking her advice about curing one illness or another. Umm Hasan couldn't bear any of this and quarreled with her so vehemently that all the neighbors could hear. But Umm Hasan's incessant protestations and her attempts to bring her daughter back into the fold of proper housewives who please their husbands with sons and daughters, with kohl-painted eyes, made-up faces, and bodies perfumed with musk and jasmine, fell on deaf ears. After months of waging a fierce battle with her daughter, Umm Hasan retreated and left the matter in God's hands.

Umm Jaafar, on the other hand, reacted in a different manner, accepting what Saleema was doing, however grudgingly. She wasn't at all convinced, but she accepted it. Perhaps she was too old to engage in such a battle. In her heart of hearts, it wasn't so much what Saleema was doing that bothered her as it was her neglecting Saad. She could see him dejected and withdrawn, and so she treated him tenderly and showered him with affection, insisting on inviting Naeem to the house, knowing that he could lift Saad's spirits and ease his pain in these trying times. Saleema's rejection tormented Saad, and he complained to his friend of his misery.

"Whop her," suggested Naeem. "Give her a good whopping until she comes to her senses."

Then he changed his mind. "Treat her kindly, Saad. The poor thing is grief-stricken over the loss of her baby. She needs sympathy and understanding."

Finally, he gave a third piece of advice. "Get up right now and smash all the jars and vials she fills with those strange brews she's concocting. Tear up those books that are poisoning her mind and throw out all those women who come seeking her advice and cures."

Naeem's suggestions were both numerous and contradictory, but Saad wasn't able to act on any of them. He was too emotionally tied to her, and he longed to be close to her as though she were his mother and had rejected him. She sat absorbed in this new occupation that seemed to have befallen her like the plague. But he was patient, speaking kind words to her, trying to catch her attention with a question, an observation, or a piece of news, only to have her keep her distance, beyond the reach of anyone, as the sadness of an abandoned orphan overwhelmed him and the tears swelled in his eyes until sleep would bestow mercy on him.

One day it happened that Saad's long-suffering patience reached its limit. Umm Jaafar heard his voice rise in utter anger and Saleema replying with equal vehemence. The quarrel erupted in explosion, and when Umm Hasan heard it from the kitchen she came rushing out to find out what was the matter. "Let them fight it out a little, and then they'll make up," cautioned Umm Jaafar.

Umm Hasan couldn't take her mother-in-law's advice, especially when the shouting reached such a pitch and it appeared that Saad was striking Saleema. Umm Hasan shouted furiously, "This is the last straw. We take him off the street and put a roof over his head, and he mistreats our daughter and beats her!"

She rushed toward Saleema's room and Umm Jaafar followed her frantically and out of breath. "Your daughter deserves everything she's getting, Zaynab. Saad isn't the first nor the last husband to strike his wife to keep her in line. Keep your composure, Zaynab."

Umm Hasan stormed into the room, adding her screams to those of Saad and Saleema. Umm Jaafar couldn't make out exactly what was going on when she was suddenly stunned by Saad rushing out of the house with his clothes in a bundle. Saleema stood stone-faced and grating her teeth but without a tear in her eye. When Maryama came home, Umm Jaafar asked her to go and sit with Saleema and calm her down. Later when Hasan returned, she asked him to go look for Saad and win him back. He agreed, but before he left the house he went into Saleema's room, cursed and slapped her. Maryama started to cry, as did Umm Jaafar, as well as Umm Hasan and all the children. Then Hasan stormed out, cursing mindless women, burdensome children, and the jackass of a man who thinks of getting married and raising a family. Umm Jaafar was convinced that an evil eye had cast its spell on the household, and she asked Maryama to go out and fetch her the best incense she could find to ward it off.

As he anticipated, Hasan found Saad at Naeem's. He tried to convince him to go back with him to the house. When Saad refused, Hasan swore that he would divorce his own wife if Saad didn't return with him.

For the next three days, Saad and Saleema didn't exchange a word. Then Saleema broke the silence. "You were wrong to strike me, Saad. You struck me and then Hasan did the same. No one has ever raised a hand to me in my life, neither my father nor my grandfather." She remained silent for a short while and continued, "But I too was wrong when I insulted you and said that this is my house, and that if you didn't like it, you could leave. It was a hurtful thing to say and I said it in a moment of anger." She was looking at him directly as she spoke, and he could see in her blues eyes the light that had bewitched him several years ago. He took a deep breath with great difficulty and spoke.

"I didn't mean to hurt you. But these ointments and brews you concoct day and night are driving me insane. I can't bear the fumes, and they're giving me nightmares." He gulped and then added, "Nightmares upon nightmares."

"If you want, I'll move them somewhere else, Saad, but I beg you not to ask me to give it up. I need to do this and I need the books you're making such a fuss about. I must have them."

Saad sensed the tears swelling in her eyes and the determination lurking behind them. He knew then that he could never stand in her way. It wasn't only that he couldn't break her determination, but that he really didn't want to.

13

As Umm Jaafar made her way through the twilight years of her life, she drew closer to Naeem. She actually counted the days that separated his visits. She had known him since he was a boy and followed him as he grew up, often guiding and sometimes scolding him in the process. But the closeness that had developed between them during the past few years had grown into a deeper intimacy, and she gave him her full attention whenever he spoke to her. His stories carried a certain warmth and colors that shattered the forlornness of leafless trees, cloudy skies, and the occasional chill of the winter of life that settles into the bones. Their talks began ever since the day he told her that King Ferdinand and Queen Isabella were cursed in their offspring.

"How so?"

Naeem was working in the service of a learned Castilian priest. He helped with household chores and manged his library by collating and binding manuscripts. What he didn't hear directly from the priest he learned from the priest's conversations with visitors, and that's how he came to learn what he told Umm Jaafar.

"I heard from Father Miguel that before they died the king and queen lost their oldest child, Prince Don Juan. Then his younger sister, Princess Isabella, followed. She had been married to a Portuguese prince who died himself only several months after the wedding."

"Then God really did punish them. For what good is winning

wars and expanding one's kingdom only to suffer the loss of one's own flesh and blood?"

The story Naeem related to Umm Jaafar gladdened her soul not out of vengeance against the king and queen, who forced all the people of Granada to taste the bitterness of defeat, but because she finally found the divine justice that had eluded her and filled her with a doubt that at times briefly appeared to her in the voice of Abu Jaafar after the burning of the books. But then she would ask God to forgive her. God in His exaltation was wise and just, and so He punished the king and queen in their own lifetimes for the sins they had committed. A defeat in war was not harsher than the loss of a child. Truth had shown its face, and in that she found some inner tranquility. And so whenever Naeem came to visit her, she wanted to hear more of his stories.

"They were cursed, Umm Jaafar, and God did not lighten their punishment, nor did He wait until the Day of Judgment. He handed down their sentence in this world, and now that they have departed, He will inflict eternal punishment upon them."

Whenever Naeem visited Umm Jaafar, she would bring him what food she had and sit beside him, fixing her eyes on him and pricking up her ears to listen to his stories. "Listen, Umm Jaafar, to this latest news that not a soul in Albaicin knows about. Juana, the daughter of Ferdinand and Isabella, is stark raving mad!"

"There is no god but God!"

"I heard that she married a prince from another land known as Philip the Handsome."

"Mercy me! And so then what happened?"

"His name is Philip the Handsome because he's handsome, and any woman who lays eyes on him is immediately smitten with love for him."

"And so?"

"And so, my lady, that doesn't please Princess Juana, and jealousy devours her soul."

"I don't blame her!"

"When she expresses these feelings of jealousy to Philip the

Handsome, he strikes her violently, but she still loves him. She's caught between her love for him on the one hand and her jealousy and his abuse on the other, and as a result she loses her mind. After that, Philip the Handsome dies."

"There is no power or strength save in God!"

"He dies, and so what do you think Juana does?"

"Naturally, she mourns for him even though he may have cheated on her, because she loves him."

"That's not the point."

"What is the point?"

"Patience! I'll tell you all the details. It seems that Queen Isabella's mother was also demented, and she passed down her insanity to her granddaughter."

"Praise the Lord! Have we reached the point where we're all being ruled by a family of lunatics?"

"I heard all this from the priests while I was serving them dinner. They talked on as though I wasn't there or as if I were a piece of furniture standing behind them. Anyway, Philip the Handsome died in the prime of life, and Juana went totally mad. She had his body exhumed from the grave and brought to her bedchamber as though he were still alive. And if the affairs of state required her to travel, she would take his corpse along with her. And since she couldn't bear to let any woman come close to him, she had all her handmaidens replaced with butlers to clean her bedroom and serve her on her travels."

"The corpse must have rotted and surely Juana died from the putrid odors."

Naeem laughed before divulging the latest piece of gossip he was sure would shock Umm Jaafar and knock her off her chair like a bolt of lightning.

"In fact, Juana didn't die at all but instead inherited the throne of Castile when her mother died and the throne of Aragon when her father died. And now she's the ruler of both kingdoms."

Just as Naeem expected, Umm Jaafar's mouth dropped and she stared at him incredulously. "Do you mean to tell me that the current queen, daughter of Ferdinand and Isabella, is that same madwoman?"

"She's the very one. Father Miguel even said it himself, 'Juana La Loca,' which means 'Crazy Juana.' Just think, Umm Jaafar, we're being ruled by a woman who's out of her mind!"

Naeem grinned from ear to ear while Umm Jaafar roiled at the very thought that God punishes the wicked king and queen with the death or madness of their children, and still they rule over us, forcing us to reap the fruits of their insanity. How difficult it is, she thought, for anybody to understand God's judgment, such a profoundly complicated mystery, much less for an old woman like herself.

When Naeem departed and after much thought, Umm Jaafar found an explanation to all these unjust laws in that whoever enacted them was a madman. What harm would be done to a person if someone else refrained from eating pork, or dyed her hands with henna, or conducted his daughter's wedding ceremony inside a church or outside? And what threat would there be to a ruler if some of his subjects purchased books written in the language of the Arabs and not in somebody else's language? And why should it anger him if someone like herself wore an Arab-style dress instead of a Castilian one, or laid a wreath at the tomb of her dearly departed husband?

She didn't understand the wisdom of God in allowing a madwoman to rule over His subjects, but she came to realize that those strange and oppressive laws were the result of a deranged mind. Were it not for Naeem, God bless him! she wouldn't have understood a thing. And were it not for his wonderful anecdotes, she would find herself passing her days and nights alone, talking to no one and no one talking to her. Saleema was up to her ears in jars and vials, and Umm Hasan was always in the kitchen cooking meals for the children. Maryama was constantly picking up after them, and the children were content to be left on their own to play and chatter among themselves. And when they tired from playing, they gathered around their mother who would tell them stories. Whenever Umm Jaafar called them to tell them a story, you could see a hint of mockery glimmer in their eyes because the sounds she made just weren't the same since her teeth had fallen out and the words became garbled in her mouth. When Hasan came home exhausted after a hard day's work, he occupied himself with his children and wife. So Umm Jaafar only had Saad to pour her attentions on, and she looked forward to Naeem's visits, which lifted her spirits as he entertained her with his stories.

She only had to take a quick glance at Naeem before Umm Jaafar knew he was bringing her a juicy bit of news. He would approach her, flashing a broad smile that he adjusted with pinpoint accuracy and control. But then he would lose control and the smile led to a shimmer in his eyes and the divulgence of his secrets.

"Best of mornings to you, Umm Jaafar," he greeted resoundingly.

"Good morning to you, too. You brought me a strange and wonderful story, right?"

The smile gave way to a hearty laugh. He stretched out his hand to give her a needle and thread. "Could you thread this needle for me?" he asked.

Umm Jaafar was taken aback since it wasn't in Naeem's nature to mock her. She looked at it with an odd and reproving look. "Just try, Umm Jaafar, just give it a try," he begged.

"What's gotten into you, Naeem?" she asked with annoyance. "You know I can't do that."

"But you will thread this needle," he insisted. He placed the needle in her left hand and the thread in the right. Umm Jaafar was at a loss to understand what was going on, but she yielded to Naeem expecting the worst. Naeem pulled out of his pocket a small envelope and opened it gently. He took out something quite odd and unfamiliar. It was two flat circular pieces of glass joined together and framed in a delicate gold wire rim, with a small slender handle attached to one of the pieces of glass.

"What's that?"

Naeem held the handle and lifted the two circles of glass close to Umm Jaafar's face until they reached her eyes. She shut them tight and asked, "What are you doing, Naeem?"

"Don't be afraid, Umm Jaafar. Open your eyes and thread the needle."

Umm Jaafar opened her eyes slowly as she muttered, "In the Name of God, the Most Compassionate and Merciful." Then she uttered the same thing with exuberance when she looked through the pieces of glass and saw clearly the eye of the needle she had been unable to see for some years now. She tried to thread the needle a few times but couldn't do it because her hands were trembling.

"Calm down, Umm Jaafar, and concentrate on threading the needle."

"Have you taken up magic, Naeem?"

Again she tried and when she passed the thread through the eye of the needle she handed it to Naeem as she listened to the hard, fast pounding of her heart. Naeem lifted the glasses from her eyes and spoke joyously. "This instrument, Umm Jaafar, is used by people when their sight grows weak and they can't see small things. It belongs to Father Miguel."

"Does the priest need it to thread a needle?"

"He needs it to read all those books that have fine print," he answered in laughter.

"Where did he buy it?"

"He asked one of the Genoese merchants to buy it for him."

"Then it's sold in Genoa?

"I don't know."

"Is it expensive?"

"I have no idea."

"If it's not too expensive, I'll ask Hasan to buy one for me. There are lots of merchants from Genoa who pass through Granada. Hand it over and let me try again, Naeem." Umm Jaafar stretched out her hand and took hold of the delicate gold handle and raised the glass circles to eye level. She looked through them toward all the corners of the room.

"Strange!"

"What's strange, Umm Jaafar?"

"The things that are far way I can see better without it."

"I think it's to see things close up. I see Father Miguel using it only when he's reading."

Umm Jaafar called out to one of Hasan's daughters to go and bring her aunt Saleema. "Let's see what Saleema will do with it when she reads a book."

Before the little girl reached her aunt's room, she managed to spread the news of the strange instrument to her mother, grand-mother, and sisters. They all came running and surrounded Naeem, looking on with intense curiosity and asking questions all at once, while Naeem refused to let any one of them get close to it or touch it.

"Does this thing let blind people see?" asked one of the children.

Umm Hasan shook her head in relief. "Such a wonderful piece of news I must tell our neighbor who's lost her sight. Now she'll be able to see again." She got up to go out and tell her neighbor the news without even looking at Naeem who was trying to explain that the glasses only magnify small things but do not give sight to the blind.

When Saleema entered the room, she inquired about the in-strument, then she picked it up and held it to her eyes. She took it off, and when she started to go to her room and get a book Naeem stopped her. "Bring the book here," he said. He took the glasses away from her, and she went and came back with a book with small print. She took back the glasses from Naeem and started to read with them. Those small letters that always exhausted her and made her pull the book away from her as she squinted her eyes now seemed so clear to her, and she could read them with astonishing ease.

"Naeem, where did you get this thing?"

"It belongs to the priest."

"Will you leave it for me just for tonight?"

Naeem jumped up from his seat and grabbed the glasses from Saleema's hands. "That's impossible," he answered. "When he asks me about it, what will I say?"

"Since you've brought them here, it's obvious he's away."

"He's away, but he'll be back tomorrow."

"Leave it with me, and I'll give it back to you tomorrow morning."

Umm Jaafar, Umm Hasan, Maryama, and all the children joined together in trying to convince Naeem to leave the glasses with Saleema, "Just for one night," they repeated. After going back and forth several times, Naeem finally accepted his fate and gave in, handing the glasses to Saleema repeating over and over again to be extra careful, and he showed her how to hold and use them so they wouldn't break.

"Tomorrow morning, I'll be back tomorrow morning to get them."

Naeem returned the following morning to pick up the glasses, but Saleema had already made up her mind. "What you were afraid would happen, happened," she told him. "The glasses broke."

"Broke!" Naeem shouted out this one word and then grew silent. Several moments passed with him not knowing what to say or do. Then he spoke. "How did they break? Let me see them."

"They fell and smashed into pieces. I was afraid the children would step on the gláss, so I threw them away."

At first he was suspicious, but then he became certain. "You're a liar, Saleema. You decided to steal the glasses."

"Hold your tongue, Naeem."

He was seething in anger. He shouted at Saleema, and she shouted back. They got into a heated argument that neither Umm Jaafar nor Maryama could pacify. Umm Hasan took offense at Naeem's accusation of theft and took her daughter's side. As she shouted at Naeem, he shouted at her daughter.

Naeem stormed out of the house, repeating over and over again: "I'm going to complain to your husband and your brother, and God willing they'll beat you savagely until you tell us where you put the glasses you stole."

14

I n times of trouble, men's hearts soften and seek the solace of others, and the long years in which Saad and Hasan shared the same roof only strengthened their friendship as they spent long hours in conversation, more often than not seeing eye to eye on most matters. Hasan treated Saad with kindness and affection, not only because he was his friend and his sister's husband, but because he had descended upon his grandfather's house as a guest. And he continued to take care of him well beyond the many years when he was no longer a guest and no one could remember that he was living in a household that wasn't his own. Even the problems with Saleema only fortified the strong bonds between the two men, especially since Hasan deep down blamed his sister and felt a kind of gratitude toward Saad for not mistreating or divorcing her, and especially for not taking another wife.

So what happened that day when a whispering conversation between the two friends flared up in dispute and ended in a ferocious exchange of words? Umm Jaafar rushed to them as fast as her advanced years allowed to find out what was the matter only to have Hasan snap at her. "I beg you, Grandmother, go away. This is a conversation for men only. Take Maryama, my mother, and the children into the inner courtyard, and leave us alone!"

Even as far away as the inner courtyard, you could tell that what was going on between the two men was a fight although the exact words couldn't be detected. Umm Hasan said that an evil eye, the same one cast upon Saleema, had struck again. Umm Jaafar nervously muttered, "May God protect us!"

The children went to sleep, and Umm Jaafar, Umm Hasan, and Maryama sought refuge in their beds although none of them could sleep a wink. They wondered what was going on, what possibly could have provoked such an outburst.

In the wee hours of the morning, Saad came into Umm Jaafar's room and sat down next to her. "I'm going away, Umm Jaafar," he said.

The thought never occurred to her.

"Going away? Where and why?" she asked.

He was hesitant in responding.

"Are you leaving Granada and leaving us alone to fend for ourselves?"

His eyes welled in tears, and he leaned over, took her hand, and kissed it.

"I'm going to the mountains. I have comrades there who need me. I'm not leaving Granada, nor am I abandoning you. You're all the family I have. Everything will be fine, my mother."

He got up and she followed him like his shadow as he went out to bid farewell to Umm Hasan, Maryama and the children, and then to Saleema.

"Saad's going away, Saleema," announced Umm Jaafar to her granddaughter.

"I know."

Saleema seemed upset to her, and she noticed a nervous twitch in her face. But Umm Jaafar mustered enough courage to speak up: "Stay with your wife, Saad. Stay with us even if Hasan has offended you. He was wrong to do so." As she said this, she went up to him and kissed him on the top of his head as a gesture of conciliation.

"Say something, Saleema."

"I already told him."

"Told him what?"

"I told him to stay, and that he can come and go as he pleases. I told him this is my house and Hasan's house, and that it was his house as well. I told him to stay and do whatever he wants."

Then the problem was with Hasan. Umm Jaafar hurried to his room, woke him up, and scolded him as if he were a little boy. "What did you do to your sister's husband? What did you say to him? Why did you make him angry?"

Hasan sat up and took a deep breath. His face was white as a ghost.

"Saad is planning to leave," she shouted.

"I know that."

"What did you do?"

"I didn't do anything!"

"Then why is he going away?"

"Leave him be, Grandmother. He's already made up his mind, and there's nothing we can do to stop him."

Everyone began to cry, Umm Jaafar, Umm Hasan, and Maryama. Seeing them, the children burst into tears as well. Saleema stood still, as though the man who was leaving was not her husband. Hasan didn't budge either. Umm Jaafar thought to herself that it wasn't true that the two of them did not care. She stared at Hasan and noticed his body trembling from beneath his summer robe, and she looked at Saleema who was so pale that she looked, God forbid, ill.

Neither Hasan nor Saleema, who both knew the reason for the fight and the reason for Saad's leaving, divulged a word to anyone in the household. Hasan insisted that Saad was not leaving the country and that he would be back to visit them from time to time. "Perhaps . . . ," he never finished the sentence but instead left the house.

Two weeks later Naeem came to the house and learned of the news. He flew into a fit of anger so violent that the children all ran off to hide from him.

"He went away? What do you mean, he went away? Why? How could he leave and not say anything to me, without taking me with him? What am I supposed to do now? He had a fight with Hasan? It's not Hasan's nature nor Saad's to quarrel like that. You

must be lying to me. What happened to my friend? Did he die?"
Naeem was screeching frantically, with a pitch wavering between
anger and fear.

"Where's Hasan?"

"He's not home."

"Where's Saleema?" He burst into her room as though he was
one of the household or a little boy not yet prohibited from going
into women's quarters. He stood in front of her, seething in anger,
at a loss for words. Finally he shouted out, "Are you happy now?
He's gone away. Isn't that what you wanted?"

She stared him straight in the eye just as he was doing to her. "I
had nothing to do with that."

The devils were dancing in his eyes. He was overcome with a
powerful desire to smash all the pots, bottles, and vials and throw all
the powders, fluids, and ointments on the floor, and then to strike
Saleema as hard as he could to release the anger toward her that had
been building up inside of him for several months. Instead, he just
spat on the floor and stormed out.

Umm Jaafar called out to him but he paid no attention. He left
the house with his thoughts and emotions in turmoil. He was livid
and frightened, and he didn't understand a thing. Had he taken his
advice and left Saleema to punish her? A bit late for that, he
thought. But why punish him? What did he have to do with it? And
were Umm Jaafar and Hasan at fault? He fought with Hasan? How
and why? Did some horrible catastrophe befall his friend and were
they hiding it from him?

He hurriedly raced back to Abu Jaafar's house. "Has Hasan returned?" he asked.

"Not yet."

Once again, he went outside of the house, squatted on the
ground, and waited for him to come back. When he noticed Hasan
coming from a distance, he jumped up and ran toward him.

"What happened, Hasan?"

"Can you stay the night with me?"

"I can."

"Well, then, come with me."

Dawn crept up on them without either one having a moment's sleep. Hasan told him the whole story and Naeem listened without interrupting, except for one time. "Saad never said any such thing to me," he lamented. "Did he really say all that?"

"Not at the beginning, but I figured it out because I live with him under the same roof, and I know when he comes and goes, and when strangers I've never seen come to visit him. Finally, I confronted him about what was going on, and he told me. We disagreed and ended up in a fierce argument. Do you think I was wrong, Naeem?"

Naeem didn't answer the question, but left that very moment since he had to get back to his place of employment before the priest discovered his absence. "If I find Father Miguel awake, I'll tell him I woke up early and went out for some fresh air," he said as he was leaving.

He went back taking quick steps thinking all along how and why Saad kept all of this a secret from him, and why he went away without coming to say good-bye. His pace slowed down and he stopped dead in his tracks. He went over to the side of the road, sat down on the ground, and burst into tears.

Hasan spent the next few weeks in a state of depression, which of course was no secret to the members of the household. The children were unaware of what was going on even though they bore the brunt of their father's quick temper, his scolding and spanking that was not his usual way. Umm Jaafar and Umm Hasan blamed his behavior on his quarrel with Saad, which had a devastating effect on everyone. They counted the days before Saad's return so that Hasan would calm down. But the mystery of why Saad left and why Hasan let his friend and brother-in-law do so was known only to Saleema and Hasan. But Saleema didn't utter a word of it, so engrossed she was in her herbs, and she didn't have much to say anyway. Not even Maryama could say anything because Hasan had made her swear on the Quran to keep it a secret after she persuaded him to tell her what had happened. Hasan himself was in a state of bewilderment, and he couldn't sleep, tortured by the question of whether he behaved rightly or wrongly. At the time it seemed certain, as though he had made up his mind and the subject was closed. "I can't stop you from taking the road you chose for yourself, but I'm responsible for the safety of my family and I'll do anything to protect them."

"It's not protection you're giving, Hasan," replied Saad. "If every one of us shut the door of his house and only cared for the safety of his family, we would all perish, once and for all!"

"Are you accusing me of cowardice?" Hasan asked in an agitated voice.

Saad didn't answer but shot Hasan an accusatory look that only increased the tension.

"I don't have to defend myself," protested Hasan. "It's not wrong to protect one's family, even by means of deceit. Life goes on and you have to provide them with food and a roof over their heads. The Castilians show no mercy, as you can see with your own eyes every day. The least suspicion they have of someone leads to an arrest, an investigation, abuse, and torture to extract a confession that is only fabricated to ease the torture. The prisoner may be sentenced to death or he may die in detention before sentencing, leaving a whole family without a provider, and the wife takes to the streets to feed her children. Even an honorable woman will do whatever she can to feed her hungry children."

"It's correct what you're saying, but what are you suggesting to confront this scourge? If every one of us said that he feared for his wife and children, then what would become of us?"

"God is our supporter," said Hasan after taking a long, deep breath.

"This shows passivity and indecisiveness."

"There's no need to be hurtful, Saad," shouted Hasan.

Saad stubbornly repeated what he said. "Passivity and indecisiveness, while our brothers on the Moroccan shores cross the hostile sea and face the greatest obstacles to wage attacks on these shores to inflict whatever losses they can on the Castilians, and while our own men hiding in the mountains launch a resistance from above.

And if they were to ask us for some help or protection, should we mention our women and children as an excuse, and tell them, 'Go away and God be with you? When you achieve the victory that we're all hoping for, we will hoist you on our shoulders and shout out our thanks and gratitude?' "

"I'm not a freedom fighter, Saad," retorted Hasan with a bitterness tinged with sarcasm.

"Nor do I claim to have that honor, but I will cooperate with them. If they ask me for anything, I will give them whatever I have or do anything I can."

"But you're receiving them here in my house, and you go to meet them leaving from this house, and in the process, you threaten everyone in it, my mother, grandmother, sister, wife, and children."

"What do you want, Hasan?"

"I want you to refrain from dealing with the freedom fighters."

"And if I don't agree?"

"You must agree because you're not living by yourself."

"Then I'll go away and live alone. Will that give you any peace of mind, Hasan?"

Hasan had a pained look and he shouted back. "Why do you want to humiliate me, Saad? Do you think I don't care? Do you think all this doesn't weigh heavily on me and tear my insides out? I can't sleep at night. I've consulted more than one faqeeh, in fact, I consulted three. Wait!"

Hasan got up and came back a few minutes later carrying three sheets of paper that he spread out in front of Saad. "Look," he said, "I copied this letter in spite of the danger in doing so. I copied it so that you can see and hear for yourself what's in it, and you'll know that I'm not a coward or a derelict, nor am I abandoning our religion. But God wishes ease for us and not hardship, as the Quran tell us.[1] Listen to this fatwa of one of the most eminent Maghrebi jurists

---

1. The reference is to Quran 2 (The cow), verse 185: "as God wishes ease and not hardship for you."

who permits us to use concealment and dissimulation to protect ourselves and our children. It says:

"*Thanks be to God, and prayers and blessings on our Prophet Muhammad, on the members of his household and all his companions. Our brethren who hold on to their faith are like those who hold on to live embers, the most deserving of God's rewards for what they encounter and what they suffer of themselves and their children to please God. Though they live in exile, they are yet to be brought close to His prophet in Paradise, in the highest heavens. They are the inheritors of the traditions of the pious ancestors in bearing the burdens of the faith even in the face of death. We ask God's kindness and protection for ourselves and for you. May He help us all preserve His righteousness with pure faith and truthfulness. May He lift from us our burdens and ease our difficulties.*

"*Greetings upon you from the author of this fatwa, from the most humble of God's servants and the most needy of His forgiveness, the servant of God, Ahmad bin Bujum'a al-Maghrawi of Oran. May God shed His kindness and protection on all. May I prevail upon you in your state of pure heart and your presence on distant shores to pray your best prayers so that God grant us a safe and happy ending to the perils of this life. May He gather us in the company of those pious folk on whom He has shed His grace. Hold on dearly to your faith and instruct your children who come of age to do the same, even if exposure to the enemy is no longer a danger to you. Blessed are those who follow the right path when others have been corrupted. For praying to God amongst the heedless is like living among the dead.*"

"The shaykh didn't say in his fatwa that you should turn your backs on those who were forced out of their homes and have become freedom fighters."

Hasan's face contorted, and he exploded in anger. "Just listen until I finish, and don't interrupt.

"*Pray, even if by outward gestures. And give as though you were giving to the poor and destitute, because God does not look into your faces, but rather into your souls. Wash yourselves from any ritual impurity, even by swimming in the sea. And if you are prevented, pray at night to make up for the day prayers, even if you are compelled to use unclean water. You may perform your ablutions with fine sand by rubbing your hands on a wall. If it is not possible, you are absolved from performing the prayer for lack of water or fine sand, unless you can point with your hands and face to pure earth, a stone, or a tree with which to clean yourselves. Then you may go through the gestures . . . "*

Hasan read on in a soft voice with a slight tremor and a grim expression on his face.

"And if they coerce you into denying your religion, and if you can do so deceivingly and with trickery, then do so; and if you cannot, then rest assured in your faith even if you utter something false. And if they force you to insult the Prophet Muhammad, then do so with the devil in mind."

Tears rolled down from Hasan's eyes and his voice quivered and cracked as he continued to read until he reached the end.

"Whatever hardship you face, seek counsel with us so that we guide you in the right direction, God willing. We ask God to end all coercion against Islam so that you may worship Him with His grace without intimidation and fear, but with the aid of our co-religionists, the noble Turks.[2] And we bear witness to you in the eyes of God that you have been truthful and you have accepted Him. We must respond to you, and send you our sincerest wishes for your safety. May those in exile return, God willing."

Saad looked at Hasan despondently but responded with resolve: "This is a fatwa about something else. I'll be leaving at the crack of dawn."

2. It was widely believed among the Muslims of Spain and North Africa at the time that the Ottoman Turks would defeat the Christians and bring al-Andalus back into Islamdom.

15

Umm Jaafar was waiting for Saad to return when she died in
her sleep. She passed on with no one in the household
aware of any trace of illness. She took to her bed because
she was weak, and she never complained of any ailment. When they
found her in the morning, she had already died during the night.

"What shall we do?" asked Umm Hasan, wiping the tears from
her eyes.

"Take Maryama and Saleema inside and wash the body according to our tradition, then dress her in her embroidered dress. I'll go
and call the priest to come and read whatever prayers he wishes to
read and let him go. Then I'll let Abu Mansour and some of the
neighbors know. We'll conduct the prayers of the dead here in the
house, then we'll carry the body out and walk in procession and
bury her according to their tradition."

"We bury her according to their way?" she asked Hasan.

"Yes, according to their way." He replied as the color faded in
his face and a stern look shot from his eye. He spoke as though he
had rehearsed what to say and was exhausted from repeating it, and
he delivered his lines quickly so he wouldn't stutter or waver. His
mother stared at him, and he averted his eyes. "I'll perform the ablutions and get the Quran."

The women did exactly what he asked them to do. They were
sobbing quietly while they poured warm water over the lifeless
body. When Maryama brought the embroidered dress to the corpse,

Umm Hasan leaned over and kissed Umm Jaafar's forehead and whispered, "We never wanted to deprive you of your shroud. Forgive us!"[1]

The sobbing grew louder, and Maryama wept uncontrollably. The crying turned to wailing and didn't stop until the priest arrived. He muttered his prayers and placed a small wooden crucifix between the deceased's hands. The men came in after he left and recited the prayers of the dead over her body. Then they left the house and formed a procession to take her to her final resting place next to her husband. Umm Hasan, Maryama, and a few neighborhood women remained at home to wait for the men to return. They prepared the meal for the mourners as they bemoaned the loss of Umm Jaafar and lamented the passing of time that took with it the right of good decent folk to shroud their dead and pray at a Muslim funeral.

Saleema participated neither in preparing the meal nor in the women's mourning rituals, but withdrew to her room. She was thinking about death and how it oppresses and humiliates, and that before it human beings stand powerless, and she thought about God in the highest heavens. Is He watching all of this in silence and indifference? Isn't it He who takes life away? Why does He take it away and why does He place it in the heart only to recall it after a while, leaving its warm nest a wasteland? God seemed so obscure to her, incomprehensible, a tyrant who burdened His servants with unbearable things. She contemplated the image of her dead grandmother, and a shiver ran through her body. A lump swelled in her throat, and she held back the tears from her eyes. Her grandmother was dead like her infant son and the gazelle. How could all this be? She couldn't do to the grandmother's corpse what "Hayy" in the story had done to the gazelle, the mother who nursed him, when he ripped open her chest to look for the thing that animates the body, after he had called out to her and she did not respond. He looked at

1. In the Muslim tradition, the body of the deceased is undressed, washed, and wrapped naked in a shroud.

her eyes, her ears, and all her limbs, and he didn't see any defect or disease, but he found her nonetheless incapable of moving.

Saleema brought out the book and opened it exactly to a page practically worn from constant use. She read:

He examined the heart and saw that it was totally still. He wondered if there were some discernible defect, but he didn't see anything. He pressed it with his hand, and he felt a cavity. He said, "Perhaps what I've been looking for has always been inside this organ, and I've never been able to reach it."

He split it open. He noticed that there were two cavities, one on the right side and one on the left. The one on the right was filled with coagulated blood and the one on the left was completely empty. He said, "I only see coagulated blood in this chamber on the right. It must have clotted when the rest of the body became in this condition." For he had witnessed that whenever blood leaves the body and flows out, it clots and congeals. "And this is blood like any other blood, and that this blood is found in all the other organs, and that no organ has the sole possession of the blood over the other organs. But what I've been seeking, my ultimate goal, does not have this quality, but rather something that uniquely distinguishes this state in which I find myself. It is that without which I cannot do, not for a single moment, and to which I at- tribute my first emanation.

"How many times have I been wounded by wild animals and rocks and much blood flowed from me, but that hasn't caused me any serious danger, nor has it affected my actions? This chamber does not contain what I seek. I see that the chamber on the left is empty, but that must not be without rea- son. I've seen that every organ has a function that is uniquely its own. How can this chamber be worthless from what I've seen of its prominence? And what I've been seeking can only have been inside of it, but now it has de- parted and left it empty. And that's when what happened to this body hap- pened. It lost consciousness and the ability to move."

When he saw that what was residing in that chamber had gone away before its demise and left it as it is, he became almost certain that it could not return to it after the breakage and destruction that had happened inside. And now Hayy considered the body as base, and having no significance in relation to what he now believed inhabits the body for a period of time and then de- parts. And so he focused his thinking on that one thing, but what is it? And how so? And what connected it to the body? What's become of it? From which portals did it depart the body? And what was the reason that so disturbed it and forced it to leave? And why did the body arouse such aversion in it that it separated from it, even if willingly?

His mind was befuddled by all of this, and he thought no more about that body and cast it aside. And he realized that his mother, the one who showed him affection and nursed him, was that thing that went away, and that all her actions issued from it, and not from this useless body. He also realized that this body in all its parts is like an instrument for that thing, like the stick that he took in hand to fight off the wild beasts, and his attachment to the body was transferred to the owner of the body, its animator; and the only longing he had left was for that thing.

The *Epistle of Hayy Ibn Yaqzhan*[2] was one of only five books that Saleema had taken from Ainadamar when her grandfather died. A few years later, Naeem started to bring her one book at a time, always on the sly, and each time he would emphasize that she read it quickly, during those few days Father Miguel was away on one of his brief trips. He would give her the book, and she would stay up at night reading, exerting her mind to understand everything in it, and writing down notations until it exhausted her and she dozed off. Even in her sleep the ideas would pile up in her head, and the fear of having the book taken away from her would wake her up in the wee hours of the morning and coax her to resume her reading. Then Naeem would come by to retrieve the book and return it to its exact place in the library.

What kind of student is this whose reading list includes only a handful of books? she thought over and over again with bitterness and annoyance. She resorted to consoling herself with the thought that among her books was a book worth a hundred volumes, penned by the most eminent of scholars and philosophers, Avi-

---

2. *Risalat Hayy Ibn Yaqzhan* is a philosophical romance about a foundling who grows up alone on a deserted island, and, through the powers of an uncorrupted mind, attains the highest intellectual and spiritual levels. It was written by the Andalusian Muslim philosopher Muhammad Ibn 'Abd al-Malik Ibn Tufayl (d. 1185).

cenna, and that she studied his great medical treatise, the *Qanun,* as
though under his direct tutelage.[3] But however fanciful the
thought, she was depressed just to think about the miserable times
in which she lived, when buying books is a punishable crime, where
studying demanded caution and secrecy, not only from the prying
eyes of the stranger lurking about, but from acquaintances as well.
She couldn't read in the daytime and have Hasan, her mother, and
the children all watching her as she put on the glasses she had taken
from Naeem. She waited until the dark of night when everyone
went to bed to light the lantern and read. And the narrow confines
of her prison would gradually expand, and the iron bars of her cell
would be pried open to the sunlight that shone from the book and
from her mind. What kind of student is this whose reading list includes a handful of books? Saleema repeated the question in her
mind resentfully as she recollected the good old days when people
could pick up any book from any shelf in one of the great libraries,
when a wise mentor gave guidance, and when travel to study at the
feet of an illustrious scholar in Egypt or Syria satisfied the heart's desire. Whether you stay or travel, in both cases the points of light
from a thousand books are your lessons and your teachers. How is it
possible from the confines of her Castilian prison to discover the secret of that bird that departs on the order of an inscrutable God? She
wavered between hope and despair, as she contented herself with
Avicenna's *Qanun,* but then she was not satisfied, and so she added
to the margins her questions and observations, as well as a summary
of the findings her experiments led her to. She complied with these
miserable times and Hasan's adamant decisions to protect the family,
and then she didn't comply, whispering to Naeem the titles of
books she wanted, or discreetly asking a woman who knows someone who knows a third person who can bring her a certain book for
which she will pay a year's worth of earnings.

---

3. Abu 'Ali al-Husayn, b. 'Abdallah Ibn Sina (d. 1037), a philosopher of Per-
sian origin who combined Aristotelian and neo-Platonic theories with Islamic
mysticism. His *Qanun* is a voluminous medical encyclopedia.

If her mother or her grandmother, or even Maryama who knew about her book buying, had any idea how she obtained Ibn al-Baytar's *al-Jami'*[4] and how much she paid for it, they would accuse her of being insane. Her mother would most likely faint upon hearing it. The day the book with all its parts was brought to her, she held it to her bosom and her heart beat so fast that it felt like it was breaking free from the prison walls of her chest and dancing its way out uninhibitedly. What's money when you have such an encyclopedia that details the effects of every herb and plant? The wise man is he who buys, and the fool is the one who sells, like those who squander their days and nights racking their brains in an attempt to transform cheap metals into gold. And even if they succeeded, what have they accomplished, since death lurks about, dispatching its emissaries to pierce the walls with fatal diseases, only to make its appearance to strike down and crush the body under the hooves of his stampeding horses? They haven't succeeded, but merely wasted their lives and their minds.

Saleema was now so bullheadedly certain that illness was in the body. But the thing that subordinated the body to it, that animated it, what could it be, from where did it come, and where did it go? These questions tormented her, but she never lost her resolve. She brought these questions into the realm of her daily research on the many diseases that afflict the body. She would stalk them and produce an array of effective weapons, seeking inspiration from her books and burying herself in her experiments. Her pots, jars, vials, and trunks were full to the brim with fresh and dry herbs, mixtures, ointments, and medicines that sometimes cured and other times failed. She smiled in satisfaction, but never forgot completely the bitterness that sat crouched in the corner of her heart, a bitterness of knowing that any victory she achieved was only partial because death can at any moment unleash its powerful sword and flash its victorious smile.

4. Ibn al-Baytar was born in Malaga and died in 1248. His work *al-Jami'* is a medical compendium.

16

Maryama was famous throughout the neighborhood for her amazing surprises. Her natural intelligence always came to her rescue with good, quick thinking that transforms the bitterness the weak feel when subjugated by the powerful into uproarious laughter, when the tables are turned and the strong becomes weak and the weak holds the upper hand. The neighborhood women exchanged stories without ever tiring of what Maryama said or what Maryama did. Why not, since every story about her filled them with joy and entertainment that filled the drudgery of their lives with humor and laughter.

The latest story to circulate among the women concerned Maryama's visit to the schoolmaster at the missionary school to convince him that Arab boys are born "like that," telling him, "And if you don't believe me, sir, then ask any one of these little boys to pull down his trousers and you can see for yourself. This is the way we Arabs are made, with thick black hair and, please don't be offended, deprived of that little extra thing your boys are born with."

Maryama had made the visit after one of her neighbors came crying to her and seeking her advice when her six-year-old boy slipped on the ground while playing and his private parts were exposed. It just so happened that the schoolmaster was standing close by, and when he saw what he saw he flew off the handle. He vowed to notify the authorities at the Office of Inquisition so that they would punish the boy's family for violating the law. Maryama calmed the woman down and reassured her, "There's nothing to worry about. I'll take care of it." On the following day, Maryama went to the school and requested a meeting with the schoolmaster. When she told him what she told him, he shot her a dismissive smile and asked in a stern tone of voice, "Are you trying to mock me?"

"Why would I try to mock you?" answered Maryama with confidence and resolve. "I'm telling you the truth that you don't know because you're a Castilian and you don't know much about Arabs. And because you're a schoolmaster, it pains me that some Arabs may mock you and accuse you of being ignorant. But if you would be so kind as to come and visit us at home, my husband will be more than happy to show you our son's private parts and you'll find it exactly like all the other children even though he's only three years old. I can also bring you to a neighbor of mine who just delivered a baby boy two days ago, and you will see the same thing. Or, if you prefer, go into the classroom right now and ask the children to expose themselves to you, and you'll be convinced what I'm telling you is true."

The schoolmaster was somewhat taken aback by this woman who was sitting in front of him, speaking with such confidence and force of conviction that he surmised she was telling the truth. But to clear any doubt from his mind, he got up and went into the classroom and ordered the boys to lift up their shirts and pull down their trousers. His eyes rotated from one boy to the next and what he saw was a repetition of the same thing. They differed in size or thickness, and some were crooked and others round-tipped. But the boys were similar in that they all lacked, without exception, what the lady called "that little extra thing." He instructed the boys to cover themselves and he left the class. He went back to the lady who was waiting for the results of the examination. Before he could utter a word about what he had discovered, she blurted out with a satisfied look on her face: "Didn't I tell you? And you didn't believe me! You didn't find a single boy different from the others, right? Now, you must believe me, sir, that just as your skin tends to be white and our skin is darker, your boys are born with that little extra thing and our boys are not, unfortunately."

"But I heard that Arabs circumcise their children?" he muttered somewhat sheepishly.

"That's correct. In the old days we used to circumcise girls. But that was a mistake and we mended our ways. But the boys, well, how do we circumcise them?"

Maryama arose from her seat and the schoolmaster bade her farewell, thanking her with profuse apologies for the misunderstanding.

All of Albaicin had a good laugh for the next two weeks, but Hasan was not amused. Rather, he scolded her, telling her that she was putting herself in danger and threatening the safety of the family. "Don't rely on always being so lucky," he warned.

But she always seemed to come out of any predicament intact. She maneuvered her way through every situation with quick thinking and intelligence. The neighbors recounted the stories of her antics and they laughed, but not always without a tinge of apprehension: "What if good fortune abandoned Maryama?" The mere thought sent shivers down their spines, but they always laughed. They all loved her simply because she was Maryama, and because her actions gave them moments of pure joy. Many of them were indebted to her for helping them or their children out of a difficulty; God only knows how they would do it without her. These feelings of gratitude were not limited to friends and neighbors, but to people whom Maryama hardly knew at all. Such a situation would sprout an acquaintance and a visit that always blossomed into affection.

Maryama did not know the little boy or his family. She spotted him near the souk in Granada. He looked about eight years old. He was walking merrily with a beaming face, and he was reciting the feastday prayers that he undoubtedly heard from the grown-ups at group prayer meetings held on these days. He was chanting in a melodious voice, "Allah is great, Allah is great, Allah is great, there is no god but Allah. He was true to His promise, He gave victory to His army, and His enemies were defeated."

Maryama shot a look in every direction like a threatened hawk and spotted two Castilian guards and a few passersby. She ran toward the boy and slapped him across the face. He was stunned and speechless as his eyes widened in shock. But he only started to cry when she grabbed him by the hand forcefully and started to scream at him in Spanish.

"Didn't I warn you about playing with the Arab children? Now here you are learning sinful things from them!"

Maryama continued her shouting, bemoaning her bad luck, as people gathered around her including the two guards. She began to address the crowd.

"Tell me, what can we do? Isn't there a way to protect our children from those evil people? Here you see before you my son, the fruit of my womb, and me, a pure-blooded Castilian woman, and he's singing Arabic songs and saying 'Allah is great'!"

She turned around and started to scold the boy once again when some of the people tried to calm her down, saying that he was only a little boy who doesn't realize what he's saying. Maryama noticed a man from Albaicin whom she knew, and in his eyes she saw a gleam that encouraged her to go on with the trick she was playing on the Castilians. One of the passersby reprimanded the boy, while a guard patted him on the head and spoke to Maryama. "Don't be so harsh with him. He's still young, and he doesn't understand what he's doing."

The boy was terrified, and he had no idea what was happening to him. She took him by the hand and walked away. On the way back home she asked, "Where do you live, son?"

He stammered and then he answered.

She brought him back to his mother. "You should teach your children to be more careful outside the house," she advised.

Maryama did exactly what Hasan wanted her to do in raising the children. At home they spoke Arabic and they lived their daily lives as their fathers and grandfathers had lived. But on the street and in school they spoke Spanish, and they conducted themselves in the manner prescribed by the authorities and the Office of Inquisition. This is what Hasan wanted, and this is what Maryama carried out, but in her own way.

"Whoever speaks Spanish at home or does what the Castilians do will turn into a baboon."

"Has any child ever been turned into a baboon before, Mummy?"

"Many have. Tomorrow, I'll take you to the market and show you the baboons and how their owners make money off of them. The poor things, they used to be children each with a face like the moon, then they all turned into baboons."

"And those who speak Arabic outside the house?"

"Whoever speaks Arabic outside or reveals one word of what goes on inside the house will be lost on the street, and won't be able to find his way home. He'll wander from one neighborhood to the other unable to find his house, as though it vanished into thin air."

Maryama did her best to cope with the times, and her days, although fraught with worries, were bearable and sometimes happy because her heart was strong and full of love for her children and husband. She didn't dwell much on his behavior, and she learned how to find excuses and justifications for his angry outbursts. She told herself he was putting on this harsh facade, and that his overprotection, which some saw as weakness and lack of courage, was nothing more than his attempt to secure the safety of his family and shield them from problems. Sometimes she felt him distant and distracted. And when he was present, she noticed that he would easily become annoyed with the children or with her as though they had all become a nuisance he tried to avoid. She thought to herself that he didn't want her or her children, and she was entrapped by the thought that some other woman had stolen his heart, and that he had returned in a rage against his life with her. These thoughts nearly consumed her, but she would shake them off as lies, seeking solace in the memory of other moments when she saw clearly Hasan's intimacy and affection that revealed his tender heart. Then she would blame herself for increasing his burden in these difficult times.

It was a visit that brought nothing good. Her two brothers knocked on the door at sunrise. She put on her clothes and she and Hasan followed them out. Her father had died during the night. Maryama lifted the sheet over his face, looked at him, and covered him again. She stood over him for a long time, motionless as though her soul had retreated and her body had broken down. Then the tears poured out.

"We will do what's befitting us and him," insisted her brothers. "Let the Castilians go to hell!" Hasan tried to caution them not to rush into anything in order to avoid problems. But the brothers were adamant. Maryama was too grief stricken to say anything.

They washed Abu Ibrahim's body, wrapped it in a shroud, and escorted the corpse in procession from the house, through the alleyways, to the secret mosque where they recited prayers over him, and then brought him to the graveyard to bury him. That evening, the mourners gathered and the brothers took turns reciting the Quran. The voices reverberated throughout the neighborhood with the relentless sounds of longing.

On the third day of mourning, Maryama returned home. By week's end, the Castilians had forced their way into her father's house and arrested her mother and brothers. She wondered where they took them and what they would do to them. Would the Office of Inquisition stop at staging a public trial and imposing a fine, or perhaps a mere sentence of a year or two in prison? Or would they take it further? Would she ever see them again, or would life for all of them come to an end without ever having their eyes meet one more time?

Maryama had no recourse but to regularly attend the auto-da-fé processions, thinking she might see her mother or one of her brothers, or perhaps all of them together. She indulged in the hope that they would be found innocent or simply be obliged to pay a fine. She even wished that they might get off with being paraded in the sanbenito, the robe of penitents, or even be forced to perform the ceremonial circumambulation with a donkey, or have their names inscribed on a banner and hung in public to remind the neighbors of their sins and penance.

On one particular morning, Maryama left the house early and waited outside the church with a throng of people whose hearts were in their mouths just like hers. There were also crowds of Castilians who came to watch and listen. She stretched her neck, and her heart began to beat fast when she noticed the procession approaching. There was a line of the accused dressed in liturgical garb, walking barefoot, with ropes around their necks and a candle in hand. They entered the church to perform the rituals of penance. The crowd was blocking her view, so she rushed inside and occupied a place where she could see everything. This is what she always did, whether in the burning heat of summer or the bitter cold of winter, she waited. She waited until she heard the beating of drums and the blowing of bugles, and she saw the clerics, the officers of the Inquisition, and the town notables approaching as the penitents marched behind them. The officials sat in places designated especially for them while the penitents sat in rows close by. Her eyes searched in every direction, oblivious to the increasing crowds and the rising clamor. She strained to listen as all her senses descended upon her ears and followed what the official read of the accusations and the sentences. He moved from one name to the next, from one sentence to the next until he finished without mentioning any of her family. She dragged herself back home disappointed. She hadn't gone there to see a man whipped or a woman burned as a sentence. She left with the courtyard behind her bellowing with the shouts of the Castilian masses who had come to participate in the festivities and watch the exciting events. There were even among them people who had a brother, a daughter, or a neighbor found guilty.

Maryama always came home from these occasions drained, eyes lowered, and often so weak that she took to her bed for several days, exhausted and defeated. She would tell herself or Hasan that she would never go back again, but as soon as an announcement of a new ceremony was made, she would prepare herself and count the days until she left the house early in the morning.

"I see you're not getting ready for Mass," Hasan said to Maryama one Sunday morning.

It was the day after one of the auto-da-fé processions. "I'm exhausted, Hasan, and I'm not up to it."

"They're watching us, Maryama," he insisted. "They took your mother and brothers, and they're keeping an eye on us. Pull yourself together, and let God give you strength."

She obeyed him, and the family all went to church. Except for Saleema, who had made up her mind years ago that she would never go to church, even if they bound her hands and feet and dragged her with a team of horses. Hasan no longer broached the subject with her, even though he insisted on taking his wife, mother, and children with him, if only to throw dust in their eyes. The family took up a whole row of seats in the church. Hasan sat on the aisle seat, next to him was his mother, and after her the children. Maryama sat at the opposite end of Hasan.

The dim light, the ancientness of the church, and the faint voice of the priest only added to Maryama's sadness. She sat with her head bowed and a grave expression on her face. Her torso was bent somewhat forward, and she looked as though she were staring at her two palms opened and resting on her lap. She wasn't staring at her palms, but rather at the faces of those whom she saw the day before at the penitents' procession. They were pale, frowning faces with lowered eyes and absent looks, made all the more gaunt by expressions of worry and fear. Underneath the long, flowing liturgical garments that concealed the body, the emaciation was evident on their bodies, not to mention the vestiges of the torture and suffering of those lonely nights in the dark dungeons inhabited by rats and by the ghosts of those killed by loneliness or burned at the stake. Among those pronounced guilty was a young girl her daughter Ruqaya's age whom she couldn't keep her eyes off no matter how hard she tried. Even after she left, Maryama couldn't stop thinking about her, and she would even see her in her sleep that night. Maryama was startled when the organ music rang out suddenly. A shiver ran through her body and the tears welled from her eyes. She lifted her head a little and through her tears she saw him. He was so close she could practically touch him if only she held out her hand.

He was directly to her right. She stared at him closely. She looked first at his bare feet and dangling legs and then lifted her eyes toward his thin, naked torso to his narrow shoulders. Then she saw his tilted head and the crown of thorns he was wearing. She stared at his ribs bulging from his rib cage, and at his eyes shut tight in humbling pain. His arms were stretched out on the wooden cross, and her eyes fixed on each of his palms with a nail driven through his flesh and onto the cross. Then she looked at his face once again. It was sad and dejected, worn out by suffering. Its only communication to her was the slight tilt of the head.

Maryama stood up and took two steps forward. She knelt and stretched out her hand to touch the two bare feet. It appeared as though she was going to ask for his intercession, but when she got near and touched him, her heart grew heavy and she murmured, "There was peace on me the day I was born, and will be the day I die, and on the day I will be raised from the dead. This was Jesus, son of Mary—a true account, they contend."[1] The two arms stretched out on the cross were like wings he spread out to her in love and mercy. Maryama asked for nothing, but opened her arms and wrapped them around his legs, and she tilted her head forward and kissed them.

1. Quran (Mary 19): 33–34.

17

ather Miguel proposed to Naeem that he accompany him on his journey to the new world. The invitation came as a surprise to Naeem, and he didn't know what to say. He asked his employer to give him a few days to think it over. Had Saad not left him in such a callous way, he wouldn't give a second's thought to leaving. But he felt like a branch severed from its tree. Why shouldn't he travel to a new world, or even an old one, or to hell for that matter? What's the difference between one place and another? he thought. He didn't have a wife or children, and he didn't have his friend. Even Umm Jaafar had passed on and now lies in the folds of the earth. Besides, Father Miguel is a kind and gentle man. He doesn't mistreat him. In fact, he roils whenever he hears news about the Office of Inquisition and its oppressive treatment of Arabs and other people. The priest speaks of the new world as if it were Paradise in its beauty and riches. So, why not travel? But what if Saad came back? Why hadn't he returned, three years later, without a trace or a word?

Naeem lived his life injured by the wound of Saad's sudden departure and burdened by a constant worry that led to endless questions. Did Saad go to North Africa, or is he in the mountains? Is he working with the freedom fighters from the attack ships, or is he hiding in some mountain cave plotting in secrecy with his comrades? Did something horrible happen to him? Did he take a second wife, and did God bless him with a son or daughter? He wondered where he was and what he was doing at every moment. Did he ever think about his friend Naeem, or did he forget him the day he left Granada without even saying good-bye?

Naeem accepted Father Miguel's proposal. Two days before departure, he paid a visit to Hasan and his family to bid them farewell. Umm Hasan greeted the news in tears, but the children were fired up and bombarded Naeem with questions about the new world he was going to. Naeem laughed and explained to them that he hadn't seen it yet to tell them anything about it. "When I return, God willing, I'll bring back lots of stories and lots of gold as well! They say it's a land paved with gold and silver." He was laughing because he didn't believe a word of these fanciful rumors.

Hasan sat in silence, watching Naeem closely. The idea of his departure was more than he could bear. He thought about Saad's departure and dreaded the thought of going on with his life without any support. "When will you be back, Naeem?" he asked.

"Probably in a year or two. Father Miguel says that the purpose of the trip is to write a book. He wants to see everything himself and document his findings in a book." Naeem dug into his pocket and pulled out a folded piece of paper and gave it to Hasan. "If Saad should return during my absence, give this letter to him. You know how much I miss him and how hurt I was when he left. Tell him I won't be long in my journey. Tell him . . . well, don't tell him anything. I've written it all down in the letter. Could I say good-bye to Saleema?"

One of Hasan's daughters ran ahead of him and told Saleema he was coming. He went into her room but stood there fumbling for words. Finally, he spoke. "I'm going on a trip to the new world with Father Miguel."

Saleema looked straight at him, and he thought he detected a gleam in her eye or perhaps a twitch in her cheek. She didn't say a word, but she extended her hand and shook his. As he turned around to leave the room, he heard her call out, "Don't be angry with Saad, Naeem. You know how much he loves you." He turned around to look at her and saw a tear trickle down her cheek. He then rushed out of the house so that no one would see him crying.

Did Naeem cry out to Saad that night so loud that Saad heard him from a distant village? Does the voice of a man reach his friend across the mountains and plains? On that very night, Saad saw his friend in a dream. They were together, along with Hasan and Saleema, all standing around Abu Jaafar whose imposing stature towered above them. His face radiated light as he guided the children in their work. Hasan was arranging the folios of a manuscript and measuring the leather for the binding. Naeem was leaning forward meticulously sketching a series of letters for the title page, drawing them in floral designs alternating between fine and broad strokes. "Where ever did Naeem get such beautiful penmanship?" Abu Jaafar would ask. Saad was looking over his shoulder, and Saleema stood at the door of the workshop with her gazelle, reminding everyone that the book will be hers. "Patience, Saleema," cautioned Abu Jaafar. "We need to finish it first, and then we'll give it you."

When Saad awoke the next morning recalling the details of his dream, he wondered whether he missed them so much that he dreamed of them and whether this dream was a vision or an omen for a reunion. The thought even occurred to him that they were calling out to him and that his heart had heard the call. He decided it was time to go down to Granada to see them.

Three years had passed since he first went to live among the young freedom fighters in a mountain village far from the eyes of strangers. He crossed the rugged and unpaved mountain roads the Castilians didn't know about, carrying supplies and letters to the freedom fighters who launched their attacks by sea, inflicting casualties on both the Castilian army and its government. He also helped in expediting the safe arrival to the coastal areas of the villagers who chose to emigrate. When they received word from a certain village, they would sneak off in the dark of night and meet with the elders to make all the necessary arrangements. On the appointed day, Saad and his companions would guide all those who wanted to leave through untrodden mountain passes, like silent phantoms feeling their way under the protection of darkness, as the hearts of the nocturnal travelers pounded in their chests, without a murmur, a song, or a chant. And when the specter of the shore loomed before them, the children grew wild with excitement and jumped for joy, and the grown-ups moved eagerly to load their children and their possessions onto the ships. Their eyes shone with the hope of salvation, and then became clouded by the memory of an olive tree they left behind and basil stalks they'll never lay at the graves of their fathers. They climbed aboard and are rocked by the small boats that will take them out to the big ships that will take them far away.

Saleema was seated as usual with her head buried in a book, absorbing its every detail by the light of her lantern, when she heard a voice. She turned around and then went back to her book, thinking to herself, "I must be imagining things!" When she heard the voice again, she was certain it was Saad calling out to her. She ran outside the house and saw him in the dark courtyard. He stretched out his arms and embraced her as she embraced him. They kissed, and she took him by the hand, and he followed her into the house as the rest of the household slept.

In her room Saad sheepishly sat facing her not knowing what to say. She was looking at him, clearly ill at ease. He had been gone for thirty-nine months, but it seemed to her like ten years, and she wondered whether it was because she missed him so much or because of the gray hair around his temples and the wrinkles on his forehead and under his eyes brought on by the icy winds or the burning sun. "You've been gone for so long, Saad," she said, breaking the silence.

He went over to her and they connected in a furious embrace, spurred on by a craving in the body and deprivation in the soul that not only sought, but demanded, union. He seized her and she seized him, and the wave of union lifted them high. They gasped between life and death, as one wave crashes into another, bringing to the surface deep, dark blue ripples that blaze with the heat of a hot, burning sun. They gasped as the body jolts, and the soul inside it quickly follows, and when the shore of coming looms on the horizon, the sea gulls burst forth and joyously light up the skies with their whiteness.

At the shore of coming they basked in the calm. They spoke at length, in hushed voices, and when the morning birds began to chirp, they fell into a deep sleep.

Saad's unexpected arrival brought to the house a feeling of such bliss that it seemed like a feast day. The house filled with happy excitement, and Hasan was by far the most exhilarated, laughing as he hadn't done in years. He joked with Saad, told him stories, and bombarded him with questions, soaking up every detail. The children and Umm Hasan finally had to protest, as Hasan wasn't giving them a chance to talk to Saad.

Saad could hardly believe that three years had already passed since he left them. Ruqaya and her younger sister, whom he had left as children, had become young women, and it wouldn't come as a surprise to him if someone came knocking on Hasan's door asking for their hands in marriage. And little Hisham, whom he last saw as a toddler and who only knew two or three words, was now talking effortlessly, understanding and responding to everything that was said to him. He told Saad that next year he would be going to school to learn to read and write.

"Will you be learning Arabic or Spanish, Hisham?" Saad asked.

"In school we learn Spanish, but at home my father will teach me Arabic like he taught my sisters."

Saad laughed, pleased with the boy's cleverness.

"Light some incense, and protect him from my evil eye," he said to Umm Hasan.

Hasan laughed, but his mother did not. She started to intone the expression, "God forgive . . ." but finished it with a mutter under her breath clear enough to be read on her lips.

Neither Saleema nor Maryama joined the men. They decided to go out early and buy food from the market. Maryama had convinced Saleema to go with her, saying that this wasn't any ordinary day. As soon as they reached some distance from the house, Maryama turned to Saleema and gave her a sly look. "Last night was some night, right?"

Saleema blushed a crimson red in embarrassment and answered, "So, what shall we buy for dinner?"

"I think I'll slaughter a sheep."

Just before sunset, the sheep was fully cooked and ready to be eaten. The raucous laughter that accompanied the lavish meal was not on account of Saad's return and the family reunion only, but on account of the story of the sheep that was yet another episode in Maryama's hilarious saga.

"When I told Saleema I intended to slaughter a sheep in Saad's honor, she thought I was kidding, right, Saleema? But of course, I wasn't joking. It's true that slaughtering sheep at home is forbidden, and that I could get myself put in jail for it, but I made up my mind and put my trust in God. I went into the vendor at the livestock market with such a depressed look on my face, you'd think I was carrying the burdens of the world all on my shoulder. I said to him, "I have a little boy, my only son. God blessed me with him after five daughters. A week ago he came to me and told me he wanted a sheep. When I asked him what he wanted with a sheep, he told me he wanted to play with it. So, I said to him, 'God willing.' But naturally I had no intention of buying him one. I said to myself, are we living in times that allow us to buy sheep for our children to play with? But, O, my poor heart, my son fell ill yesterday."

Hisham interrupted her story in protest. "But I'm not sick, Mummy, and I didn't ask you for a sheep."

His sisters beckoned him to be quiet, and he obeyed. They were following the story on the edge of their seats.

Maryama continued. "My son, O my poor heart, fell ill yesterday, and his forehead sweltered in fever. He spent the night delirious, calling out for a sheep. So you see why I have to buy him a sheep."

"Of course you should buy it," responded the vendor, visibly moved. "If you can't pay for it all now, sister, you can give me what you have and pay me the rest later."

"If you had seen her on the verge of tears, and the vendor as well, you'd have surely thought that Hisham was sick," added Saleema.

Maryama returned to where she left off. "So, I thanked him and told him that he was a kind and noble man. 'Do you have children of your own?' I asked. He told me, seven. I said, 'May God bless and keep them safe for you. I passed by the jeweler's and sold my gold ring. How much is the sheep?' "

Saleema finished the story. "Before we even left the vendor's shop, he had begun to tell the story of the poor woman who sold her gold ring to bring a little joy into her sick son's heart. On the way home, Maryama told the story three times, twice in Spanish and once in Arabic. God forbid, one of the people she told the story to is an employee in the Office of Inquisition."

"What if someone asks about the sheep tomorrow, or the day after?" asked Hasan.

"I'll say that the sheep died," answered Maryama with a smirk. "I'll sigh and say, 'God forgive the vendor, he sold me a sheep with a disease. If he hadn't had seven children and I didn't have a kind heart, I would have evoked the wrath of God on him. But who knows? Perhaps it was the will of God, just and merciful, that killed the sheep and restored my son's health.' "

After dinner, Hasan lured Saad away to be alone with him. Saad told him stories of the mountain village where he was living.

"It's just like what Granada use to be. The voice of the muezzin rings out, and you can hear chanting and singing at the wedding feasts and out in the fields. We speak in Arabic without any restrictions, we dress the way we're accustomed to, we sit vigil for the coming of Ramadan, and we celebrate the two feasts."

"Are there any Castilians there?"

"Not a single one."

"That's odd."

"Its an abandoned mountain village in the middle of nowhere. They probably have no idea that it exists."

"Do you plan to stay there a long time? This is your house, Saad, and you can come back whenever you want."

"That's difficult at the moment, Hasan. When I was living here, I use to help them with what little I could. I'm working with them now."

"Are you going to stay with them for good?"

"Pray with me that this nightmare ends and the need for our work no longer exists. Maybe God will give guidance to the Ottoman Turks or the North Africans to launch the final campaign we're all hoping for."

"Do you really think that could happen, or are we deluding ourselves with the impossible?"

Saad took a deep breath and did not answer the question. "How did Umm Jaafar die, Hasan?"

Hasan spoke without elaborating, but when Saad insisted on hearing the details, Hasan told him everything.

"In the morning I'll pay a visit to her grave, and then I'll go and see Naeem and tell him I'm back."

Hasan looked at him. He was just about to tell him about Naeem's journey, but decided to put it off until the next day. "Go to your wife, Saad. We've spoken too long, and it's getting late."

In the morning, Hasan accompanied Saad to Umm Jaafar's grave and they prayed for her soul. On their way back, Hasan broke the news about Naeem's journey. He handed him Naeem's letter that Saad read despondently and without uttering a word.

"Come with me. I want to show you that inn," Hasan said.

On the way to the bank of the Darro River where the inn was located, Hasan told his brother-in-law all about it.

"Two members of the Tahir clan from Valencia bought this inn. They're a big and influential family. They even say that a few years ago they were able to buy an innocent verdict for three of their younger members. They were accused by the Office of Inquisition of establishing contacts with the French and agitating a rebellion between the Arabs and the local citizens. They say that the plan was to distract the Aragonese officials in the event of a French invasion. The father and uncles of the three accused supposedly traveled to Madrid and Barcelona and contacted the Royal Court and the Supreme Council of the Office of Inquisition, and they paid large sums to secure the release of their sons.

"The point is that the two men who bought the inn are from this family, although they have no connection at all to the case of the three accused. Obviously they have a lot of clout since they were able to buy this inn and register it under their name despite the ban on buying land and buildings imposed on the Arabs residing within the province of Granada. These two men sent a messenger offering me the job of managing the inn. The messenger said that if I agreed, the two men would come personally to work out the details. So, what do you think?"

Saad inspected the place from every angle. They had just walked through a wooden gate across a corridor and into a rectangular open courtyard in the middle of which was a two-story stone structure. The courtyard was surrounded on three sides by protruding wood-latticed balconies, along which ran a wooden passageway that carried both the columns and the ceilings to the second story.

Directly to the right of the entrance was a spacious pen for the livestock, with a high covering on top and troughs for food and water running across it. Toward the left was a stone stairway that lead up to the wooden loge to which the guest rooms opened out. Hasan opened a door to a long rectangular room that accommodated a bed and a wood armoire. The room was lit by a square window that arched at the top.

"There are fifteen rooms on this story," said Hasan, "five on each wing. On the lower level there are ten rooms and a storeroom where the guests can deposit their belongings. On one side there's the stable, and a large hall for a kitchen and dining area, as well as a place to keep a fire going during the winter. For summer nights there's the open courtyard where we'll lay out carpets and wooden sofas. What do you think?"

"I think it's very nice, spacious, and can be put to good use. God help you with managing it. It'll require the energy of many men to keep it going."

"If I were made this offer before Naeem left, I would have kept him here to work with me. I also asked Abu Mansour to help me."

"Will he be able?"

"He can, but he's been drinking heavily lately. I asked him to work with me in the hope that he would have something to distract him from drinking," answered Hasan. The two men left the inn and went to see Abu Mansour, but they didn't find him at home.

Saad spent three days with Hasan and the family before slipping out in the dark of night to return to his village in the mountains. They all said their good-byes and Umm Hasan cried while Saleema stood ashen faced. He told them he would come back before the end of the summer, but if he were unable to do so, he would certainly be there in the fall to spend the feast of the end of Ramadan with them. As he was leaving the outskirts of Granada and on his way back to his companions, Saad thought about his intimate moments with Saleema, and the thought of his leaving weighed even more heavily on him. What he didn't know was that he bid farewell to his wife leaving a part of himself, and months later he still didn't know that the seed he left inside of her sprouted and grew into a black-eyed baby girl who resembled him, whom Saleema cuddled with great anxiety as she waited for her father's return to tell him that his new name is "Abu Aysha."

Despite a lingering anxiety over Saad's absence that continued well beyond the end of the summer and even beyond the end of the following winter, Aysha's birth brought a renewed joy to the household, filling it with the screams of a newborn and all the family fussing over her. The newest member of the family found more than the breast of one mother, but of many mothers who pampered her and showered her with affection. It wasn't just Saleema, Maryama, and Umm Hasan who were consumed by caring for the baby. Hasan's older daughters found in Aysha an infant on whom they could practice their early mothering skills, while his younger daughters found her to be something of a new and exciting toy to play with. Only Hisham found himself without any role in all of this. He was only five years older than the newborn, and he saw her merely as an unwelcome guest who was trying to usurp him of his throne of importance within the family. His father wouldn't tolerate his attitude and scolded him often, adding insult to injury.

Hasan was convinced that the birth of this little girl was a promise of prosperity and a good omen. Only days after she was born, good news came to Albaicin that made the people's hearts beat fast and their eyes flutter with hope. The sea commandos from the Moroccan ports launched an attack that broke the backs of the Spanish and rubbed their noses in the mud. Their ships anchored under cover of night, as was their custom, and succeeded in safely boarding six hundred emigrants. Then the Spanish armada surprised them at sea and engaged them in battle. Not only were the freedom fighters able to defend themselves, but they also launched a counteroffensive. They sunk some of the Spanish ships and surrounded others. They took prisoners, including their admirals and other high-ranking officers, and returned to Morocco safely.

The woman greeted the news with ululation. The women of Albaicin ululated in their hearts, while the wives and daughters of the freedom fighters ululated from the shores across the sea to their menfolk as their ships approached land.

"Aysha, daughter of Saad and Saleema, brings blessings and good tidings," Hasan repeated as he held the little girl against his chest. He began each morning looking at her radiant face, and he never went to bed at night without planting a kiss on her forehead, whether she was sound asleep or screaming as newborns do. When it was time to register her name on the birth certificate, he wrote "Esperanza," but they called her "Aysha." But he, himself, gave her the nickname "Amal" for the hope she inspired.

18

Naeem sat in a corner of the room as he watched Father Miguel repeatedly dip his feather pen into the ink bottle and write slowly from left to right. Naeem was hoping his patron would stop working, if only for a few moments, so that he could engage him in conversation. But Father Miguel was much too absorbed in what he was writing.

By the light of the lantern, the priest appeared to him like a feeble old man, worn down by a long life. The dark clerical robe, the straight posture, and the self-assured gait that always gave him a youthful countenance were nowhere visible at this moment as he sat in his white nightgown with his head slightly bent forward, taking with it the smooth silver wisps of hair and his pale, wrinkled, round and puffy face. Naeem wondered if the priest was as tormented by nightmares as he was, even though he didn't wake up screaming in the night, at least he had never heard him doing that. He never saw him cry, except for that one time he heard the sound and rushed to him. He saw him through the open door on his knees, with his forearms raised and his chin resting on his folded hands. He was praying and sobbing in a loud, defeated voice. On that day the two of them had witnessed the bodies of ten native women swinging from the ropes of gallows suspended onto a wooden structure high enough to leave space between the feet of the women and the ground to hang their children with the ropes that dangled from beneath their mothers' feet.

The priest cried that night, but Naeem didn't. Instead, he thought how gracious God was to the mothers in letting them be hanged before their children. Only a few days before, he had seen the horror of a baby's murder in front of its mother's eyes. She was a beautiful woman, robust and sweet, carrying her infant child of no more than seven or eight months old. He had his mother's plumpness and moonlike face, as well as her dimples. What stroke of ill fortune brought her to that place at that time? he thought. She walked along casually, carrying her child without a care in the world. When the Castilian soldier caught her by surprise, she was startled, and her sudden shrieking scream failed to prevent the baby from being snatched away from her. In a moment's flash, he had pounced on her and grabbed the infant from her arms and threw it on the ground between his feet and his hungry dog. It was a black hunting dog with a long snout, high haunches, and two big dangling ears like a goat. The dog took one leap at the baby and grabbed it by the teeth. The screams of the mother and the baby blended with the chortles of the Castilians who gathered around to watch. They were all laughing uproariously except for two of them, one of whom looked on and shook his head in disbelief, and the second who struggled to keep his arms around the woman to prevent her from getting to her child. The dog continued its meal, the men laughed, and the woman screamed until a shot rang out and she fell to the ground soaking in her own blood. Then everything became silent.

When the ships landed at port and Naeem arrived in this new world with his employer, he was more taken by the women than the lush greenness of the trees and the austere darkness of their imposing trunks. Naked women like the virgins of Paradise! He gaped at them, and his heart beat fast and his soul ignited with a scorching desire. One, two, three days, and then he saw the panting and voracity of the men as they hunted their prey until they prevailed, clawing at their flesh and raping them. He ran to Father Miguel in a panic and told him the story. The priest reassured him, "Tomorrow, I will meet with the governor and inform him. That is a sin, my boy, a mortal sin that angers our Lord. If such an action happens again, God will bring down a devastating punishment on all of us, those who committed the sin and those who denounced it."

After a while, Naeem stopped running in a panic to tell about what he had just been witness to, for the priest came to realize that any meeting he had with the governor or his deputy would be to no avail, and writing letter after letter to the king or the court officials in Spain, or to the pope in Rome for that matter, would fall on deaf ears.

Naeem would pass by the bare breasts, the slender bodies, and those ravishing eyes without staring. He averted his eyes as though these women were members of his own family whose honor he could not violate. He was afraid to make eye contact lest the shame of their nakedness and his own weakness devour him.

If only Father Miguel would stop writing and talk to him. If only he could speak the language of the natives, he could come to know and befriend a number of them. He would see them working, cutting down trees, paving roads, lifting rocks, always under the vigilant eyes of the armed Castilians. He stared at them for a long time, guessing their natures and temperaments. He would say that this one is kind-hearted, and that one is less so, or that one is self-confident and kind to his people. He wished he could approach them and talk to them, to introduce himself to them. He wanted to tell them his stories and listen to theirs. But how could he do this not knowing their language? Besides, they most assuredly thought of him as one of those whom the sea washed ashore to inflict suffering on them.

Naeem closed his eyes and imagined the middle-aged man whom he saw time after time and who by now was as familiar with his face as he with his. Naeem would smile and wave his hand whenever he passed him by. At first the man just fixed his gaze on Naeem in wonder, but then he gradually began to smile and wave back exactly as Naeem had done, lifting his hand and touching the side of the forehead. If only he understood my language, Naeem pined, if only I understood his, I would say to him, "I'm not one of them! Did you think I was one of them? I'm from Granada!" He would speak to him at length, and the man would get to know him and like him, and then he would invite him to his house. And who knows, maybe he has a daughter as nice as himself, and he could ask to marry her. Surely, I'm a stranger and nearly forty years old, he would say, and I'm not as handsome as I used to be, but I have a kind heart and I would take care of my wife and I would lavish on her both love and children. So, what do you say, uncle?

Between the time he awoke until drowsiness overcame him, Naeem saw the girl he was going to marry, the daughter of that man. She resembled the one he had seen that long-ago day near Granada. The one who stole his heart. It was astonishing how much they looked alike. She wasn't naked, but like her was dressed in a white robe.

"Your eyes are getting heavy with sleep, Naeem. Why don't you go off to bed, my son?"

Naeem opened his eyes wide and responded, "Not at all, Father. I don't feel like sleeping just yet."

Father Miguel smiled and shook his head. "You fell asleep and perhaps you were dreaming. My voice must have awakened you."

"Father Miguel, may I ask you something?

"Go ahead, my son."

"What are you writing? What exactly are you writing?"

"I'm writing, I mean, I wrote the story from the beginning. I wrote about Christopher Columbus's four voyages, the difficulties he encountered and the successes he achieved. Now, this past month, I'm writing about the island and its inhabitants. I'm describing the climatic conditions over the course of the year, and I'm writing down my observations about the different species of plants, birds, and animals. After that, I'll write about the people. I'll describe their physical characteristics, their way of life, their thoughts and beliefs."

"But . . ." Naeem stuttered. "How do you know about their thoughts and beliefs when you haven't spoken directly to them?"

"I observe their behavior, and I compare my observations with those of others, and from that I deduce their thoughts and beliefs."

"Are you writing about those other things as well, Father?"

"Yes, my son, I have written and will continue to write more and more about those painful things I saw and heard about. And I will add that it's a shame we're transforming the dream of that great man who discovered this land into this incredible savagery. Do you know, Naeem, what compelled Columbus to set sail and seek adventures?"

"To discover a new land, Father?"

"That was just a means to an end, my son, a means to achieve a noble and lofty dream that can be epitomized in just two objectives: to spread the word of God among the people who have not received it and bring them into the fold of the Church; and to obtain gold in order to unleash a holy crusade on the Holy Lands, liberate Jerusalem, and rescue the tomb of our Lord and Savior from the hands of those who do not believe in him."

"But the Muslims do not deny Jesus Christ, Father." The sentence slipped out without Naeem thinking, but he wasn't able to retract it.

Father Miguel shot him a stern look and retorted emphatically, "Yes, they do deny him!"

Father Miguel arose from his chair, which was a sign that he finished writing and was preparing to go to bed.

Naeem jumped up and said, "Thank you, Father, for allowing me to sit with you. I hope that I haven't bothered you with my questions. Sweet dreams!"

Naeem had no choice but to go to his room and lie alone on his bed, to wait for sleep to overtake him and, like every night, nightmares to ravage him.

19

The two brothers, Omar and Abdel-Kareem, arrived from Valencia to work out the details and come to an agreement concerning the management of the inn. Hasan hosted them at home, and he honored their visit not only because they were strangers who came from out of town, but because he had taken a genuine liking to them. He liked their confident manner and their intelligent conversation, and there was something else about them that he couldn't put his finger on that particularly drew him to them. It was something that he didn't see in the Arabs of Granada. He wondered if it was wealth that gives its possessor an air of self-assuredness, or perhaps power and influence that gives an individual that certain thing he saw and liked in them.

The brothers were close to Hasan in age. Omar, the younger of the two, was the more effusive. He spoke forcefully, coherently, and clearly, which amazed Hasan since speaking about political matters and delving into details required a great deal of caution. But he spoke courageously as though these troubled times were surmountable, or that these troubled times weren't troubled at all. He had a round, full face distinguished by two big, wide eyes that made direct contact with whomever he spoke. He had an impeccably groomed moustache and beard. He was tall and stocky, although not corpulent in the least, and his elegant robe added to his dignified look. Although his brother looked a lot like him, he gave a totally different impression. His quiet demeanor and his measured speech and short sentences complemented his outward appearance, reflecting in the look in his eyes and his facial features confidence, importance, and aloofness. Yet, at the same time, he was cultivated and warm.

The brothers listened attentively to Hasan as he described to them the conditions in Granada. In turn, Omar spoke about Valencia. "The conditions in Valencia are much better. The nobility are with us, and the court could be with us if we behave prudently. The Aragonese nobility are the ones who are resisting the injustices perpetrated against us. King Ferdinand had promised them repeatedly that there would be no forced conversions or expulsions for the Arabs, nor any restrictions on our interactions with the Christians of the kingdom. When Emperor Charles V assumed the throne of Aragon upon the death of his grandfather, Ferdinand, he was forced to renew this promise. The struggle exists between the nobility on the one hand and the Office of Inquisition on the other. The court is leaning toward the nobility, but it fears the powerful influence of the Office of Inquisition."

Hasan had some difficulty comprehending the idea of a dispute between the nobility and the Church. "I don't understand how the nobility can defend the interests of the Arabs when they financed wars against them and offered themselves and their men to Ferdinand and Isabella to invade Granada."

"They're not defending the Arabs, Abu Hisham, but their own interests and the interests of the kingdom of Aragon. The Arabs are a financial power the kingdom needs. More important than that is the fact that most of our people in Aragon work as farmers on the feudal estates of the nobility, and they impose on all of us, rich and poor alike, heavy taxes that exceed those imposed on the rest of the kingdom. If the Arabs were to emigrate, the estates would fall into disarray, and their conversion would mean a decrease in the tax revenues they reap from us."

"We have an expression in Valencia that goes, 'The more the Arabs, the more the profit,' " added Abdel-Kareem.

"But they don't want us to remain Arabs or Muslims!" argued Hasan.

"That's correct," answered Abdel-Kareem, "but self-interest governs everything."

"But as Omar pointed out yesterday, there are the Brotherhood of the Germania whose gangs hoist the cross and chant 'Death to the Arabs,' and wherever their banners pass, you find a trail of corpses, burnt homes, and people so terrorized that they seek baptism as a way to save their lives."

"These are hooligans whose activities will be crushed."

"Even these hooligans," interjected Omar, "and I agree with my brother that their activities will not last much longer, are not targeting us specifically, but rather the nobility. They're striking out at the Arabs to wound the nobility who protect them and depend upon them to cultivate their estates. But that's not the point. What's important is that we win over the court and convince the officials, as well as the emperor, that protecting the Arabs and keeping them here are in the best interests of the state."

"Is that possible?" asked Hasan, as it seemed to him to be wishful thinking.

"It's very possible, but the one problem is those who call themselves freedom fighters."

"Freedom fighters?"

"They're ruining everything," said Abdel-Kareem.

"How so?"

"With their extremist behavior that only complicates matters."

Omar elaborated on what his brother just said. "The attacks on the Spanish coasts and the smuggling of emigrants on the one hand, and collaboration with France with the aim of weakening the emperor's power on the other, reinforce the attitude that the Arabs of the country have no allegiance to the kingdom, and therefore the only solution is forced conversion or expulsion. This makes our task more difficult."

This was the oddest thing Hasan had ever heard. The people of Granada were afraid to publicize their sympathies with the freedom fighters or their clandestine cooperation with them. It's true they feigned their support and allegiance to the kingdom, but he never heard that what the freedom fighters were doing harmed the interests of the Arabs. The brothers' position confused Hasan, and when he retired in solitude to his room that night he thought about it long and hard. After a night of tossing and turning and mulling the matter over and over again, he came to the conclusion that they were correct, especially since they were influential and in a position to be in contact with the nobility and the court officials, or at least with those who were in contact with them.

The day before the brothers were to depart, Omar spoke to Hasan. "Listen, Abu Hisham, we came to you from Valencia to reach an agreement on managing the inn, but apparently the Knower of All Secrets has foreordained something further. We have met you and come to know you well. We have seen your family and told ourselves that there is no finer man with whom we would like to bond through marriage. What do you think?"

Hasan was stunned and speechless. Omar continued, "Your daughters, Abu Hisham, are a credit to our Maker. I have a son, and Abdel-Kareem has two sons. What do you say to that?"

"I would say, with God's blessing."

Hands went outstretched and they recited the opening chapter of the Quran. After the initial moment of shock, Hasan began to feel immense satisfaction and joy. Where would he find such noble stock, he thought, with breeding, wealth, knowledge, and influence. He rushed off with the happy news to Maryama but was taken aback by her reaction. She was not pleased, and she screamed in angry protest. "What's gotten into you, man, that you banish your daughters to some faraway place?"

"Lower your voice! The two guests are still in our house, and it's not right that they hear this!"

"How can I give my daughters over to a family I know nothing about?"

"It's a good family, of good stock with wealth and influence. What more could you want?"

"I want to rest assured of my daughters' safety and security. I want them to visit me from time to time. I want to be able to go to them if need be. How could you, man? Shame on you."

"Calm down, Maryama, and listen to me. This marriage will protect your daughters from the evil of poverty. Besides, the people of Valencia are not subjected to forced conversion. Your daughters will never be forced to give their children names other than their own, and they won't have to live their lives practicing one religion in public and another in secret."

Maryama responded with a scoffing smirk on her face. "Why don't you marry them off to men from North Africa or Egypt or Arabia?"

"If an honest and decent man from North Africa came and asked for one of my daughters, I would give her to him."

"I'll die of grief if my daughters are far from me."

"Valencia is not that far away. Both countries are ruled by one emperor. Besides, the law that prohibits the Arabs of Granada to travel to other provinces within the kingdom may be changed within a year or two."

"It's bad enough you give one away, but why did you give them three?"

"I recited the opening chapter of the Quran, and the matter is settled." Hasan turned his back to Maryama, closed his eyes and went to sleep. This only increased Maryama's anger, so she got up and left the room to go and complain to Saleema.

"Saleema . . ."

"What's wrong, Maryama?"

"Your brother has lost his mind. I swear to God, he lost his mind. He's deranged."

"Calm down and tell me what happened."

"Those two men who descended upon us like a death sentence."

"You mean, the guests?"

"Exactly. I wish they had never come to this house and I had never laid my eyes on them."

"Did they insult Hasan?"

"They asked for three of my daughters to marry their sons."

"And go to Valencia?"

"Yes, they're going to Valencia!"

"Why did Hasan give his consent? He may have found the two men to be good people, but who knows if their sons are as good as they?"

"Exactly, who knows? I'm going to Hasan right now and telling him that." Maryama rushed into the bedroom. Hasan was plunged into a deep sleep, and she woke him up.

"How do you know that the sons are as good as their fathers? They could be evil, drunkards, deformed, or ill-tempered. How could you give three of my daughters to strangers I know nothing about and who'll take them away to a faraway place where they'll be miserable?"

Hasan rubbed his eyes as he listened to Maryama. He was still half asleep and couldn't grasp everything she was saying. When she repeated her argument a third time, he finally understood, and said to her sternly, "Calm down, woman, and let me get some sleep!"

When the news was revealed to the three daughters, they were elated in spite of their mother's anger and distress. They were going to get married and travel to Valencia where there was going to be a wedding, just like those grand occasions Umm Jaafar never tired of telling them about. There was going to be the trip to the bathhouse, the henna celebration, the ululations, singing, and the banging of the tambourines. It all seemed so exciting, like dreams that come true before you even dream them. The girls' happiness only increased Maryama's sadness, which was mixed with scorn and self-pity. She was crying when Ruqaya, her oldest, came to console her. "Why are you crying, Mother? We'll be together, the three of us. We'll take care of one another and keep each other company all under one roof. That's better than if each one of us married husbands unknown to one another, each one living in a separate place and seeing each other only on holidays and special occasions." Maryama looked at her with tear-soaked eyes but didn't say a word, but when the thought sunk into her head, she calmed down.

A month later Abdel-Kareem and Omar returned in the company of their mother, their wives, and the three young men. That night when Hasan was alone with Maryama, he asked her, "Has your mind been put to rest now, Umm Hisham?"

He was alluding to the good impression the young men gave to everyone in the family, with their good looks, refined manners, speaking only when spoken to, and doing it intelligently and courteously. Hasan had no idea that his three daughters had fallen in love with the young men as soon as they laid eyes on them. They were attracted by their svelte physiques, their finely chiseled, olive complexions, their black eyes, and the attention and care they gave to their appearances. But what he did know was that his mother, his sister, and even Maryama found no fault whatsoever in them. In fact, Maryama even began to retract from her bitter opposition, although her fears were not appeased.

The women of the Tahir family came bearing gifts and greetings of affections and pampering for their future daughters-in-law. It was so profuse that Maryama heard one of her youngest daughters say to the other, both of whom were under ten, "I wish the brothers had two younger ones to ask us to marry them." Maryama grabbed the broom by the handle and spanked the two little girls, the one who spoke and the other who listened. Just as they were about to let out a loud cry, she lifted the broomstick and whispered to them in a soft but threatening voice to be quiet. "Not a sound! There are guests in the house!"

Quietly and secretly, the family celebrated the engagements and the signing of the marriage contracts. Their closest and trusted friends and neighbors were invited to the wedding feast with abundant food and low-keyed singing that stayed within the neighborhood walls.

Umm Abdel-Kareem, the grooms' grandmother, was at a loss to understand this strange way of celebrating a wedding. The women did not go to the bathhouse accompanied by the beating of tambourines or festive music. Nor did they cry out, "Allah is great!" when the sheep were slaughtered, or adorn the door of the house with the imprints of their palms soaked in sheep's blood. Apart from Maryama's distress and Umm Abdel-Kareem's annoyance, the house of Hasan glowed with happiness, affection, and the excitement of children until it was time to think about making preparations for the journey to Valencia.

Two days before departure, Umm Abdel-Kareem fell ill. She woke up that morning with a pallid look on her face and wilting eyes, along with shivers and a fever. The poor thing would return to her bed after spilling her guts from vomiting and diarrhea, only to have to make the trip once again.

Umm Hasan whispered to Maryama, "I hope the woman doesn't die in our house and then have them say that Hasan's daughters brought us bad luck. That's all we need. Ever since I first laid eyes on that woman and her sour puss, my heart sank. She's a jinx!"

Saleema gave Umm Abdel-Kareem a thorough examination. She checked her chest, her stomach, eyes, throat, pulse, and the color of her fingernails. She determined that it wasn't serious. The old woman grew more pale, as though she had just put one foot into the grave. The blood in her arteries coagulated in fear whenever Saleema touched a part of her body. The truth is that when she first saw Saleema she made mental note of her strange appearance, her disheveled hair, and her distracted look. Her suspicions were confirmed only two days later when she passed by her room while the door was open and caught a glimpse of the bottles, jars, baskets, and books and got a whiff of the strange odors. She moved away as quickly as possible and muttered some Quranic verses under her breath to protect her from the evil spirits.

She thought of the expression that says, "Like aunt like niece," as she reminded herself that her family was being afflicted with not one, but three of them. That's all she could think about. Did Valencia lack young girls? Surely there were thousands of girls there, more beautiful, and more noble of birth and prestige than these.

There was no choice, so Umm Abdel-Kareem submitted herself to the will of God and awaited His decree. Even her resistance to any medications Saleema gave her could no longer continue since her sons and their wives stood around her and scolded her for her behavior. "Do you think it's right at this age to act like a child?" She put herself in God's hands and took the medicine. At first Saleema gave her some boiled pomegranate rinds mixed with ben-seeds. The old woman knew this remedy, and when she took it she stopped vomiting and the diarrhea stopped. But her suspicions didn't abate. When Saleema came in with a new mixture, she asked, "What's this?"

"Medicine."

"I know it's medicine, but I'm asking what's it made of?"

Saleema paid no mind to her suspicions and thought the question was asked merely out of interest. She sat down next to her and started to explain.

"This is a mixture that cures stomachaches. It's extremely effective, and I concocted it myself. I took a small amount of pure iron dust and soaked it in clean vinegar. I strained the liquid several times. I pulverized it and took a little bit and mixed it with some ground clove and a paste of ginger and honey. Then I brewed it with musk and amber, and God willing, you'll be cured."

The only thing that Umm Abdel-Kareem's mind could comprehend was the pure iron dust that stuck in her head. She refused to take it in spite of the insistence of Saleema, Maryama, and even her daughters-in-law. Finally, Abdel-Kareem came in and forced her to take the medicine. She drank it as though she were drinking a cup of poison.

Although she arose from her bed five days later in robust health, and despite the fact that everything turned back to normal just as it was the day they arrived, Umm Abdel-Kareem was convinced that she was cured only because God gave her victory over that woman possessed by demons. He had listened to her prayers day in and day out beseeching Him not to leave her alone in this time of affliction. With Umm Abdel-Kareem's convalescence over, the Tahir family was able to take the girls and travel to Valencia, along with the prayers and best wishes of the family, and the tears of Maryama.

20

They wondered how Saad would feel if word got to him that
Saleema carried the seeds of his loins and bore him a daughter whom they named Aysha. Would he jump for joy at the
news, or would it only increase the misery of his imprisonment and
reinforce the walls of confinement around him? When he had told
the family that he intended to return by summer's end or at the beginning of autumn at the latest, it had seemed both possible and
probable to him. But time does not disclose its secrets to hu-
mankind, and the possible turned impossible.

Saad was assigned to receive a shipment of gunpowder from a
deserted spot by the coast. He received it under the protection of
night, loaded it onto his mule, and took it through whatever deserted roads he could find, passing through whatever villages he had
to. Whenever he came into a village, he claimed he was carrying a
shipment of wheat to the inhabitants of his village, and that he was
merely a cart driver whose task was to deliver goods. Then he entered the ill-fated village where he encountered what he was
doomed to encounter. Some of the villagers told him, "We will buy
some wheat." He answered, "It's not mine to sell. I don't own the
shipment. I'm only transporting it from the vendors to the buyers
who already paid for it." Saad felt uneasy about the suspicious look
some of them gave him, and he proceeded to leave the village as
quickly as possible. His anxiety increased when he realized that provisions in the village were meager, and that they were in dire need

of flour. He had to repeat over and over again to the many who asked him to buy wheat that the shipment didn't belong to him and refused their request. He was exerting all his effort to spur on the mule to move faster when he was accosted by a number of men who knocked him to the ground with the intention of taking what they thought was wheat. Saad stood up in protest and tried to keep them away, but their hands had already ripped open the sacks. When he heard someone shout, "It's not wheat, it's gunpowder," Saad dashed off like the wind.

He was running through open roads conscious of how exposed they were, and that only increased his anxiety of how vulnerable he was. He anticipated at any moment that the ground would fall from beneath him and that a pack of barking and panting Castilian dogs would be running on his heels as he sped forward in fright, picking up speed in search of safety. But when he arrived at a spot under some trees in a densely wooded area, he decided to continue running like a madman until he could run no more. He collapsed to the ground, out of breath, but with his ears wide open. The beating of his heart, his panting, and his gasps for air jumbled the silence he was hoping for. After sitting for a while, he grew somewhat calmer, and he began to think about the shipment of gunpowder that was lost, along with the money that was paid for it, and the hopes that were attached to it. He started to bang his head against the tree he was sitting under, asking himself over and over again, "What am I going to do?" The only responses to his question were the throbbing sensations of defeat and disappointment. He sat motionless for some time, unaware of how long, but after a while he grew certain that his only recourse was to look for a way back to his companions.

He walked on until he reached the outskirts of a village he didn't recognize. But he had a good feeling about it, and he assumed he could ask the inhabitants for directions. He also hoped he could find some safe haven to spend the night, drink some water, and perhaps get a bite to eat. When he went into the village, he was taken by surprise by an unusual clamor and a great deal of nervous commotion, and he wondered what was going on. When he made inquiries, Saad learned that the rebellious Brotherhood of Germania were approaching the village and that their leader had just scored a victory in a neighboring village. He knew he had to leave the place as quickly as possible, but where could he go, and in which direction? He stood confused, fearing that his feet would lead him back to the village where they discovered the gunpowder, or to a village where the Germania were in control, men more vicious toward Arabs than the military authorities. Saad finally sought directions from an old man who was preoccupied with organizing people rushing toward the citadel for protection. The old man directed Saad to the safest road and indicated to him those controlled by the brotherhood.

Saad walked along a road that would bring him down to the valley and beyond the village. Every so often he would lift up his eyes and stare at an ascending winding road the villagers were rushing toward with their children and a few provisions on their way to the citadel. The road was jam-packed with throngs of people forcing their way up along the side of an old stone wall.

Throughout the following few months Saad often recalled those moments, not of his running in panic, or his confused steps on mountain passes he was unfamiliar with, and on which he stumbled frightened and hungry, not even of his arrest four days later. What he did recall was that human wave rolling alongside the stone wall of the citadel, first ascending then descending. He actually saw them go up, and he assumed they came down. He only knew for sure when he heard the Castilian soldiers who arrested him and brought him to the interrogator at the Office of Inquisition talking about it. Then he saw through the eyes of his imagination the villagers coming down from that very road, waving in terror the white shreds of their garments to signal their submission as they headed toward the church to seek the waters of baptism and save their lives.

Was the past repeating itself? Saad wondered every time he thought about that scene. Whenever the image of that day came to mind, he couldn't help but recall al-Thaghri and his men, among whom was his own father. They stationed themselves in the Citadel of Malaga where they mounted a brave and steadfast resistance until the enemy got the upper hand. Since al-Thaghri and his men were well armed, they continued to put up a fight. But the inhabitants of the village were defenseless. They were poor farmers whose hands only knew how to operate plows and sickles. And so they sought the refuge of the old stones of a fortress, and for a while they were sheltered. But when the steady pounding brought down the fortress and the people in it, they raised the white shreds of cloth and they departed. Was the past repeating itself?

But reflection does not last long in the thick of torture, and terror mangles images and thoughts into pieces when the body is inflicted with wounds and the soul convulses like a slaughtered bird. The inquisitors in their black cassocks surround you, and their eyes pierce your innermost being as they bombard you with questions and inflict upon you their instruments of torture. They chain you to a wooden staircase and squirt water into your body, water that quenches thirst, cool, sweet water from God, water that your soul savors, but then enters you like a burning fire. You fill up, you bloat, you suffocate, and you try to suppress a scream, but it insists and comes out like a rattle in the throat as though it is your soul exiting in pain. They stare at you. Their eyes are mute and their faces expressionless. Their hearts are armored with black cloaks. The hot iron prongs burn the bottoms of your feet. The scalding stone scorches your back, your stomach, and your buttocks. The wooden instrument, the essence of the pangs of hell, crushes your bones. You bellow like a slaughtered bull, and the heart inside of you is wrenched as though the hand of death is grabbing at it, and it dies. They stare at you without batting an eye. They throw you into a dungeon, into solitary confinement, where you can't even cry. But when you do, the tears gush out in torrents, not because the body aches, but because you're thinking about all those human shreds that you know you are. You cry for your own condition and for the abandonment of a Loved One in the highest heavens who left you alone to suffer excruciating pain never promised to His pious people. Alone in your dark prison, you are surrounded by solitude with no light but the pale flicker of a candle whose shadow dances on the wall next to the phantom of the inquisitor who haunts you even in his absence. A feverish imagination exaggerates the ascending shadow on the wall, tracing the lines of the colossal vampire that spreads its blackness against the cold stone wall. Alone in your prison shared by rats you befriend because they're alive and they remind you of life. A few months later they remove you to a place where your loneliness dwindles, where you now have cell mates who share your nights and days. Sad hearts bond together, a source of light against the dark walls.

There were three of them. One was a Franciscan priest who, despite his advanced years, maintained his fiery eyes that scintillated with a vibrant deep blue like the waves of the sea. He spent long hours talking about Jesus as a young man, of his poverty, his beauty, and his suffering. He spoke about his mother who loved him deeply, and who carried him to faraway Egypt. He talked about his youthful days in Galilee, where he carried his message to a land that embraced him and denied him. He spoke about the cross he died on and his immortality. As the priest spoke, the blaze and purity of the sea gushed forth from the blueness of his eyes, and the dark dungeon opened up as though it were an open expanse along the seashore where the seagulls flew freely and the breeze of God softened the soul and warmed the heart. It wasn't just his stories that compelled them to him but something deep within him that filled their souls and created a space in which they dwelt in tranquility and peace of mind.

Even Antonio Solinas, the young Lutheran whom torture made more volatile and violent, and who fought for a reason or no reason at all, sat calmly as he listened to Father Juan Martin's stories. Antonio Solinas was as thin as a rail, ashen faced, and smiled rarely. He got into a fight practically every day with Muhammad BuSiddeeq, a young man yet to sprout hair on his face, who was accused by the inquisitors of practicing black magic and mastering sorcery that caused the death of his feudal master's livestock. The young man had eyes that flashed with a mischievous intelligence, and they sparkled even more whenever he outwitted Solinas. He would laugh at him mockingly whenever Solinas flared up in anger, because that's exactly what he wanted to do all along. When the fighting reached a high pitch, they would grab each other by the collar until Father Juan Martin or Saad intervened. Saad was quite fond of Muhammad. He enjoyed his sarcastic quips and his sense of humor. He was amazed by his emotional strength, which was not shattered by torture despite his tender age. He always reprimanded him in public for antagonizing Solinas, but in private he always apologized to him, saying that he only wanted to stop the fighting.

"I know you didn't mean to insult me," Muhammad would say, "but I get great pleasure in picking a fight with that jackass. He thinks his blood is blue because he's a Spaniard. Actually, it may have turned blue because of his stupidity. Have you ever seen such a self-important ass?"

Saad would laugh and thank God that Solinas didn't understand Arabic, or else a fresh quarrel, fiercer than before, would flare up.

Despite the daily skirmishes between Antonio Solinas and Muhammad BuSadeeq, the four of them bonded together. Each one told his story while the others shared in both the sad and the humorous details. At times they told stories and at others they just laughed together. Once in a while they would feel defeated and retreat, each one of them, into the darkest chambers of his soul. Saad was a part of all of this, and he was able to bear his nights and days because they were there, and because that strange little box in the head held some sparkling gems that glowed in the darkness of imprisonment. The faces of those he loved came to him clearly, throbbing with life, as though they were the faces in those astonishing colorful pictures in which, God only knows how, light and darkness and radiant colors capture human faces. Those faces that seem as though they're about to come out of the frames hung on the wall behind some inquisitor or another, and exchange a word or two with you, alleviating the gloom of the investigation and softening the oppressive and stern look of the inquisitor.

Saleema's face came to him, with its leanness and olive complexion. Her blue eyes mesmerize as they gleam with a defiant boldness or perhaps only an incisiveness that claims to be defiant.

Her lips are full and luscious, and thick, curly hair cascades down her shoulders. In prison Saad saw Saleema more clearly than he ever saw her before. He envisioned her face and her figure, and a slight bend in her torso when she walked as though she wanted to race her own steps by any means. In prison he heard her voice as she talked, as she laughed, as she yelled in anger, and even when she didn't utter a word. He saw her as a child during Abu Jaafar's lifetime and as a young woman who occupied his heart and caused his sleepless nights. And he saw her as a woman who would approach and give, but then would turn away for no reason.

He pictured Abu Jaafar just as if death had not taken him many years ago. He saw him as plain as day, with his imposing stature, his flowing robe, and a subtle smile that could almost be detected on his lips. But it wasn't detected and it left something of his soul in the bewildering look in his eye, something between a kindness that came from the heart and a reproachfulness that reined in the excess flow of the heart's gentleness.

And the face of his friend Naeem came to him, bright, luminous, like the rays of the sun beaming directly on him, bestowing to him something of its glow emanating from his honey-colored eyes, the fairness of his hair, and the impetuousness of his walk, his talk, and his raucous laughter. In the solitude of your prison, you see your loved ones more often because in time there is spaciousness and because they come to you, lovingly, during your darkest hour, and they let you take pleasure in watching their faces as much as you want.

Regardless of the torture and confinement Saad suffered, he never betrayed his heart, and his tongue never betrayed him. He was careful in what he said, even to his cell mates. He never pointed to anything, close or far away, that could harm him. And when the sentence was passed down on him, it was light. The only proof against him was that he had left Granada and unlawfully associated with the inhabitants of villages near Valencia. The court cleared him of the charges of heresy, sedition, and apostasy that his inquisitors had filed against him.

21

Hasan was hoping on his way home from the inn that this journey would be a long one. His day had been heavy and cumbersome, and he was shut indoors all day long. He took breaths of the fresh, cold air and followed the lightly falling snowflakes as he settled himself along the bank of the Darro River beneath the hanging branches of the trees. His heart began to calm down in the silence of the snowy night. It wasn't just this day that wore him down, but day after day after day when a crisis or complication of the day before pales in comparison to the next. But these days accustomed him to latch on to a scrap of hope or a flicker of light, even one as small as the eye of a needle. He held on to it, looking forward, selling illusions to himself before selling them to his friends and family, telling himself that "patience is a virtue," that "tomorrow is another day." But what came after that was the gloom and the dark abyss of a drowning man. When they posted the announcement that non-Christians of Valencia must convert or face confiscation of property and expulsion, Maryama burst into tears and rebuked him with words and looks. She said, "You sold my daughters, Hasan. You said, 'I will marry them off to faraway Valencia so that they can live secure in their religion, their land, and the vast wealth of their husbands.' But now they have no religion, no land, and no wealth!" He scolded her and said she didn't understand a thing. He reminded her that the nobility were protecting the Arabs of Valencia, and that the wealthy and influential Arabs would be going straight to the Royal Court to overturn the edict. But when the disturbances beset Valencia and the fires of anger and civil strife ignited, he kept the information to himself and hid it from Maryama. He followed the news through the Genoese merchants, the travelers, and muleteers who were constantly going back and forth. He sent his daughters five written messages and only received one back, orally. It said, "Things are not going very well, but we are all fine. You have become a grandfather to six healthy and happy children." Hasan relayed only the news of the grandchildren to Maryama, his mother, and Saleema. When Maryama asked their names, he replied, "I don't know." When his mother asked him if each of the girls gave birth to two children, or if only two had children and not the third, he replied, "I don't know." When asked if they were boys or girls, he also replied that he did not know. Maryama had nothing more to say, but she spent the next few days and nights in tears.

What fault is there in a drowning man latching on to a piece of wood or the branch of a tree? What crime is it to make for yourself a stained-glass lantern to brighten up the darkness of your days? Where is the sin in looking forward to a new day in hope and optimism?

Hasan saw it as a good sign the day Granada was bedecked in celebrations and fanfare, when the Alhambra Palace was awash in lights to welcome the emperor. Like many others, he went out to await the results of a meeting between the emperor and a delegation of the Arab community's most esteemed nobility. They met to review a list of grievances and demand an investigation into them. Until only yesterday, Hasan was still basking in the light of his lantern, clinging to its flicker of hope, when the town criers made the rounds announcing more restrictions added to the already existing ones. It is forbidden to use the Arabic language and Arabic titles, to wear Arab clothing and jewelry, or to patronize Arab bathhouses. All books must be submitted for inspection, and those that contain nothing harmful will be returned. It is unlawful for Arab midwives to assist in giving birth, and the bearing of arms is prohibited. All families must leave their door open on Fridays, Sundays, holy days, and feast days, to make sure that only the sanctioned practices are followed. Adults must perform all the rituals of their new religion, and children must attend catechism classes to wean them from their fathers' religion.

Hasan was neither able nor willing to go home that night. He walked on until he felt his nose and his extremities turning to ice. He veered off the road toward a tavern and went in.

The patrons of the tavern were seated in a main hall, huddled around a wood stove that gave the place a warm glow. They were eating and drinking, chatting and laughing boisterously. There were three women in the hall, each one holding a tambourine. At times one of them sang alone, at times they all sang together, and sometimes the patrons sang along.

Hasan took a seat with some men he didn't know and joined them for a drink. His eyes were fixed on one of the three women. She was tall and full-figured, and her dress revealed her upper chest and arms. Her thick, wavy, black hair fell across her half-naked shoulders. When she got close to him, he began to trifle with her. When she set her wide, kohl-stained eyes on him, he told her how captivating they were. She laughed heartily and her laughter was music to his ears. When she finished her song, he pulled out a chair for her next to him. She sat down, and they ate and drank together. Then she invited him to her room. He followed her, leaving behind him his worries and his usual shyness with people he didn't know.

Back in her cavelike room, she brought him some more wine. He drank and laughed until the tears rolled down his cheeks. She flirted with him, and he flirted back with a boldness he never knew he had. She took off all her clothes and stood naked before him. Her body was hot and sumptuous, and it took his breath away. He ran his fingers all over her body, from the tips of her shoulders to the bottom of her legs. He pressed his face against hers, kissing and softly nibbling on it with his lips. She purred like a wild cat, arousing him with uncontrollable lust. He guided her over to the bed and covered her with his body as the fires of passion ignited inside him.

When their desire was appeased, they lay wrapped in a repose as though they were the first creation at the beginning of time. There

wasn't a sound or an echo, nothing old, nothing new, no recollection or memory, nothing except the mixture of orange and green.
There was nothing but a silver liquid, a water or a sky, where the
clouds touch. One cloud had released its water, but others were full
and promising more.

In the morning he couldn't remember how many times he had
made love to her. The only things he found were her scent and
some of her clothes strewn across the room. He got dressed quickly
and headed out toward the road. He sneaked into the house. When
his mother caught sight of him, she ran to him and asked him the
reason for his absence. She was pale and her eyes were red and puffy.
"We said to ourselves, something bad must have happened to him.
Maryama's been out since dusk asking about you all over the place."

He raised his voice and berated her. Then Saleema came out
and spoke to him harshly. "Thank God nothing horrible has happened to you. Next time you intend on staying out all night, let us
know so that we don't stay up worrying ourselves sick, only to have
you greet us in the morning with shouting and rebuking."

He felt ashamed at what she said and he didn't say a word. He
went inside and doused his head in a basin of cold water. He asked
his mother to heat him some water to take a bath.

Soon thereafter, Maryama and Saleema, reassured of Hasan's
safety, went back to whatever was keeping them busy. But Umm
Hasan spent the better part of her days and nights thinking about
Hasan's absence. She had asked him openly about it, but he never
gave her a straight answer. She wondered if he took a second wife.
And if he indeed had, why would he keep it a secret from his own
mother? She would certainly understand and sympathize with how
much he has to put up with that miserable Maryama who annoys
him with her constant whining about her mother and brothers who
disappeared, and with her ceaseless nagging for marrying her
daughters to strangers who took them away where she can never see
them.

Whenever Umm Hasan complained about Maryama and dis-
played her annoyance over her shortcomings, Umm Jaafar, God rest

her soul, used to say, "Be patient, Zaynab, she's still a young girl with no experience. She'll grow up and learn." But here she was now grown up and still hadn't learned, and Umm Hasan had to interfere in every matter, big or small, to set her straight. She tells her, "The children prefer this dish, not that one," or "They like it cooked this way, not that way." When she finally had had enough, Umm Hasan threw up her hands and vowed never to set foot in the kitchen again. "Let's see what this daughter of a drummer will do," she said to herself. But only a few weeks later she discovered that this was precisely what Maryama had wanted all along. She wanted to banish her from the kitchen and take sole charge of it, as though she inherited it from her father. Umm Hasan was convinced that her daughter-in-law was the kind of woman known for her cunning and tricks. She quickly changed her mind and went back into the kitchen so that the drummer's daughter wouldn't get the best of her. Hasan would be totally justified if he did take a second wife because he had had no luck at all with the first. But then Umm Hasan realized that they were all Christians on paper and that Hasan couldn't have a second wife, that he would have to divorce the first to marry the second, but that divorce wasn't easy, and most likely it wasn't possible. Poor Hasan, she thought, without a wife to make him happy, and no way to make himself happy. Maryama interrupted Umm Hasan's thoughts when she suddenly walked into her room, carrying a basket.

"Look at this fish, Umm Hasan. I bought it this morning at the market. It's very fresh. The fishmonger swore that he just brought it in from the shore."

Umm Hasan looked into the basket and saw the glimmering silvery and reddish fish. She picked up one of them and examined its eyes and gills. She squeezed the head gently. "He wasn't lying. It's nice and fresh."

"The children and Hasan and Saleema say that nobody prepares fish the way you do. So, what do you say, will you cook it for us today?" asked Maryama with a smile.

"Why don't you cook it yourself?"

"Because they prefer the way you do it!"

Umm Hasan let out a sigh and stood up, feigning annoyance, to prepare the fish. Maryama followed her into the kitchen with the basket and then announced to her that she was going to the souk with Saleema and they would be back later. "We may be a little late if we have to go to more than one druggist to find what Saleema's looking for."

Maryama and Saleema went out of the house and walked to the square next to the Church of San Salvador where a cart and driver were waiting for them as prearranged. They exchanged greetings and the two woman got into the cart. Ever since the edict demanding that all Arabic books be turned over for inspection was announced, the thought of being investigated terrified Saleema. She knew full well that "inspecting books" meant confiscation, and that Hasan would comply with the new decrees. She also knew that any attempt to persuade him would end in failure.

"What can we do, Maryama?"

"Let's hide the books."

"How?"

"Let me think about it." Maryama spent night and day until she thought of a solution and proposed it to Saleema. "Let's go to Ainadamar and remove the books. When Hasan insists on turning them in, you can tell him that you sold them. He won't believe you and when he comes to get them, he won't find them. He'll blow up in anger, but then he'll calm down."

"But where will we take the books?"

"To this house."

"Here? How?"

Maryama had it all planned in her mind. She laid it out to Saleema, starting with buying the fish and coaxing Umm Hasan into cooking it, and ending with bringing in the books without arousing any suspicion.

They went to Ainadamar and put the books into five sacks. They tied them up tightly, and the driver helped them put the sacks onto the cart. They got on and returned to Albaicin.

Maryama went into the house first and passed by the kitchen. She found Umm Hasan standing in front of the stove with a large frying pan and the splattering hot oil. She was just starting to fry the fish when Maryama popped her head in, greeted her, and left her in peace. Then she gathered all the children together and asked her oldest daughter to tell them a story. "I bought some sweets," she told them. "If you sit quietly and listen to the story, I'll give you some." Then she rushed off toward the front gate of the house and gave a hand to Saleema and the driver in carrying the sacks into the house. They paid the driver and he left. Then they moved the books, one sack at a time, into Maryama's room.

Maryama had emptied out her chest of everything that was in it. She opened it and opened the sacks. She and Saleema then carefully stacked the books in neatly arranged piles inside the chest. When that was done, Maryama put the padlock back on and locked it. She started to laugh. "If Hasan has any suspicion that we removed the books, it will never occur to him that they're hidden right under his nose in this chest that is the first thing he sees in the morning and the last thing he sees at night. Are you happy now, Saleema?" Saleema put her arms around her and hugged her tightly. She didn't say a word but her eyes were swelling with tears.

22

Naeem spoke to Father Miguel. "Tell me, Father, what do you think of my Spanish?"

"It's excellent."

"When I speak, does it seem that it is anything but my mother tongue?"

"Not in the least. Why do you ask?"

"I learn foreign languages quickly. And I wanted to surprise you with something that will please you. I've learned many words of the native language, and I can express myself in sentences and I understand what's being said to me."

"This is indeed a surprise."

"Do you know why I want to learn this language, Father? I want to help you."

"Help me?"

"Yes, help you. If you had a translator to convey to you the thoughts of some of these people, your task in writing about them would be all the easier. Isn't that correct?"

Father Miguel gave Naeem a look that made him uneasy, as though he was trying to pry into his soul and expose his secret. "But learning a new language requires a long time, long after we will have returned to Spain and I will have finished my book."

"Not at all, Father. I've learned quite a bit of the native language over the past several weeks. I'll be able to master it in two or three months, but I only need . . ." Naeem stopped. It was now time to ask the question right out. But what if the priest refused?

"What is it you need? A teacher?" Father Miguel laughed as he asked the question.

Naeem responded in laughter as well, but only to hide his nervousness.

"The only thing I need is to speak more with the natives."

"So, what's preventing you from doing that?"

"Nothing's preventing me, but I only speak to them in passing, to this group or that one, usually slaves too busy with work. But if I were given the occasion to sit with them sometimes, to go and visit them in their huts for an hour or two every day, I swear to you, Father, I would learn their language in a short time. I would then be able to tell you what you needed to know of their ideas, their legends, and the meanings of the songs they sing."

Father Miguel remained silent as though he was pondering the matter. "You want to be away from the house an hour or two every day?"

"You needn't worry, Father. When I leave the house, I'll make sure everything has been prepared, and you won't feel my absence at all. But . . ."

"What?" Father Miguel interrupted.

"If you were to notify the regional governor that I was going to learn the language in order to assist you with your book, then none of the soldiers will think I was frequenting the huts for some dubious reason."

"I agree, it would be more prudent to do that. When I meet with the governor tomorrow, I'll bring up the matter."

"Rest assured, Father, that I will do my utmost to master the language in the quickest time possible."

Barely had Naeem left Father Miguel's study than he leaped for joy. He got exactly what he was looking for. He would see her every day, he would go and visit her at her hut, and perhaps she would take him inside to meet her family. And maybe God will even ordain . . .

Naeem had first laid eyes on her only two weeks ago. He was bathing in a stream behind the house when she drew near him. He was embarrassed by his nakedness and dove in the water. When he came up, he looked around and found her standing there and watching him. He noticed she had sharp features, a dark, round face, a wide forehead, black eyes that came to a slant on the sides, a big nose, thick lips, and long silky black hair that shimmered in the sun. He stayed in the water until he saw her move away, and he quickly jumped out and put his clothes on. And then suddenly she reappeared. She wasn't at all a young girl but a woman, perhaps thirty years old, with a voluptuous body and a well-developed bosom. She had wide shoulders and buttocks. Naeem averted his eyes and attempted to look up at the sky, but he was fully aware that she was staring at him and his face couldn't hide his embarrassment. He looked at her and covered his shyness with a smile. She smiled back. He pointed to himself and said, "Naeem," and repeated it several times. Then he pointed his finger toward her inquiring about her name. "Maya," she said. He repeated her name a couple of times while he pointed at her, and then his own name as he pointed to himself. He laughed and then she laughed. Her face radiated with such sweetness that it warmed his soul. He asked himself where this heavenly woman came from. He wanted to give her a present. He fished in his pockets but came up with nothing. He raced back to the house and grabbed one of the two pies he baked that morning. He came back running and found her exactly where he left her. She had sat down by the edge of the stream. He sat down next to her and set the pie in front of them. He invited her to eat, but she didn't understand what he was saying. He broke off a piece of the pie and put it in her hand. Then he broke off a piece for himself and began to nibble at it. She did the same. They ate together, but couldn't do much else besides exchange names and smiles. When she got up to leave, Naeem had a great urge to embrace her, but he didn't have the courage. He stuck out his hand bashfully and patted her on the head. He never took his eyes off of her as she wandered off gracefully, with her voluptuous body swaying gently from one side to the other.

On the following day at the same time and the same place they met again. Naeem had saved his lunch for them to share. As they sat and ate, she repeated his name and he repeated hers. He pointed to a tree and said "tree." She repeated it and then taught him the word in her own language. He went home ecstatic with his accomplishments of the day, ten new words of her language, the ring of her voice in his ear, the rhythm of her laugh in his soul, and the quick peck on the cheek he gave her. At night the more he thought of her the more aroused he became.

On the third day Maya did not come. He had every hope she would. He thought she might be late, but was convinced she'd show up. It was inconceivable that she wouldn't. After waiting a long time, he gave up and went home, disappointed and depressed, with no way to console himself except to wait for the next day. The hours passed by torturously slowly, from evening until night, from night until dawn, from morning to midday. He ran to the stream and paced back and forth, looking in every direction until he saw her from a distance coming in his direction. He ran toward her calling out her name. When he reached her, he conveyed to her how worried he had been. "Where were you? I nearly died thinking that I might never see you again. Your absence scared the wits out of me, Maya. Why. . . ?" Naeem then realized he was speaking in Arabic while she smiled at him curiously, wondering what he was saying. He put his arms around her and hugged her tightly and affectionately. He began to kiss her head, her neck and shoulders, and then their lips met.

Beneath the trees and the rustling of the leaves at the edge of the stream, the woman gave herself to him. She gave him what he had been longing for ever since he was a young man but never attained. What did this woman do to him? Naeem was neighing like a wild colt that sprinted furiously as the earth quaked beneath it, stamping the ground and making it shake, as he gained speed and gasped for breath. The sharp point of a knife and the shiver of life conjoined in his soul as it drank from the waters of Paradise while his body burst in flames.

When Naeem withdrew from inside of her, he cuddled up next to her, holding on to her in embrace. He was unaware that tears were flowing from his eyes until he felt her wiping them off with her fingertips and saying something to him he didn't understand.

The sun dipped toward the horizon and then disappeared. The moonlight lit up the skies as Naeem held her hands. When the priest asks him where he has been, he'll respond by telling him to go to hell. And to hell with Saad. Don't ever tell me I don't know life and how to live. Damn you, Saad. When he heard himself thinking all this he started to laugh at himself, and Maya laughed as well. He looked into her eyes, then jumped up.

"Now, I'm going to give you a present."

It wasn't important that she didn't understand at first. Now she would.

Under the light of the moon at the edge of the stream that reflected its light, in the presence of Maya, the most beautiful of women, Naeem lifted up his arms, moved his shoulders, and leaned over, first to the left and then to the right. He stiffened his body, clapped his hands, and tapped his heels on the ground. He jumped high in the air as though he were about to fly away. He landed on the ground cross-legged and shook his thighs in consecutive motions. He jumped up and stood clapping his hands, bending and twisting his body in circles, leaping up and down. He moved over to Maya as she was watching him and he wrapped his arms around her waist. He spun her around until they both got dizzy and fell to the ground. They laughed for a long time before Maya leaned over and kissed him on the mouth.

Naeem was unable to concoct a new story every day to explain his absence at a given time. His imagination couldn't come up with enough alibis that would be convincing and not arouse the slightest suspicion. Besides, one hour was no longer enough time to be together, neither to make love nor to learn each other's languages, nor to communicate so little with so many hand gestures and simple phrases, or words he was able to pick up of her language. If only God would bless him to be able to go to sleep one night and miraculously wake up the next day speaking her language fluently. He wanted to tell her a thousand things and hear as much from her. She was his woman, so how could she not know who he was and where he came from. He wondered if Father Miguel would be happy with his story and allow him to marry her. Father Miguel was a kind man but he was Castilian, and the Castilians have strange habits he found difficult to understand. He decided that it would be best not to tell him. He would learn her language and then go to her father and address him as "Sir," as would be appropriate. He would tell him his story and explain to him that he was not one of those Spaniards who kill the inhabitants of his land or brutally rape the women. Her father would surely take a liking to him and welcome him into the family. Perhaps he would learn Arabic from him because they'll be relatives. And who knows, perhaps God would enable him to take Maya back to Granada. "God have mercy on your soul, Umm Jaafar," he prayed to himself. "If only God had granted you a longer life, I would have brought you a daughter-in-law the likes of which you never imagined. I can hear you saying, 'She looks strange and her language is stranger.' But I would respond that she's a good woman, kind-hearted and beautiful."

"What's gotten into you, Naeem?" asked Father Miguel.

"Do you see something wrong with me, Father?"

"You look so sullen, and sometimes you talk to yourself. You go on like that oblivious to my presence."

"Do I really talk to myself?"

"Yes, you do. I caught you several times, and I'm thinking it may have something to do with your repeated visits to the slaves' huts. Those people practice witchcraft, and they could have put a spell on you."

"I swear to God, Father, those people are very kind and they like me a lot. But now, I remember, did you hear me speaking to myself in Arabic? The truth is, Father, I miss Granada and my friends I left back home. Sometimes I find myself talking to them. Do you realize, Father, that there's only one other person of Arab origin in all this region, and he's the carpenter who works on the other side of the settlement, and I only run into him once in a blue moon. Since there's no one to speak Arabic with, I speak it out loud, imagining that I'm talking to one of my friends back home."

"You should refrain from doing that, or else you'll be stricken with madness," commented the priest in all seriousness. "Also, the devil could creep into your soul at any moment and turn your words into his favor since what you're saying is not directed to any-one in front of you. If you miss Arabic, then you should read the prayer book I gave you that was translated into Arabic. Didn't you bring it with you?"

"Sorry, Father, I forgot to bring it with me from Granada."

"How negligent can you be!" he said with a reproaching look on his face.

"I'm sorry, Father. I promise I won't talk to myself any more."

Naeem only spoke with Maya in these daily conversations. His desire to speak to her couldn't wait until they mastered each other's language. Even at night in bed, he spoke to her. During the day, while he cleaned the house, prepared the meals, or did the laundry, he spoke to her. He talked to her incessantly, telling her everything about his life, from the time Abu Jaafar stretched out his hand to him and asked him his name until the moment he first saw her while he was bathing by the stream and dove into the water to cover his shame.

Somehow, Naeem communicated to Maya that he wanted to marry her, to meet her family and ask their permission for her hand. She tried to explain to him that her family lived far away, but he wasn't sure whether or not he understood what she was telling him. He asked her repeatedly, but her response was no different from what he understood. After two whole days of painstaking and inter-rupted conversations, the matter became clear to him. She had come to this region with her husband who had since died. She was left alone. Going back to her family would require a horse, or sev-eral weeks of traveling by foot, in either case exposing her to prob-lems with the Spaniards. He thought about asking Father Miguel to give him his horse, but then he would have to tell him the whole story. He may or may not agree. Most likely he wouldn't, Naeem thought. But he had to act.

Naeem cleaned the house from top to bottom, washed Father Miguel's clothes, waited for them to dry and then folded them, and cooked enough food to last the priest three or four days. After that, he went outside the house, picked a bunch of wildflowers, put some of them in a vase with water, and set them in Father Miguel's library. He tied a bow around the remaining few flowers, and packed them up with a small Quran, a few provisions for the road, and a straw-colored hat he had made secretly and was intending to give to Father Miguel for a Christmas present, but decided instead to give to his bride's father. He certainly couldn't go to him empty-handed.

Just before sunrise, Naeem crept out of the house quietly. He mounted his master's horse and rode it to the stream where Maya was waiting. He mounted her on the horse behind him, and they rode off into the distance.

23

It dawned on Hasan as he lay in bed huddled under the covers trying to get warm that his life was much better now. The storm that Maryama raised had calmed down, and their life together had gotten back on course. Her family was released from prison. Her mother was declared innocent of all charges, although her brothers were sentenced to pay a substantial fine that they could not afford. When the Castilians confiscated Abu Ibrahim's house in lieu of payment, Maryama suggested to Hasan that her mother and brothers come and live with them.

"Your mother is more than welcome to come and live with us," he replied. "But your brothers will have to find their own place to live. I have my mother and sister in this house, and they are not blood relatives."

Maryama looked at him suspiciously. "Tell me what's really on your mind, Hasan. No need to think up excuses. You've hosted Omar and Abdel-Kareem before, for several weeks at a time when they were still strangers from Valencia, and not related to you through marriage."

He looked at her in annoyance and didn't respond. When she continued to glare at him, he spoke. "You know what the other reason is, so why bother to say it? But since you want to hear it, then listen! Your brothers have just been released from prison, and they're being watched. I don't want myself or my family to have anything to do with whatever problems may arise."

Maryama said nothing. She no longer broached the subject or alluded to it. But throughout the next three months, she was on edge and easily irritated, yelling at the children for one reason or another, or for no reason at all. She spanked Hisham and she cried at the slightest incident. She met all of Hasan's needs in the way of food and clothing, but she wouldn't engage him in conversation or let him near her in bed.

But patience prevailed and in the passing of weeks and months, she calmed down. One night in bed, Hasan thought about how pleased God must be with him. The state of his affairs and those of his family were stable at a time when stability was rare. Even Saleema, whose defiance and choice of such a strange life caused him so much anxiety, began to fill their house in Albaicin with prestige and gratitude because she had the power of healing, and her treatments cured both the body and the soul—at least that's what people were saying. She inherited Abu Jaafar's high-mindedness and noble heart, and she never refused a request for help, even if there were no means to pay a fee for her services. Maybe that's the reason, Hasan thought, why God rewarded her, and why people lavished their money on her when they had it, and why they lavished their affection when they had money or didn't have it. God bestowed on Saleema wisdom, knowledge, the affection of people, and that little angel, Amal, who filled his house with her joy, her radiant laughter, and her enchanting presence. "What will you give me today, Amal?" The little girl opens her arms and gives him a big hug, saying, "I love you more than the sun, the moon, and Mummy." Hasan beams with pride as the tears well from his eyes. He wished only that Saad would return to complete his peace of mind, that he marry off his remaining daughters, and that Hisham grow up and marry Amal so that he may see their children before he dies.

Hasan spent several hours every day thinking about his welfare and that of his family, or about this thing or that. Even if he went to bed late, he always woke up at the crack of dawn, two or three hours before Maryama, who lay sound asleep next to him, and the other family members. Only Saleema was awake at that time. The only thing he could do was to lie awake in bed with his thoughts, waiting for the others to get up.

Sometimes he found it difficult waking up in the dark. He would light a candle and follow the shadow of its flicker against the wall or the ceiling. Sometimes he would get up and go into Saleema's room, knock on the door and go in. He would feel comfort in her company and in watching Esperanza's angelic face as she slept.

"What's keeping you up, Hasan? Why can't you sleep?" Saleema asked.

"Nothing, really. I just seem to need only a few hours of sleep."

"Are you sure that's all?"

Her question made him uneasy. He didn't respond.

She lifted her head from the book she was reading and asked, "Do you remember the day you, Saad, Naeem, and I all went to see the Christopher Columbus parade?"

"The day Naeem suddenly disappeared and we didn't know where he went?"

Hasan began to recall some of the details of that day, and a half smile cracked on his face. His features expressed something between sadness and joy.

"We were so young then, Saleema, and we had no idea what was in store for us."

"I sometimes ask myself how our grandchildren will live a hundred years from now."

Hasan had never given it a thought. "God only knows. I never get further than a day in the future when Saad and Naeem come back, and when we marry off our children and see their children." He stopped talking for a moment and then decided to tell Saleema what he wanted to tell her for months. "Would you accept Hisham as a husband for Amal?"

Saleema laughed so loud that the little girl stirred in her bed, but then rolled over and went back to sleep. Her laughing made him uncomfortable and he asked her with a slight tone of annoyance, "Why are you laughing?"

"Because my Aysha is only three years old, and Hisham isn't even nine yet."

"Before you know it she'll be a young women of ten, and Hisham a tall and strapping young man."

"It's premature to be talking about such things, Hasan. And when the time comes, we'll have to face the problem of the Castilian edict banning marriage between relatives."

"They can all go to hell! I'll never give Amal away to a stranger who'll take her away from my house."

Saleema smiled and pretended to go along with Hasan, feeling as if she were participating in an amusing game whose outcome would be in some distant future.

"How will we get the official papers? And when they have children, won't the Castilian law declare them illegal?"

Hasan fidgeted as though he had to solve the problem then and there.

"I will find a way out. Saad is from Malaga and Amal bears his name. I will deny on paper that I'm her uncle and you are her mother."

This time Saleema laughed softly so that she wouldn't wake up the sleeping child. "Why don't you arrange for the marriage contract now?" she asked with playful sarcasm. "Then all we need to do is wait a few years for the children to come of legal age and announce the wedding."

Hasan was offended and brushed aside Saleema's poking fun at him. "What's gotten into you, Saleema? I swear by the Lord of the Kaaba that I love your daughter more than Hisham and all my daughters, those here and those in Valencia whom I miss with all my heart. Good night!" He left her to crawl into bed as was her habit at that early hour in the morning, and went and woke up Maryama to prepare his breakfast before going off to work.

Hasan enjoyed his work at the inn. The only cloud over his head was Abu Mansour with his short temper and lack of self-control. Hasan really didn't need his services when he asked him to work there, but the man was without a job and nothing to keep his mind occupied. Instead he stayed home and abused his wife and alcohol. He would sit and take one drink after another until he couldn't breathe and his face broke out in red blotches. His verbal abuse would turn physical and the sounds rang out throughout the neighborhood.

When he came to work at the inn, Hasan showed him a small room by the entrance. "Why don't you work here, away from all the commotion? You can register the names of the guests and take what they want to keep in the safe. You can put their belongings into the safe yourself, and return them once they settled their accounts."

In the beginning, it seemed that the job suited Abu Mansour. He put his mind to it, and he seemed to be pleased with it. He didn't drink excessively. But that didn't last long. After a while, the drinking got the better of him, and he would stumble out into the courtyard looking for a fight. Hasan had to stand on guard and be ready to prevent a brawl at any moment. Whenever he needed to be away, he cautioned his employees to keep an eye on Abu Mansour and make sure he didn't stir up any trouble.

Business was bustling at the inn, especially during the summer months. The rooms were always full, especially with traveling merchants, and many people stopped by for an evening of entertainment. The clientele were Arabs and non-Arabs. Some came from the villages surrounding Granada who needed to stay over a day or two to finalize a business deal. Some came from long distances, like Aragon and Valencia, or even as far away as the cities on the Italian coast, mostly merchants coming to buy or sell. During the day they would conduct their affairs, and at night they would sit and chat, or have dinner and drink. In the summer the guests stayed up late into the night, and the inn's employees wouldn't get to sleep until the wee hours of the morning.

Hasan was busy settling accounts with the chef when he heard Abu Mansour shouting. He jumped up and rushed out to the courtyard where he found him with a sullied face and fire raging in his eyes. Hasan put his arms over his shoulders and spoke to him in an attempt to lure him away and toward his room. "Everything's fine, Abu Mansour. Tell me, what happened?"

Abu Mansour wouldn't budge, so Hasan spoke to him in a stern, measured tone.

"Come with me inside to your room, and we'll talk calmly about what's bothering you."

Abu Mansour paid no attention to Hasan, but yelled out and pointed his finger at one of the patrons: "May we be rid of your kind, you dog!"

The young man Abu Mansour was pointing at was strikingly handsome and impeccably groomed. He sneered at Abu Mansour and turned his head away in disgust.

"I beg you, for God's sake, come with me," Hasan shouted at Abu Mansour as he tried to push him inside.

"This boy is the son of Yaseen the stoker. His father, may God have mercy on his soul, used to work as a stoker in my bathhouse. I just heard him now with my own ears bragging that he's a Castilian, born and bred, and that he's of pure blood. Where in hell did you get pure blood when everything about you reeks of being a filthy sodomist?"

The young man jumped up from his seat and shouted at Hasan. "Are you going to allow this senile old goat to insult people? Since you manage the place, you're responsible for making sure your guests are treated with respect."

Before Hasan could even open his mouth to apologize for what had happened, Abu Mansour stretched out his hand to grab the man by the collar. But just in time, Hasan jumped between them and ranted at him furiously. "Abu Mansour, conduct yourself like a gentleman. I've had enough of what you're doing to yourself and to other people!"

But Abu Mansour was like a raging bull as he tried to set himself free and charge at the young man. "Pure blood?" he repeated, "you son of a whore."

In a panic, not knowing what to do, Hasan punched Abu Mansour in the stomach, which quieted him down. Silence prevailed for several moments before Abu Mansour spoke.

"Hasan, whom I carried in my arms as a baby, hits me. Don't worry, son of Yaseen the stoker, you're not the only son of a whore in this place." All the clamor that had erupted in the courtyard in loud bursts ended in a whimper. Abu Mansour turned around and staggered in slow heavy steps until he vanished from sight.

Despite Hasan's attempts to offer an apology to the guest and kiss his shoulder, making the excuse that Abu Mansour was an old man prone to excessive drinking, he found it difficult to forgive his own behavior. When he found himself alone in bed that night, he was tormented by what happened. Abu Mansour never dared to insult or harm him in any way, so why did he raise his voice and strike him in front of all those people? In the morning Hasan went to him and tried to apologize, but Abu Mansour couldn't even look him in the eye. His face was crestfallen, and the only thing he could say was, "Go, Hasan, don't make matters worse. Times are hard enough."

Hasan went away, but came back to visit on the holidays. On both occasions Abu Mansour motioned to his wife to offer him whatever food or drink they had, but he sat without saying a word, as though he forgot how to talk. After that Hasan stopped visiting. He told himself that when Saad comes back he'll patch things up between them. But Abu Mansour didn't wait for Saad. When Hasan joined Abu Mansour's funeral procession, he sobbed so profusely that the others berated him. "Control yourself, Hasan. It's not right to weep like a woman."

24

S aad came to the realization that going back to work with his comrades, the freedom fighters, was virtually impossible. What good would there be in a man who walks slowly and cautiously with the help of crutches? How could he climb up or come down from that village suspended in the highest rungs of the mountain, with its roads winding and unpaved? Even if they found him some other job or duty to fulfill, how would that suit him, especially since the court extended his sentence beyond the three years of prison by placing him on probation and house arrest in Granada, restricting his movements outside the home to attending mass on Sundays and holidays, including Christmas and Easter. He could not mingle with other people without wearing the sanbenito, the yellow vest with the red armband that called attention to his past sins.

If Saad could have chosen what to do upon his release from prison, he would not have gone directly to Granada. How could he go back to Hasan and Saleema and say to them, "Feed me and take care of me because I don't have a job and the court won't allow me to go and work." How would he bear that look of pity or the suppressed gasp of dismay that reveals itself in the quiver of lips the moment the door opens and he see on their faces his own reflection, his impotence and his crutches?

He knocked on the door. When Umm Hasan opened it, she called out his name, and then yelled out, "Saleema!" and started to weep. It wasn't what he was expecting. His immediate reaction was that something terrible had happened to Saleema. He was stunned by fear and his tongue and body froze. As he started to whisper something, Maryama came rushing out and greeted him. "Welcome back, Saad. Saleema is fine. She bore you a daughter, so beautiful and radiant. Come, Aysha, come and say hello to Saad, your father."

He stared at a little girl of three years, with a bright face, and with his mother's features and her big deep-black eyes. He was looking at her in such awe that it seemed as though he was witnessing a miracle and couldn't believe his eyes. She was the exact age of his sister Nafeesa, and she had his mother's name, Aysha. Just looking at her brought back their memories, as clear as though the years had never passed, or as if he traveled back in time.

"Her name is 'Aysha'?"

"Yes, 'Aysha', but on paper her name is 'Esperanza.' But her uncle only calls her 'Amal.' "

"Amal?"

Saad bent down to the extent his crutches would allow him. "Come here Aysha, come here, honey." But the little girl was frightened and burst into tears.

Saad didn't sleep a wink that night. He couldn't even lie on his bed. He spent the night between staring at the little girl and rummaging through whatever remained of Saleema's things. In the morning and throughout the day, the little girl remained aloof from him. She stopped crying, and even though she sometimes stood still and gazed at him, she kept a safe distance just in case he tried to get close to her. But slowly her interest in him grew as she followed him with her eyes more and more. In the evening, Maryama picked her up and told her a story. When she dozed off, she put her in her mother's bed and looked over to Saad and smiled.

"So that you can sleep next to her, Saad."

The little girl was sound asleep, and the only thing you could see of her was her round moonlike face and the rings of black, curly hair moistened by sweat that covered her forehead. He couldn't keep his eyes off of her, and he listened to his heart pounding from all these new events. He thought about how he now had a daughter, not a seed that grows in her mother's stomach day after day, not an infant you watch nursing and crying, smiling and taking those first steps, uttering that first word or sentence, but a complete human being who knows her name and how to say "yes" and "no." This is your daughter, he thought, right before your eyes, ready and complete. But how was this possible? They say this is Aysha, your daughter, but then they say your wife isn't here, because the men from the Office of Inquisition came a few days ago and took her away. What did she do to make them do that? he wondered.

Maryama told him the story. "They came and searched the house, every corner and inch. They tore the place apart. It was as if some son of a bitch concocted a rumor that we were stashing secret weapons or a buried treasure. They turned the whole house upside down, Saad. It never occurred to me that they were targeting Saleema. What on earth would the Office of Inquisition want with a woman like her? But it was her they were looking for. They spent more time searching her room than they did the rest of the house. One of them had a pen and notebook and was writing down the names of all the herbs, the jars, and books. They put everything into two huge sacks. They handcuffed Saleema and carried her off in a large basket. Can you believe it, Saad, they carried Saleema off in a large basket? It's the strangest thing I've ever seen. I still can't get over it. For a while I thought they were lunatics who escaped from the insane asylum. But Hasan assured me later on that they were, in fact, officials from the Office of Inquisition."

The more Saad listened to Maryama, the more frightened he became. He was hoping that there would be some accusation charged against Saleema other than practicing witchcraft. But carrying her off in a basket meant that they were afraid to touch her. Saad was sure that they had arrested her and charged her with this, the most serious crime. His body began to shake in short, quick convulsions, then he bit hard on his lower lip to suppress the word "No!" that was surging from inside of him so that Maryama wouldn't hear it.

Should he rejoice over his little daughter or give himself over to the sadness he felt for his wife? How could he cope with all these events that unfolded in the course of one day? He now understood what Umm Hasan's face said to him when he knocked on the door and she opened it. When she saw him, she was inundated in a wave of fear and she called out for help. Whether he had aged or not, whether he was with or without crutches, she had seen him as Saad, the husband of her daughter, and she cried out to him to save her. But here he was sitting on his hands, powerless, unable to enjoy his daughter without grief, and unable to fear for his wife's life without thinking about the existence of this little one who was stealing his heart that only knew at that moment utter bliss and affection.

As Saad sat and gaped at his daughter while she slept and thought about his wife who wasn't there, he couldn't hear a thing that was going on in the next room between Hasan and Maryama as they engaged in a heated conversation that never rose above a whisper.

"I don't know what I'm going to do now," he said in great agitation.

"Concerning Saleema?"

"No, about Saad."

"What are you getting at?" she asked with a disturbed look on her face.

"Not only has Saad come to us having just been released from prison by an Inquisition tribunal, but he's coming having been placed on probation. And he has to wear the sanbenito."

"So what does that mean?"

"It means that he's being watched, that the authorities have their eyes on him, and that puts this house and everyone in it . . ."

"That puts this house and everyone in it in a position of honor! All of Albaicin respects those whom the Inquisition have persecuted, and that vest raises their heads in awe." Maryama was highly agitated and the sparks flew from her eyes.

"I'm aware of that, Maryama, and I'm not saying I don't respect Saad. But I've spent too many years guarding the safety of my family."

Maryama interrupted him and answered in a tone full of deri-sion. "I know—you've been overly cautious, you wouldn't even allow my mother and brothers to come and live with us after their house was confiscated."

Hasan didn't respond to her charge and paused for a few sec-onds before he spoke again.

"I think I'll let him know my true feelings on the subject. Saad is very astute, and he more than anyone will understand that living away from here is safer. He won't have to wait and hear me tell him that I honestly prefer that he not live with us."

Maryama gave him a long, hard stare without saying a word. She stood up and calmly went off and brought back a Quran. She set it in front of him and placed her right hand on top of it. "Listen to me well and watch, Hasan. This is the book of God, and I swear upon it. I swear to Almighty God that if you bring up this subject with Saad, either openly or by dropping hints, I will leave this house before him and I promise I will never set foot in it again as long as I live." She picked up the Quran and put it back in its place. Then she went over and lifted the cover from her bed and carried it out of the bedroom.

Umm Hasan felt Maryama next to her in bed, and she asked surprised, "Are you sleeping here?"

"I don't know what on earth Hasan ate tonight," she answered. "His snoring is very loud. Yes, I'm sleeping here."

Whenever Aysha asked for her mother, Umm Hasan burst into tears. Maryama, on the other hand, thought up ways to keep the lit-tle girl occupied. She would tell her a story or invent a new game, or she would call out to Hisham to come and get on his hands and knees and neigh like a horse. "Would you like a ride on the pony, or should I ride him?" she'd ask.

"He's a donkey, not a horse," the little girl would answer teas-ingly. Then both she and Maryama would chuckle, after which Hisham would jump up in indignation and protest that he wasn't a donkey. His mother would scold him and tell him to get back on the floor so that his cousin could have a ride. He would obey grudgingly, but get his revenge.

"My father says that Aysha is a good luck charm, but she's been bad luck ever since she came in to this house. Her father became sick and has to walk on crutches, and the police came and took her mother away."

His mother chides him with a threat. "I'll kill you if you ever say anything like that again." But the boy doesn't balk, and his mother gives him a good whack. Then she goes over to console him and calmly tries to make him understand that he has to be nice to his cousin because she is his cousin and because her mother is away from her.

Saleema's absence was a source of enormous stress and sadness to everyone in the household. Umm Hasan's eyes would swell in tears as she clapped her hands together in frustration and repeated over and over again, "There's nothing we can do!" This only exacerbated the misery as she walked around with her head held low. Hasan and Saad felt the same thing, not in words, but through that hopeless look in their eyes.

Only Maryama racked her brain to think of a strategy, some way out, even though she didn't let anyone know. She could at least find out what was happening with Saleema, what the charge was, and how long she was to be imprisoned. She poked and prodded and made inquiries until she stumbled upon a Castilian woman whose husband worked as a secretary at the Office of Inquisition. She met her at the souk by chance. They exchanged a few passing words and she left. Two days later there was a short conversation. Eventually, as the woman came to know Maryama and enjoy talking to her, they spent more time together at the souk. She would ask Maryama how she cooked something, or ask for a recipe for meat pies. After several weeks of their acquaintance, Maryama broached the subject.

"My husband, may God give him a long life and good health, is so good to me. He doesn't deprive me of anything. The only problem is that his sister doesn't like me or my children, and never wishes us well. But thank God for punishing her for her jealous heart and rewarding me for my kind heart. The officials at the Office of Inquisition arrested her, but for the life of me I have no idea what evil she conspired."

"Since she's an evil person, there's no doubt she committed acts punishable by law."

"That's what's bothering me. If only I knew exactly what she did so that I could tell my husband and he'll know the truth about his sister. And then he'll realize that in all my quarrels with her I was the victim and she was the troublemaker. Of course when she's released after the investigation, she'll claim they erroneously arrested her thinking she was some other woman, and she'll insist on her innocence."

The woman didn't seem at all interested in this part of the conversation. She asked Maryama if she was going to buy some eggplant.

Maryama let out a sigh. "I think I'll buy . . . but my sister-in-law is on my mind. Do you have any relatives or neighbors who work at the Inquisition?"

"My husband works there!"

Maryama stood dumbfounded as she tried to crack a smile of joy. "How lucky I am, for sure! Your husband will be able to find out why they arrested Saleema, and when I tell my husband why, he'll begin to believe me over his sister."

"I'll ask him, but what do you think of these olives? Are you going to buy some?"

"Don't bother. I'll bring you some much better than these. My husband has some olive trees that have the best olives. When you bring me the news, I'll bring you a couple of containers of olives."

At their next meeting, Maryama's heart sank in dreaded fear when she saw the gloating look on the woman's face when asked about Saleema.

"I brought you news worth a whole tree of olives," exclaimed the woman. "Tell your husband that his sister is a witch who practices her evil craft on living human beings. My husband tells me that they're using the most extreme measures of torture on her to extract a confession, but so far she hasn't confessed. That only proves the devil is living inside of her and helping her."

Maryama's face grew sullen, her eyes swerved, and her head spun so violently that she looked as though she was on the verge of fainting.

"What's wrong?" asked the woman. "Are you feeling sorry for her?"

Maryama stammered before she was able to catch her breath. "Not at all! I was just frightened by the thought that she could scheme to poison me and my children, but . . ."

"But what?"

"But I just don't think she's a witch. I lived with her for many years, and I've never seen her leave the house at night. Tell your husband they're mistaken. Tell him that the Office of Inquisition must know her real crime, that perhaps she stole something that wasn't hers, or she told lies about some people. She is a liar and she only cares about herself. But she's not a witch!"

The Castilian woman put her arms around Maryama. "You shouldn't be so kind. You told me how nasty she was with you, and now God is punishing her with what she deserves. Don't worry about her. Let's go finish our shopping."

Maryama excused herself from walking through the market on the pretext she forgot her money at home.

"I'll go back home."

"And the olives?"

"What olives?"

"The olives you promised me?"

"I'll bring them next week."

25

Saleema was ordered to enter the main hall by walking in backwards. This was not the only unnatural act to which she was subjected since they carried her off two days before.

She looked around and saw them. There were four men staring at her with scrutinizing eyes. Three of them were seated side by side behind a black lacquered table directly in front of her. In a corner at somewhat of a distance sat the fourth, with an inkwell and a stack of paper in front of him, and a feather pen in hand. One of the men sitting behind the table cleared his throat. He was old and had a wrinkled face. He tilted his head slightly backward and folded his hands. Saleema noticed the thick brown blotches on the back of his ivory hands. He cleared his throat again, and the scribe dipped his feather into the inkwell to record what the old man was about to dictate.

"In the name of the Father, Amen.

"In the year of our Lord and Savior Jesus Christ 1527, on the fifteenth day of the month of May, in the presence of we the undersigned, Antonio Agapida, presiding judge of the Office of Inquisition, and Alonso Madera and Miguel Aguilar, investigators of the Office of Inquisition. This investigation commenced when it was called to our attention that Gloria Alvarez, formerly known as Saleema bint Jaafar, engages in the practice of black magic, and accumulates in her residence suspicious and alarming quantities of seeds, plants, and potions that she uses to cause injury to people, and that . . ."

Saleema had to listen very carefully so that she could understand everything that was being recited in Spanish, especially with the loud scratching sound of the pen as it recorded frantically what was being dictated.

". . . and that she, by perpetrating these crimes, threatens the Catholic Church and the security of the state."

The judge beckoned her with his index finger to come forward. He squinted his eyes to the point that they seemed to disappear beneath their puffy lids. She approached the table. He asked her to put her hand on the Bible that was set in front of her and to swear to tell the whole truth about herself and others as well. She did as she was told.

The judge continued his dictation and the scribe continued to write.

"Having asked the accused to take an oath and swear on the Holy Bible, we directed to her the following questions:
— Your name?
— Gloria Alvarez after my baptism. Before, Saleema bint Jaafar.
— Where do you live?
— In Albaicin.
— What are the names of your parents and are they still alive?
— My father is Jaafar Ibn Abi Jaafar, the Paper Maker. He died before the Castilian conquest of Granada. My mother is Umm Hasan before baptism, and after Maria Blanca. She is still alive.
— Have any of your relatives ever been tried for practicing sorcery?
— No.
— Are you married?
— Yes.
— What is the name of your husband?
— Carlos Manuel after baptism. Saad al-Malaqi before.
— Where is your husband?
— I do not know.
— What does that mean?
— We had a quarrel, he got angry with me, and he left home. I don't know where he went."

The three inquisitors exchanged glances that bewildered Saleema; she was sure she had given them the wrong answer. She got a lump in her throat and slowly released the deep breath that had been lodged in her chest.

— When did you husband leave home?

— A few years ago.

— How many, to be exact?

— Approximately six years ago.

— Do you have children?

— Yes.

— How many?

— One daughter.

— What's her name, and how old is she?

— Her name is Esperanza, and she's three years old.

— Didn't you say that your husband abandoned you six years ago?

— He came back one time. We patched things up, but then he left again.

Once again the inquisitors exchanged glances, and this time she was startled by a leering look in the eye of the younger one who was sitting to the right of the judge. She also noticed a smirk on the scribe's face as he bared his front teeth.

— Do you practice witchcraft?

— No, I do not.

— How do you explain all the paraphernalia that was found in your house?

— They are seeds, herbs, and solutions I used to cure people's illnesses.

— Who taught you that?

— I taught myself.

— By yourself, or through books?

Saleema paused before she responded.

— Where am I going to get the books? I don't read Spanish, and Arabic books are banned by law.

— The books we found in your possession.

— Neither I nor anyone else in my household owns or purchases books.

— Then you admit that you practice witchcraft and that it is the devil who taught you to make what you call medicine?

— I never said that.

— Do you not believe in the existence of black magic and witches who have the power to induce storms, kill livestock, or infect people with deadly illnesses?

— I believe that all those things, I mean storms and the death of livestock and people, have natural causes that we don't know about because our knowledge as human beings is insufficient. No, my lord, I do not believe in witches.

— Then why do people resent you?

— People resent me?

— Why do they resent and fear you, and why do they avoid your stare? You once told somebody, "Do not speak to me in that manner," and you gave him a look that made him writhe in pain all night long. You put your hand on the stomach of a pregnant woman who died two days later. A woman sent for you to come and cure her ailing son, and you made him bleed so profusely that his bedroom floor was soaked in blood, and he died.

— I have no recollection at all of the first incident. When somebody insults you or talks to you rudely, you say, "Don't talk to me in that manner," but I do not remember when I said that or to whom, and his illness that night is pure coincidence. The second incident is correct. A woman I encountered on the street, a New Christian, that is, an Arab like me, sought my advice. "I can't understand why I don't feel the baby moving inside of me." I felt the woman's stomach, and I deduced that the baby was dead in the womb since there were no signs of life stirring within even though her stomach was huge. It was clear that she was in the final weeks of pregnancy. I was right; the woman died because the dead baby inside of her poisoned her body.

As for the third incident, well, that's correct as well. A Castilian woman came to me in tears. She begged me to go with her because her little boy was very sick. Against my brother's orders that I never visit the houses of strangers, I accompanied the woman home. When I arrived, I found the boy hemorrhaging, he had no color in his face, and his fingertips had turned blue. He was on the verge of death, and my prognosis was that he was bleeding internally, and that there was nothing I could do to save him.

— Do you know how to perform witchcraft?

— I told you I don't believe in witchcraft.

— And you don't believe in the devil?

— I don't know.

— Do you believe in the existence of Satan, or not? Answer yes or no.

The inquisitors were all looking straight at her. The judge's eyes peered at her from behind his thick, puffy eyelids. The thin, frail one to his left ogled her with two gleaming, lascivious eyes, and she couldn't understand why. The one to his right, the one with the waxen face and sharp features, looked at her with a stone-cold expression. Even the scribe lifted his eyes from the pen and paper and looked at her amused.

"I do not believe that the devil has existence," she answered in a faint voice. Once she said it, she quickly corrected herself when she detected a look of victory reflected in their expressions. "Yes, I do believe that Satan exists."

— Do you worship him?

The thought never entered her mind.

— What do you mean, worship him?

— Do you believe in Satan over God?

— Of course not!

— Then how do you explain this?

The judge waved in front of her a piece of paper the size of a palm of the hand, but she was unable to make out the details. He raised it as though it was the final piece of evidence that would seal her guilt. His two assistants nodded their heads approvingly.

— What's this?

— Come closer, and have a look at this piece of paper. Look at it closely.

She looked at it. On it was a drawing of a sheep or a gazelle. She examined it closely and then she remembered. "Ah, it's a bad draw-ing. I'm not good at drawing pictures."

— Then you admit that this is your drawing?

— I used to own a gazelle I loved very much. I tried to draw a picture of it.

The judge burst into a raucous laughter and his colleagues fol-lowed suit. Even the scribe joined in.

— This is a billy goat, not a gazelle.

— As I said, Your Honor, I'm not very good at drawing.

— This is the billy goat with which you copulate and to which you travel by night.

— The billy goat I copulate with?

— Yes, the billy goat that drew you away from your husband and caused him to abandon you. It is the devil in whose service you are employed.

The judge raised his voice to a shrill pitch as his face contorted and he pointed his accusing finger at Saleema. He tilted his neck forward, carrying with it his head inflamed in anger.

Was this a nightmare, Saleema thought, that shoved her into an absurd game directed by three strange, demented men? The judge accuses her of copulating with a billy goat and faults her for drawing a picture that didn't mean anything. Even those men who came and arrested her acted strangely. One of them tried to fiddle with her books, and when she reached over to stop him, he jumped away in a panic and screamed at her, "Don't touch me!" as though she were some kind of snake or scorpion that could kill him in a second. Then they tied her up as though she were a raging bull, and they put her into a large basket. You don't put a raging bull in a large basket. Maybe a lamb, a chicken, or a rabbit. But this was only Saleema bint Jaafar whom they were taking away, tied up and in a basket! When-ever she recalled the scene, she would laugh a laugh that verged on sobbing, and then she would laugh no more.

Prior to presenting her to this three-man tribunal, they brought in a huge, stern-looking giant of a woman who cut off all her hair and ordered her to remove all her clothes until she stood in front of her naked as the day she was born. The woman inspected her body and ran her fingers under her arms, between her legs, and into all the holes of her body, her nose, mouth, and ears, and even her private parts. But what was she looking for? Saleema wondered if this was all somehow a joke, or just sheer madness. And on top of it all, the judge sticks his finger in her face as though he's about to pluck out her eyes and screams at her, *"the billy goat with which you copulate!"*

Saleema was terrified as she sat alone in her cell because she didn't understand what was happening. At first she thought it was Saad they wanted, but now that the investigation started she knew it was she they intended—but why? She wondered if they were going to charge her for failing to attend mass on Sundays and holy days of obligation, but the judge never mentioned anything of the sort. She needed to be clear-headed in order to ponder, reflect, and understand everything that was happening. She needed to remain calm, but how could she be calm with all that humiliation? The woman threw at her a woolen rag that was supposed to be her dress, and then led her into the main hall and forced her to walk in backwards unlike all God's creatures. "Turn," the woman said, and Saleema turned around only to face three interrogators, with their waxen faces, curved noses turned upward, and their scrutinizing eyes piercing her very soul. She couldn't understand what they wanted from her. She was confused, and she felt both utter fear and bitterness. She was seething with an anger that could only be mollified by attacking these men, the scribe and the giant woman, tearing off their heads and shredding them to pieces. But how could she ever erase the humiliation? There was nothing that could undo that. *"The billy goat with which you copulate!"* She wondered whether to laugh or cry, or bang her head against the wall and smash it instead of smashing their heads that she couldn't stand. *"The billy goat with which you copulate!"*

As her insides roiled in anger, Saleema not for a moment harbored any illusion that the judge might be a man of integrity, with the sufficient knowledge and learning to weigh the facts judiciously, and the strength of conviction to rein in his colleagues from any belligerence or excessiveness that he might deem uncalled for. And

there they sat taking turns, acting as though they were men of learning, schooled in the textbooks of the Ancients, steeped in the
knowledge of the facts and details of theological sciences.

The youngest inquisitor, Alonso Madera, consumed by the fer-
vor of maintaining the sanctity of the faith and protecting it from
any harm or injury, spoke in a resounding, passionate voice, and the
fiery gleam in his eyes masked his pinched, severe face, his crooked
nose, and his thin, tight lips.

"We should seize the little girl since she carries the seed and
soul of the devil. There's no doubt or confusion in what the accused
said. Her husband went away six years ago, and she gave birth to the
girl three years ago. Therefore, the girl is the product of the physical
union between the accused and the devil who came to her in the
form of the billy goat."

Judge Agapida smiled. All along he was patient and supportive
of his two assistants. He never doubted for one moment that their
enthusiasm, which at times pushed them to extremes, was deeply
rooted in their steadfast faith and an ardent desire to render service
to their religion.

"My dear Alonso, the devil is a spirit and not a body. He is incapable of producing one seed of human life."

"But Your Honor, Satan, as is well known and proven, roams
the earth and crosses it from one end to the other to gather seeds,
including human sperm, to produce whatever he wants. Saint Au-
gustine emphasized that in the third chapter of his book *On the Trin-
ity*, when he said that devils collect human sperm and preserve it in
the bodies of humans. In his commentary on the Book of Exodus,
the scholar Walahfrid Strabo[1] wrote that the devils scout the earth
and gather all kinds of seeds that they can activate to produce various creatures. Likewise, Your Honor, the commentary on that very
work, which has a reference to the sons of God who attempt to se-

1. Walahfrid Strabo, 807–849, was a German scholar who wrote on Biblical
exegesis and early Christian liturgy. His evocation enhances the irony in that he
wrote extensively on botany and the medicinal use of herbs and plants.

duce young girls, says that the giants were produced by lecherous devils who shamelessly copulate with women."

At this point Miguel Aguilar interceded. He was a seasoned lawyer with extensive knowledge and experience, and when he spoke he exuded trust and composure.

"The devil is a spirit, as Father Antonio said, and the birth of a child is a function of the living human body. Despite their extraordinary powers, devils cannot endow with life the bodies they inhabit, nor can they give them the capacity to produce life. Devils can fill the world with plagues, cause storms to happen, inflict men with impotence, and wreck havoc wherever they go. They can enter the bodies of those who cannot resist their temptation and cause destruction in the life of human beings. All these things they can do, but they cannot produce one seed of human life that will create a human being made of flesh and blood."

"Do you mean to say that this little girl is not related to the devil?" asked Alonso with disappointment.

"No, but she must be related to another man whose sperm the devil removed directly, or by way of another devil, because there are many degrees of devils, and the most noble of them are those who see themselves above fornicating with women; therefore, they collect sperm, as they do other seeds, and give it to the lesser devils who consort with women and plant the seed in the right place. In this instance, the devil does what he's supposed to do to impregnate the woman, but the power to impregnate itself does not come from the power of the devil or the body it invades, but rather from the power of life that comes from a certain man in a certain place. Therefore, this little girl is not the offspring of the devil but of a man neither we nor the accused know."

"Then she won't be burned?" asked Alonso with a tone of defeat in his voice.

"She will not be burned," responded Agapida with resolution. A moment of silence passed before Agapida resumed speaking. "This has not been a question of our immediate concern because there are clear answers to it in the writings of both the Ancients and contemporary scholars. The question that does warrant discussion is, do we torture the woman to extract more information she may be hiding, or does it suffice that we undertake another round of interrogations to secure her confession?"

"Today we have heard from her three confessions. In the first she admitted that she did in fact draw the picture of the billy goat. She stated but then retracted the second one when she said that her husband had been away for six years and that her daughter was three years old. The third proves her unbelief in God and her apostasy, since she openly declared that she does not know whether the devil exists or not."

"This denial alone allows us to condemn her of heresy," said Alonso Madera. "Her statement that she doesn't know whether the devil exists or not is a rejection of one of the fundamental principles of Catholic doctrine. In light of that, I believe that torture is necessary because she most surely harbors other heretical views." He then turned to Father Agapida. "Didn't you say, Your Honor, before asking me to join you the first time in an inquisition, that witches who consort with the devil speak softly and are not prone to tears because they rely on the power of Satan to support them and convince them they have the power not only to withstand the suffering of a trial but to come out of it unscathed?"

"This is correct. And I did observe just that today. The accused did not cry, she did not plead for mercy, nor did she lose her composure. This can only confirm that she is a consort of the devil. Do you recommend that we use torture or undertake another round of interrogation?"

Miguel Aguilar cleared his throat before speaking.

"In my estimation, it would be more appropriate to further the interrogation, to ask her again some of our previous questions and be certain of her answers. We should also ask her some new questions, and in the light of those decide whether or not to impose torture."

This response seemed to satisfy everyone. They all stood up to go and have dinner and to relax their minds and bodies after a long and grueling day.

26

Saleema tries to calm herself as she sits in solitary confinement. She doesn't sleep because only with open eyes can she keep the rats away from her and repel the nightmares she cannot repel when she's sleeping, only to awaken in a seizure of terror. She lies awake wondering what it is that will give her peace of mind. The giant woman who brings her food told her she was a witch, that it was proven and declared, and like all the hundreds of other such trials conducted by the Office of Inquisition, this one would end with her being burned at the stake. She ran the scene through her mind. They would tie her up, lead her into a public square packed with curious spectators anxiously awaiting the stack of wood to be set afire, like the burning of the books . . . How did her grandfather Abu Jaafar bear to watch the blaze of fire as it ravaged one book after another, to see the pages curl up on themselves as if the fire were warding itself against them and continuing on its path of destruction, consuming, burning, snapping off, and turning into coal everything in its way until nothing remained but dust and ashes? And what was written in them, where did that all go? Saleema wondered. Weren't human beings inscribed sheets, strings of words having meaning that, when put together, connote the whole that a person signifies? She is Saleema bint Jaafar, and in one split second she wanted to defeat death, but then she changed her mind and accepted a mission less impossible. She read books, treated the sick, and deliberately disregarded the injustice of the Castilians. When she walked through the markets, she didn't concern herself with the shops like other women did, but rather with the face of a woman she prescribed a remedy for but did not heal, and she would examine the face and the symptoms, and run them through her mind and think of a treatment.

"Saleema bint Jaafar," the inquisitors asked, "why do people resent you?"

They lie. They never asked the people of Albaicin. Will they be able to look her in the eye when they light the fire beneath her? Will they be able to endure what Abu Jaafar endured, but what she could not, the day they burned the books? And Aysha? She tried not to picture her or think about her, pushing away what can defeat the body and soul and bring the mind to the brink of madness. She conjured the image of her grandfather, Abu Jaafar, the grown-up who inscribed the first word in her book. It wasn't her father or mother who did that, but the grandfather who announced that he would provide her with an education just as he would for Hasan, and who whispered to his wife that Saleema would be like the educated women of Cordova. Her grandmother laughed and repeated those words to Saleema. And so it was inscribed. The only person she ever treated severely was Saad. Why, she asked herself, when he loved her and she loved and still loves him? "I made you suffer, Saad. Will you ever forgive me?" she thought to herself. She wondered if he was still alive or had he preceded her there. Was *there* an illusion or a reality? She wondered if she would encounter her grandfather, her little son who died, and her own father, if in fact *there* really existed. She thought about meeting her father. He won't recognize her because the little girl he fathered has become a full-grown woman in her forties. She would probably recognize him because he must resemble Hasan. Poor Hasan! He wanted so much to protect his family, and out of nowhere comes this unexpected catastrophe. But he's not alone. Maryama is with him. She brings life to the house and nurtures his children and Aysha as well. Saleema broke down in tears. Her body shook as she tried in vain to suppress the sobbing.

When Saleema went through the ordeal of the red hot iron and walked with it in measured steps, the inquisitors did not come to the conclusion, as would be expected upon undertaking such a trial, that the accused was truthful in her testimony. In fact, they were as convinced as ever that she was deeply involved with a powerful demon who empowered her to cause injury. On the following day, they resumed their interrogation of her, and she added nothing more to what she had already told them. She may have even aroused more suspicion when the judge asked her if she journeyed long distances at night on the back of a flying beast, to which she replied that she had never heard of any human being able to do such a thing with the exception of the Muslim prophet, Muhammad. When asked to explain and elaborate on her answer, she told them the story of the winged creature who carried Muhammad from a mosque in Mecca to a mosque in Jerusalem. When the judge asked her if she believed that this actually took place, Saleema avoided answering the question directly: "I've been baptized, and I've become a Christian."

These new details drew the attention of the inquisitors to another aspect of the case that had not occurred to them previously, that is, that the accusation of apostasy may not be limited to the accused's consorting with the devil, but could extend to the veracity of her faith. It appeared that despite her baptism she did not relinquish her Muhammadan faith, and therefore her consorting with the devil was intended to cause harm to the Catholic Church. The inquisitors tried to extract a confession from her on this point. When they failed to do so, the judge offered her a choice and a warning. "Do not take this matter lightly, for you will have to hold a bar of burning iron." She answered that she was ready, and they watched as she held the bar with her two hands and walked with it. The inquisitors shuddered at the thought of how she did this, as did the scribe whose writing table was set up in the courtyard so that he could record everything that transpired therein.

When the members of the tribunal withdrew from the main hall, the judge congratulated himself and his colleagues because they did not soften on this woman, and for taking all the necessary precautions to protect themselves from such a powerful witch. Each one of them had made a talisman of holy salt, and they wrote down the seven words that Jesus Christ uttered on the cross on a small piece of paper and hung them like scapulars around their necks and against their chests, underneath their black cassocks.

"We must proceed with torture!"

The two assistants nodded their heads in agreement. Alonso beamed in delight at the prospect of what was to befall a woman gone astray from her faith. Miguel Aguilar sat quietly resigned to the fact that these habitual proceedings were intended to extract the truth from proud and obstinate sinners whose vices transformed Lucifer from one of God's noble angels into a wicked demon.

On the day of sentencing, they escorted Saleema in fetters to Bibarambla Gate Square. The guards made a path through the throngs of people who came to hear the sentencing and witness the execution. Saleema tried as best she could to withstand the agony of walking on two feet swollen and burned by torture. She tried not to think about the chafing of her hands shackled and tied behind her back. She still had the blisters from the red hot iron bar she had been forced to carry. She didn't dare look at the people around her. She occupied her mind with her thoughts. They were going to sentence her to death, so why didn't her insides roil with dreaded fear, or why didn't she cry out in anger and fury? She wondered if it was because she wished for death, that she was imploring God to relieve her of the unbearable suffering of her body and soul. She wondered if she was submitting her fate to God, like many of the great martyrs who face death bravely even though they may not understand or accept God's will. Perhaps it was something altogether different, that she decided without any forethought not to humiliate herself by screaming or begging, or even crying out in fright like mice in their traps. She would not add insult to injury onto herself. Intelligence in human beings is a noble quality. Pride in themselves is sublime.

She could now walk to the burning stake like a person who masters her own soul. She could say, "Yes, I am Saleema bint Jaafar. I was raised by an honorable man who made books and whose heart fumed the day he witnessed the burning of the books and who walked away in silent dignity. But I did cry out, Grandfather, when they tortured me, that is correct. My mind and my body collapsed, but only for several moments, Grandfather. I never said anything you would be ashamed of. I studied the books as you taught me to do, I eased people's pain as best I could. I even dreamed that one day I would dedicate to you, Grandfather, a book I wrote from my own research and experiments. That was my dream, Grandfather, that I could have realized had it not been for the prison of time."

Saleema finally looked around her. The crowd had grown eerily quiet. The three inquisitors were seated on a dais as the judge read out the sentence in a loud voice that echoed throughout the square.

"It has been our intention to ascertain whether the charges filed against you are true or false, whether you acted in light or darkness, and we summoned you to investigate these charges. We required that you swear by God in our presence. We sought the testimony of witnesses, and we abided by the rules and regulations in accordance with the Church. In the desire to attain the highest level of justice in this inquiry, a tribunal was formed, comprised of the foremost experts on theological matters. And upon a complete examination and discussion on all aspects of the case, and a careful review of all the evidence brought forth, we have arrived at a verdict that you, the so-named Gloria Alvarez, known prior to your conversion as Saleema bint Jaafar, accused of heresy, stand guilty as charged for being an instrument and a servant of Satan, for stealing seeds for his use, and for concocting diabolic brews that cause harm to both man and beast.

"In spite of your denial of these charges, it has been proven by the testimony of eyewitnesses that you caused the death of one child in the womb of his mother, and of another who was ill before you killed him.

"Furthermore, it has been determined that you have turned

away from the very church that embraced you and wanted to save your soul. It has become evidently clear that, regardless of your baptism, you remain steadfast in your Muhammadan faith and loyal to the Muslim prophet.

"In spite of all these charges, we have tried and continue to try to bring you back to the truth, to urge you to repent for your infidelity and your loyalty to the devil who is the very essence of nonbelief. We had hoped to return you to the embrace of Holy Mother Church and the Catholic faith, so that you may escape from the punishment of both this world and the next. We have tried our utmost in all of this, and we postponed pronouncing a sentence for as long as we could in the fervent hope that you declare your regret and sorrow. But your arrogance and stubbornness, and your predilection for sin keep you in a state of denial. We therefore report with great sadness and pain our failure in bringing you to repentance.

"So that every person of sound mind and soul be warned, that every true believer shun the path of wicked infidelity, and that all people know that apostasy does not go unpunished, I, Judge Antonio Agapida, who sit before you with the Bible in hand, so solemnly declare in the name of the Holy Church, with God as my witness and the honor and majesty of our faith guiding me, my sentence as follows:

"As you sit before us in the Square of Bibarambla Gate, we declared you an unrepentant infidel, and condemn you to death by fire."

The crowd roared, and the shouts of the masses that pounded in Saleema's head like thunderous hammers mixed with the pounding of her heart and the throbbing in her stomach. She didn't want to look around her. She didn't want to look because she feared their eyes, Castilian eyes gleaming with delight and eager to watch, and Arab eyes that break your heart with their sorrowful or frightened looks. She doesn't look up, but she hears a voice that sounds like the voice of Saad. She keeps her eyes down. They unfasten some of her shackles and lead her toward the woodpile.

Maryama was worried sick over Saad and Hasan's delay, but she couldn't refuse Aysha's request to tell her a story.

"Once upon a time, Aysha, there was a big tree in the sky that had as many green leaves as the number of people there were on earth, people from all over the earth, small and big, girls and boys, those who spoke Arabic like us and those who didn't. It was a big tree that sheds its leaves and then grows new ones over and over again. Every year on the night of Laylat al-Qadr, the tree sprouts a strange and wondrous leaf. In the year this story takes place, the tree sprouted . . ."

Maryama stopped. She was at a loss at what to say. Her mind was wandering in many directions, and she was thinking about why Hasan and Saad were late. She wondered if Saleema was to be sentenced that day.

"And so, then what happened, Auntie Maryama?"

Maryama looked into the face of the little girl and she took a long deep breath. She let it out and continued her story.

Glossary

Abu: father [of]; honorific, followed by the name of the oldest son

auto-da-fé: a ceremony conducted by the Office of Inquisition to pronounce judgment on and order the execution of a heretic

bin, bint: "son of," "daughter of"; term forming part of a person's name, following the first or given name

dinar: a coin, usually of gold

faqeeh: a scholar and teacher of Quranic and Islamic studies

fatwa: a solicited legal opinion (response)

imam: prayer leader in a mosque; spiritual head of a Muslim community

muezzin: the announcer of prayer time

Ramadan: the holy month when Muslims are obligated to fast from sunrise to sunset

Sidi: an honorific equivalent to "Lord," "Master," or "Sir"

shahada: the profession a faith incumbent upon all Muslims: "There is no god but God, and Muhammad is His prophet."

shaykh: a title given to a respected elder or to a scholar of religious studies

souk: a marketplace and center for commercial and social activity

sultan: a title of power, equivalent to the title "prince"

Umm: "mother [of]"; honorific, followed by the name of the oldest son

vizier: the head of government, usually under a caliph or prince